THE BERLIN CONSPIRACY

THE BERLIN

wm
WILLIAM MORROW
An Imprint of HarperCollins*Publishers*

CONSPIRACY

TOM GABBAY

This book is a work of fiction. References to real people, events, establishments, organizations, or locales are intended only to provide a sense of authenticity, and are used fictitiously. All other characters, and all incidents and dialogue, are drawn from the author's imagination and are not to be construed as real.

HarperCollins books may be purchased for educational, business, or sales promotional use. For information please write: Special Markets Department, HarperCollins Publishers, 10 East 53rd Street, New York, NY 10022.

FIRST EDITION

Designed by Sarah Maya Gubkin

Printed on acid-free paper

Library of Congress Cataloging-in-Publication Data

Gabbay, Tom.
The Berlin Conspiracy: a novel / by Tom Gabbay.
p. cm.
ISBN-13: 978-0-06-078785-1 (acid-free paper)
ISBN-10: 0-06-078785-6
1. Kennedy, John F. (John Fitzgerald), 1917–1963—Assassination attempts—Fiction. 2. Attempted assassination—Fiction. 3. Intelligence officers—Fiction. 4. Americans—Germany—Fiction. 5. Berlin (Germany)—Fiction. 6. Conspiracies—Fiction. I. Title

PS3607.A226B47 2006
813'.6—dc22

2005047938

---

06 07 08 09 10 JTC/RRD 10 9 8 7 6 5 4 3 2 1

To Julia

for everything

The following is an account of events that took place in June 1963. I've kept these facts to myself all these years for obvious reasons, but I'm too old now to worry about any of that.

Besides, the bastards will never find me.

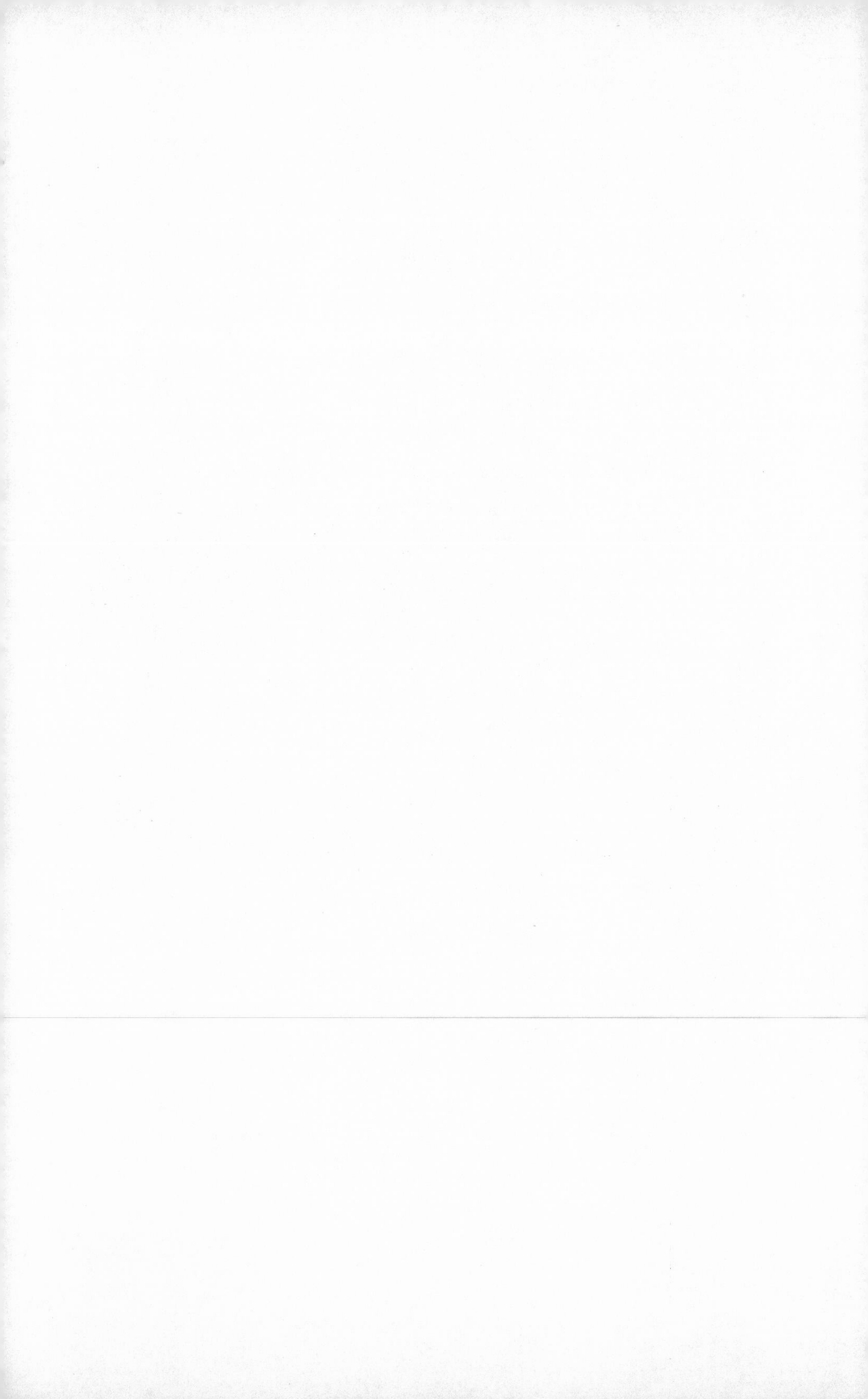

THE BERLIN CONSPIRACY

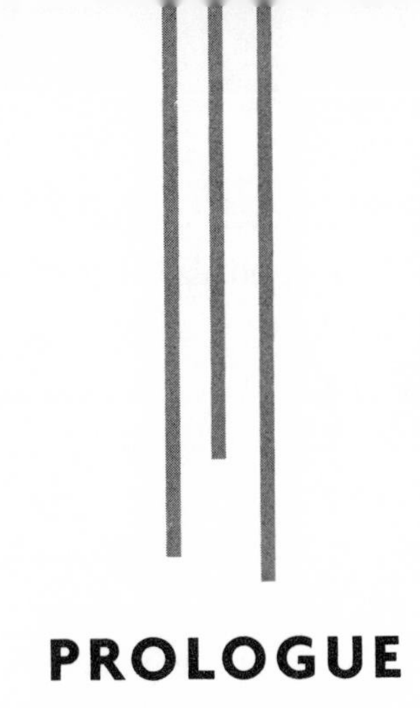

PROLOGUE

I left Berlin on the morning after my mother was buried. A few hours before she died, my brother and I were roused from our beds and told we should say our final good-byes. The memory of that night is still vivid, even through the fog of all those years.

A band of warm light spilled into the room as we entered, illuminating her face. She didn't look real, already more an angel than our mother. After a moment, she spoke, softly, on shallow breath. *"Kommt,"* she whispered. "Come. . . . Don't be afraid." She was young, far too young to die, but even I could see that precious little life was left in the slender frame that faded into the shadows.

Outwardly, nothing had changed. The dressing table was neatly arranged with lipsticks, rouge, and powders; the music box still sat on the mantel, its waltzing couple frozen in silent midstep. Next to the bed stood a formal wedding photo in a silver frame and, on the wall, a fuzzy picture of a smiling man in uniform—black ribbon and medal of honor draped over the image of a husband and father who, like many others, never returned from "The War to End All Wars." Everything was in its place, yet the room had changed in some way. The smell of medicine was gone; now there was death in the air.

I took Josef's hand and led him to our mother's side. He was only eight, five years younger than me, and probably didn't fully understand what was happening. Nobody had explained it to us, not in so many words.

She lay there, very still, for what seemed like an eternity and the thought crossed my mind that she might've died in the time it took us to cross the room. Finally her eyes lifted and turned toward us. She studied our faces for a long time, as if trying to memorize them. Or maybe she was gathering strength, determined to use those last few breaths to carry the words that she wanted to leave behind.

"Give me your hands," she whispered. I felt her weakness as she attempted to close her fingers around ours. "You see . . ." She tried to smile. "A family . . . Do you understand?"

I nodded, though I wasn't sure that I did.

"Say it," she demanded.

"A family," I responded obediently.

She slipped her hand away, leaving Josef's palm in mine. "And now—" she breathed. "Still a family . . . Always a family."

I felt that she wanted to say more but was unable to summon the strength. I wanted to say something, too, but words wouldn't come. Not because I was too emotional. In fact, I can remember wondering why I wasn't more upset. I loved my mother dearly and I knew she loved us more than anything, but for some reason I felt removed from it all, watching the scene from someplace far away, like I am now.

Not many came to her funeral. Three, maybe four faceless men in dark suits and polished shoes standing a few steps behind us, heads bowed, hats in hand. I didn't know any of them. Josef and I stood in front of the open grave with Auntie between us. The lady who came once a week to clean the house—I don't remember her name—was the only one who sobbed quietly as the priest said his prayers and remarked that although it was sad our mother had left her sons orphans, God knew best and must have needed her in heaven more than we did on earth. I hadn't thought of myself as an orphan before that.

I think Josef and I each placed a flower on top of her coffin as it was lowered into the ground, but I'm not sure. I remember that we stayed long after everyone else had gone, wanting to see that the headstone was properly placed. It read simply:

Gertrud Teller
1895–1927

On the first night she lay in her grave, I lay on my bed thinking about a cold December day, shortly before my brother was born, when she and I went to a toy shop in central Berlin. I was completely mesmerized by a display of wooden soldiers in the window, two opposing armies—complete with cavalry and artillery batteries—lined up against each other in neat rows of red and blue. She tried to interest me in all sorts of other toys and games—spinning tops, puppets, a bright red fire truck—anything other than those soldiers. But I could see nothing else. Two weeks later, on Christmas Eve of 1918, I found a small box under the tree with my name on it. Inside were two soldiers, one red and one blue.

Two full battalions now faced each other across the floor of the attic room I shared with Josef. I studied the carefully arranged formations into the early hours of that morning, until I finally drifted into a restless dream, where I joined the painted soldiers in combat and felt the gut-wrenching fear of a position being overwhelmed by opposing forces. When I woke, something had changed. The soldiers no longer came to life.

A boy's battles are fought on the field of his imagination. There's no cause, no doctrine, nothing to gain, it's just Blue vs. Red. Not so different from life, I guess, except that in life the colors can get muddied, making it hard to tell which side is which. I must have sensed that there were other battles waiting for me, bigger battles to be fought on a larger field. Or maybe it's a smaller field. Anyway, I knew it was time to put my toys away. I found an old tin box and began to dismantle my childhood fantasies.

Josef woke and watched respectfully from his bed as I carefully placed each soldier in the box. Not until I had closed the tin did he feel he could speak.

"Where will we live now?" he wondered.

"You'll stay with Auntie," I said without looking up.

"Where will you be?" he asked with growing concern.

"America," I said. "I'm leaving today." As far as I can remember, it was the first time the idea had entered my head, but it seemed as good a plan as any, so I stuck with it.

"I'll go with you," Josef quickly decided.

"No," I said flatly. "You're too young."

"So are you," he frowned.

"I'll come back for you when you're older," I said, thinking that I might, in fact, return for him once I'd established myself.

"Did Auntie say you could?" he asked, knowing full well that the idea could not have been authorized.

"You can't tell anyone, Josef. It's a secret."

"Mama says not to keep secrets."

"It depends on the secret," I explained. "Some secrets are like promises. If you tell the secret you break the promise. Then you become a traitor and a traitor is nothing more than a coward." But I understood my brother well enough to know that this lesson in ethics wouldn't keep his mouth shut. I held the box of soldiers out to him.

"Would you like to have these?" I asked enticingly.

"Until you come back?" he ventured, looking very skeptical.

"For as long as you keep our secret," I said. He let that sink in for a moment, then smiled conspiratorially and took the tin into his possession. I suppose there's a moment in everyone's life when they learn the value of a secret. That was Josef's moment.

So it was that on a sunny morning in late September of 1927, at the auspicious age of thirteen, I packed a bag and set out to begin my adventure with the world. Maybe I actually believed that one day I'd return for my younger brother, fulfilling our mother's last wish that we remain a family. But life didn't work out that way.

ONE

In 1963, the world was divided into two camps, and Berlin was on the front line. They called it a "Cold War," but one spark in that divided city and it wouldn't be cold for long—the whole damn planet would go up in flames. Of course, I'd contributed more than my share to this nonsense doing contract work for the Company through the fabulous fifties, but after Cuba the shine had gone off and I dropped out of the insanity.

I found an agreeable retirement spot in a small bungalow near Pompano Beach, Florida, about forty miles north of Miami. At that time it wasn't much more than a couple of bars and a convenience store on a strip of sand off the highway, but it suited me fine. The idea was to get rich as a bestselling author of spy novels and then find more desirable living quarters. I had a typewriter and loads of material, but nothing ever came together in my head, let alone on paper. So I did a lot of fishing.

It wasn't the first time Sam Clay had phoned in the middle of the night, but it was the first time in a while. Sam was DDP (Deputy Director for Plans, in charge of covert operations) and as near to a real friend as I had, even though I'd only seen him once since I dropped out. I hadn't left the agency on the best of terms, not that Sam held any of that against me, but when you're out you have to be completely out. I'd made my own bed and didn't mind sleeping in it, if it wasn't for the cockroaches, that is.

Anyway, I was surprised to hear Sam's voice. He didn't waste time asking how the fishing was, just got to the point, which was a ticket waiting at the TWA desk in Miami for the morning flight to New York, connecting through to Frankfurt and Berlin. There would be a car waiting for me at the airport and he'd see me in a few days. That was it. No small talk, no explanation. Not that I would've expected one over the phone.

I hung up, sat on the side of the bed, and wished I had a Marlboro. There was an ocean breeze coming through the window and I got up, stood in front of the screen to let it wash across my bare chest. It was pretty black out there, just the sound of the waves slashing onto the beach. Why had I gone along with Sam? I may not have been cutting it as a writer—or as a fisherman, for that matter—but I had no desire to get back into the game. I'd had enough subversion and betrayal for one lifetime and I certainly had no wish to revisit the city of my youth. It might as well have been someone else's childhood memories knocking around in my brain, that's how removed I felt from it. There was nothing left of Berlin to revisit, anyway. The places I once knew had been reduced to rubble and rebuilt into something else that I didn't care about one way or another. It wasn't that I wanted to avoid my past, either. I just didn't give a damn.

I guess the easy answer was that I was tired of hauling in empty lures by day and staring at blank pieces of paper by night. A change of scenery would do me no harm. And I owed Sam. Anyway, whatever the reason, I packed my bag and thirty-six hours later I was back in the business of chasing shadows.

It would've been a routine operation if not for an unusual request, made in a letter written by an unidentified East German official and dropped in the car of a State Department staffer, somebody's secretary I think it was. The anonymous official said he had important information that he might be willing to share, under the "right circumstances." Those kinds of letters were fairly frequent in Berlin and the "right circumstances" usually meant the right price, which was invariably paid, even though the information was usually pretty lame. But the author of this particular enticement wasn't interested in money or even a one-way ticket west. He had just one demand: me. I was the only person he'd talk to.

And no one, especially me, had the slightest idea why.

It would be a significant understatement to say that the guys in Berlin were unhappy about this request. The chief of station at the time was a joker named James Powell. A midforties, tall, slender, tailored-suit kind of a guy with a head too big for his shoulders, he was a Yale man who thought he was a real smooth operator. I thought he was a pretentious asshole, but that didn't matter. You came across a lot of pretentious assholes in the intelligence business. I even liked a few of them. Not Powell, though.

He didn't care much for me, either, which was understandable for a man in his position. No station chief would've liked having an outsider brought in to handle a routine letter drop, but having me show up out of retirement (they called it exile) would've really got under his skin. He must have lobbied Washington hard to keep me out of it and been overruled. Everyone knew I'd ditched the agency and thought they knew the reason why, not that I cared what they thought. I was back for a limited engagement and didn't want to get into any of that old bullshit.

Still, I was curious about my mystery man. Why the hell would some East German official single me out for contact? I'd been out of the game for two years and I'd never worked Europe anyway. It must have intrigued Washington, too. Whoever the guy was, he had access to files on me, and he'd found something in one of them that got his attention. They must've figured he was a player, and it wasn't often that you got the real thing to volunteer. Usually they'd have to be bribed, extorted, or drugged into betraying their country, which took a lot of time and planning, and more often than not you still came up empty. This was a potential gift, one that would come at an extremely opportune moment. Hence the middle-of-the-night phone call from Sam and the pissed-off Berlin chief of station.

Everyone was a bit on edge. Except me, of course. I had no bet in this game. Or so I thought.

The instructions went like this: I was to be at the eastbound Charlottenburg S-Bahn station at 8 P.M. on Saturday night, the twenty-second of June. Being a suburban station, used mostly by commuters, it would be pretty well deserted at that hour. I was instructed to sit at the most forward bench on the platform reading a copy of the *Herald Tribune.* If I was alone, a man with a cane would make contact. The letter had been very clear about me being alone, but of course I wasn't. Washington wouldn't have allowed it even if Powell had.

The station sat on a grassy bank above a small tree-lined road, where a black four-door sedan was parked up on the shoulder. It looked empty, but scrunched down in the front seat, Powell and a young field op named Andy Johnson were monitoring me on a two-way radio link. Johnson was a fresh, crew-cut kid from West Texas who wore big "Buddy Holly" glasses. Very military. I spoke to him through a microphone that I had in my shirt pocket and he communicated to me over a small, wireless speaker in my ear.

Our man was thirty minutes late when I noticed a guy on the opposite platform taking an interest in me. He wasn't the subject, but I thought he might be a scout. "There's a guy across the tracks in a blue overcoat," I whispered into my pocket. "I think he's in love because he keeps making eyes at me."

"That's 'Mama Bear,' " Johnson said in my ear. One of the sillier aspects of intelligence work is the code names. On this night Powell was "Papa Bear," Johnson was "Baby Bear," and I was "Goldilocks." Mama Bear, it turned out, was a mental case named Roy Chase, a guy I'd heard about but had been lucky enough to avoid up until now. He'd spent a lot of time in Manila, which was the main staging point for operations throughout Southeast Asia. In fact, I was kind of surprised to find Chase in Berlin. It was a very different game here and called for a lighter touch than he had a reputation for. They hadn't told me he was going to be spotting me, but the guy was so clumsy Ray Charles would've made him.

"Well, tell Mama Bear to take a walk," I said too loudly. "He might as well be wearing a fucking sign."

There was a pause, then Johnson came back on the radio, to Chase. "Uh, Mama Bear, this is Baby Bear. Papa Bear wants you to give Goldilocks some room. . . . But stay with the action." Chase shot a nasty look across the tracks, then wandered down to the other end of the platform and pretended to read a train schedule.

8:37. The street lamps were coming on as the last light of day faded away. It wasn't going to happen. Either the guy was a civilian and chickened out or, more likely, a pro who'd spotted Chase and decided to give it a miss. Either way I'd come a long way for nothing. To my surprise, I felt let down. Being back in action, even such as it was, had my adrenaline going again and my curiosity was aroused.

It started to drizzle.

"We've been stood up, guys," I said into my pocket. "Anyway, it's getting wet out here and Goldilocks needs some hot porridge."

Long pause, me getting wetter while the message was relayed.

"Papa's not ready to call it," I finally got in my ear. "We'll go till twenty-one hundred."

Powell knew the guy wasn't going to turn up. He just wanted to avoid any second-guessing from Washington, but meanwhile I was the jerk getting wet. "Sure," I said, keeping my cool. "But I'm lodging a formal complaint with my union."

"We'll be sure to put that in the report," Baby Bear assured me. "And, ah . . . Papa Bear requests that you knock off the chatter."

"No problem." Now I wanted to knock Papa Bear's arrogant head off his gray flannel shoulders.

The rain started to pick up. I was about to tell Powell where to get off when out of the corner of my eye I caught sight of a figure with a cane approaching. I buried my nose in the *Tribune,* muttered, "Heads up," into the microphone.

"Yeah, we see it," I got back from Johnson.

My heart picked up a beat.

The figure stopped, maybe fifteen feet short of the bench. I stole a look and saw it was a woman holding a closed umbrella. Mid- to late thirties, with dark hair falling out of a cream-colored nylon scarf with faded red roses around the edge. She looked tired, kind of used up. I noticed a small run in her stocking along her right calf that she had mended with nail polish. She became aware of my look, glanced back over her shoulder, and opened the umbrella.

There was no reason that our mystery man couldn't be a mystery woman. Of course, an umbrella wasn't a cane but that could've been a glitch in translation. (It wasn't that unusual. I once saw a description of an especially tall Venezuelan contact translated as "he is unusually high." The meeting never came off because our guys were looking for somebody who was stoned out of his mind. It really happened.)

I went back to the newspaper, but kept one eye on her. She was doing the same with me, but not very subtly. I could tell that she was going to make a move and after a few more peeks she did, faking interest in a movie poster to move closer to the bench. I waited, thinking we were wasting our time—this was strictly Amateur Hour.

Finally she turned to me and, in German, said, "You're getting wet."

My German was pretty rusty, but I tried anyway, saying something like, "Are you offering to share your umbrella?"

She paused for a beat, looked me over, then, in English, said, "Would you like to have some company?"

I couldn't help laughing, which took her by surprise. She turned away, looking more embarrassed than offended, which she had every right to be. I was about to apologize when I got Powell in my ear.

"For Christ's sake, Teller, get rid of the whore," in that weary Ivy League way. Fuck you, I thought, she's just trying to earn a living, probably a more honorable one than you earn. I removed the earpiece, put it in my jacket pocket, and got off the bench.

"Hey, I wasn't laughing at you." She looked at me, dubious. "I just thought it was funny that you switched to English. Is my German that bad?"

She smiled. "Terrible." It was a nice, natural smile. She had nice eyes, too. Light brown. Too bad they were massacred with mascara.

"I don't do this all the time," she said after an awkward pause. "I'm a nurse." She didn't need to explain anything to me, but if it made her feel better that was fine.

I said that in fact I wouldn't mind sharing her umbrella, and as soon as I was under she started to tell me about how she needed the money to pay for her sick mother's medical bills and how little a nurse made and how she only went with nice men. I asked her how she could tell if they were nice and she said she could just tell, like she did with me. I thought she probably said that to all her potential customers, but I didn't mind listening. At least I was dry.

I heard the door of the sedan slam and a minute later Powell was storming the platform with Baby Bear Johnson in tow. They stopped about ten feet away, like they were staking me out.

"What the hell are you doing, Teller!" A vein was throbbing violently in Powell's right temple and his head looked like it could explode any minute. He really needed to loosen his tie.

"I was just talking to—" I turned to the lady. "I'm sorry, I don't know your name."

"Rita," she responded, looking kind of apprehensive.

"I'm Jack," I smiled. "Jack Teller."

"Hello." She nodded warily.

"Zip it up, Jack. Fun's over," Powell barked.

I started to say that I hadn't actually had a lot of laughs so far, that maybe Rita and I would try to salvage the evening, but I stopped short because that's when I saw him—standing under a street lamp on the road below was our man, watching the whole scene with an expression of utter contempt on his face. He didn't move, just stood there like a statue, one hand in the pocket of his raincoat, the other holding the cane, rain splashing off his fedora, waiting patiently for us to spot him.

"Looks like we all got caught with our pants down." I nodded toward the street.

He waited for Powell to see him, then turned and disappeared into the darkness. Powell signaled Chase on the opposite platform and he took off after him, hoping to get some kind of ID—a car, a face, anything, but I knew he'd come up empty. This guy wasn't your run-of-the-mill East German bureaucrat building a retirement fund. He was for real, you could tell.

I wondered again why I would be of such interest. I'd been turning it over since I was briefed, thinking about operations I'd been involved in that might have attracted his attention. Iran, Guatemala, Mexico, or even Cuba—nothing connected. I'd been active in all that stuff and knew a lot, but nothing a lot of other guys didn't know, too. The most reasonable explanation was that I looked like a candidate for recruitment because of the way I walked out, but that didn't work, either. If they wanted to try me they'd have used a discreet approach, at the beach maybe, with a well-stuffed bikini as bait, not a letter that alerted the entire intelligence community to their intentions. No, it had to be something else that hooked him. But now it looked like I'd never know—it was highly unlikely that he'd give us a second shot.

"We won't see him again," I said.

"If that's true, you're in big fucking trouble," Powell flashed. "Hell, you're in big fucking trouble anyway."

"Really?" I answered as coolly as I could. "I'm the only one who's supposed to be standing on this platform. Besides, I'm here on a guest pass, so if anyone's in big fucking trouble it's you, Chief."

Powell signaled Johnson with a nod. The kid reached out to take hold of my arm, and without really meaning to, I laid him out pretty cleanly with a simple left hook. To be fair, he wasn't expecting it, but it felt good anyway. Powell sighed like a frustrated headmistress.

"For Christ's sake, Teller, was that really necessary?"

I shrugged, offered Johnson a hand up, and pulled him onto his feet. "Sorry, kid, you took me by surprise."

"No problem," he drawled, dabbing at a tiny spot of blood on his lip. "Would I be taking you by surprise now?"

My throat was firmly in his grasp before he finished the sentence. I knew the move, but I'd never been on this side of it. It's kind of like having your trachea in a vise—the slightest pressure will collapse the thin wall of membrane that runs from the larynx to the bronchi, blocking the only air passage to the lungs, causing the subject to suffocate within seconds. Of course, conversation is out of the question in these circumstances, so I never got a chance to say good-bye to Rita.

We adjourned to the Company car, where I massaged my throat while we waited for Chase. He finally climbed into the front seat beside Powell and reported that our man had disappeared into thin air. I was about to make a comment, but decided to shut up for once.

"Langley wants a report tonight," Powell fretted. "How the fuck do I write this up?"

"Chase got too close, let the subject make us," Johnson said matter-of-factly. "It was clumsy."

Chase turned, gave the kid an icy stare. Even in the dark you could see that this one was dangerous—the kind of guy who could snap at any moment, but you'd never be able to predict when or why. The kid didn't flinch, though. I was starting to like him, in spite of my sore throat.

"How about I say the target walked because Jack was hitting on a chick?" Powell looked to me for a reaction.

"A chick?" I forced a laugh through the bruises on my vocal cords. "Do you know how silly you sound when you say that?"

"We can't all be as cool as you, Jack."

"I guess that's right." I opened the door to get out. "Tell Washington whatever you want. Tell them I was getting a blow job. I didn't ask for this shit, you guys came to me."

"Where the hell do you think you're going?"

"To get some fresh air. Don't bother waiting up."

Johnson asked if he should stop me, but Powell was smart enough to know it would only make his report that much harder to write.

TWO

I stumbled onto a beer hall tucked away in a small side street not far from the rail station. It was called Struwwelpeter after the fairy-tale kid who never washed or trimmed his fingernails. A painting of the boy over the door brought back an image from a book my mother used to read to me. Memories of that time were pretty rare for me, so I guess Berlin was jostling something. Anyway, it made me smile.

The pub was a traditional place—high ceilings, rows of long wooden tables, large fireplace, and a warm atmosphere. About half-full with a cheery crowd. I ordered sausages and a Pilsner, found the *Tribune* in my pocket, and settled in. I felt like a smoke, decided what the hell, and bought a pack of HBs from a machine. It seemed to go with the scene.

I realized that I'd been sitting on the bench at the platform for well over an hour staring at the front page of the paper and hadn't read a word of it. KENNEDY DEPARTS ON EUROPEAN TOUR was the lead item. I read the first paragraph:

> *London — President Kennedy's European tour is taking place at a most inauspicious time, according to many diplomats here. In his speech at American University on June 10, the President set as his goal an easing of rivalries with the Soviet Union. That conciliatory gesture on East-West relations is regarded here as ruling out any possibility of a strong declaration by the United States in support of West Germany, and particularly Berlin, during Mr. Kennedy's visit. A high-ranking NATO officer said, "President Kennedy wishes to turn back the clock of warfare and stop development of nuclear weapons on earth and in space. But this cannot be done."*

It's a trick of journalism that when a newspaper wants to put an editorial on the front page, they simply write an opinion, then go out and find someone to attribute it to. What did "according to many diplomats" mean? It meant the writer had been to a cocktail party full of junior ministers who'd spent the night second-guessing American foreign policy. That's news? And the "high-ranking NATO officer" was bound to be one of de Gaulle's cronies. The French president, unable to understand why the world gave Kennedy the adulation that should have been his, took potshots at the president whenever the opportunity presented itself.

I skipped to the next item, which was much more interesting. It involved sex, drugs, abuse of power, and human betrayal. Stuff you can get your teeth into. I'd been following the story since it broke in London a few weeks earlier, thought maybe I could use it in one of my many unwritten novels.

The published version went like this:

Britain's Labour Party today demanded a full-scale investigation of War Minister John Profumo's resignation in a sex scandal that shook the British government. The opposition party called for a parliamentary inquiry into any possible breech of security resulting from Profumo's relations with a redheaded playgirl.

Profumo admitted that he lied to Parliament on March 22 when he said there had been no impropriety in his relations with Christine Keeler, 21. The party leaders said they were particularly concerned about Miss Keeler's "friendliness" with Captain Eugene Ivanov, an assistant Soviet naval attaché, at a time when she was also seeing Profumo. Ivanov was recalled to Moscow last December.

Of course, there's always more dirt if you dig a little deeper. I got the scoop from a friend at the Bureau who was keeping tabs on the case (code-named "Bowtie") for Hoover, who claimed to be interested in U.S. citizens who might've been friendly with Miss Keeler, and who might've dropped a secret or two along the way. The London FBI office had, in fact, uncovered a couple of air-force officers based at Lockenheath who'd had £100 worth of "friendliness" one night, but they were cleared after an exhaustive interview. (The highly descriptive tape of the interrogation was apparently a hot item around the Bureau.)

But my guy thought the director wasn't so much worried about the affairs of state as the other kind. The word was that maybe the current occupant of the White House had more than a passing interest in the sex scandal because one of Keeler's cohorts, a classy Czech girl named Maria Novotny, had told the Brits that she and another girl, Suzy Chang, had together serviced the president when they were working New York. My man at the Bureau hinted that the director, no great fan of the president, was collecting information and feeding it to his friend the vice president to use if the Kennedys tried to dump him from the ticket in '64, as rumor had it.

Comrade Ivanov was KGB, that's for sure. What did he take back to Moscow? Not so sure. Keeler, under interrogation, had said he wanted her to find out from Profumo if and when West Germany would be joining the nuclear club. (You'd be surprised what a responsible government official will say to a sexy redhead who has his dick in her hand.) Keeler insisted she never asked the question. Maybe so, or maybe the girl was exceptionally good under questioning. Certain interrogation techniques, well known to SIS, would've been ruled out in this case because of the media profile. My guess was that Ivanov didn't go home empty-handed. And it was certainly possible that the Brits got more out of Keeler than they cared to admit. That kind of security breach would have severely limited Washington's willingness to share sensitive information with our friends in Whitehall.

At one time I would've seen all this as a big win for Moscow, necessitating some sort of countermeasure. Now I couldn't for the life of me figure out what difference it made whether the Soviets knew if West Germany would go nuclear. For Christ's sake, they already had something like twenty-two hundred warheads pointed at Western Europe. So what if they decided to point a few more? But that was the game. If West Germany was going to install warheads, Moscow had to be ready to put them into East Germany.

The guy who intrigued me was an osteopath named Stephen Ward, the guy who'd put Keeler together with both Profumo and Ivanov. Ward, who palmed himself off as an artist, was being accused by the press of all sorts of depravity. Stories of uninhibited orgies, wife swapping, marijuana, pills, whips, and chains were good grist for the paper mill and, no doubt, most of it was true. But it was all smoke, meant to obscure the obvious. The kind of "public relations" campaign I'd run many times.

What neither side wanted to say was that the good doctor and his orgies were bait. Nothing special or unusual about it; there were dozens like him in every capital around the world, set up by both sides to see what kind of fish they could hook. But the big news was that the good doctor was *our* bait. MI5 had put him in business with the hope of getting Ivanov on film in a compromising position, then turning him. But putting a dabbler like Ward up against the Russian was like putting Fred Astaire in the ring with Joe Louis. He can dance around for a while, but sooner or later he's gonna find himself trapped in a corner and it's a pretty good bet who's gonna leave on a stretcher.

The good doctor wouldn't have fully understood his position until it was too late. A guy like him goes along for the ride, so taken with the thrill of it all that he can't see where it's taking him until it's too late. When he finally realized they owned him, he ran for cover, forgetting that the guys he was running to were on the other side now, because he put them there. In fact, Ward had no side, and no future. Not important enough to get a ticket to Moscow, but clued in enough to make him a liability to both sides. He was used up and was about to be discarded. Chumps like him always end up dead, one way or another.

I thought about ordering another drink, lit a second HB to help me decide. My throat still ached from Andy Johnson's Green Beret move, but I convinced myself that the smoke was soothing it.

"May I use a match from you?"

I looked up and was greeted by the widest, silliest grin I'd ever seen, beaming down at me from a tall and skinny bag of bones in a loose-fitting suit. Leaning over the table pointing at his Camel, he was young, early twenties, and more than a bit wobbly.

"Sure," I said, and lit him up.

"America," he winked, blowing smoke.

"Are my stars and stripes showing?"

"All Americans read this newspaper and stay at the Kempinski," he smiled proudly, indicating the hotel matchbook. He held out his hand. "Horst Schneider."

"Jack," I responded in kind. "Jack Teller."

"It's a pleasure to get your acquaintance," he said, holding the handshake a beat too long. Then, noting my amused smile: "Is it not correct?"

"Happy to *make* your acquaintance would be better, but you could just say, 'Glad to meet you.' It's less formal."

"Yes, of course. Much better. Glad to meet you. Jack, yes? May I sit with you?"

He did before I could answer, but I would've said yes anyway. He looked a little unstable and I was already starting to like him.

"We must have a schnapps together. Let me buy you one." He signaled the waitress and turned quickly back to me. "Have you seen Berlin before?"

"Not lately," I answered.

"It's quite unique. One of a kind, really. An island surrounded by no water. From which parts of America do you come? New York? Or is it Los Angeles?"

"Florida."

"Ah!" He closed his eyes, recited, "Miami Beach, Daytona Beach, Palm Beach . . ." then got stuck.

"Pompano Beach."

"Key Largo!" he exclaimed, ignoring me. "How could I forget! Humphrey Bogart is the war hero—by killing lots of Germans, of course—but wants only a quiet life now. In Key Largo lives the father of his good friend who was killed in the war, and the beautiful young wife, of course, who is Lauren Bacall, the wife of Bogie. Not in the film, but in life. Then comes the gangster, who is Edward G. Robinson, of course, Johnny Rocco, from Cuba, where is he—*verbannt* . . . ?"

"Exiled."

"Yes! . . . Ah, *sprechen sie deutsch!*"

"Just a little."

"Good—and here is our schnapps. Of course, Bogie kills the bad guy and wins the girl. To your good health." He raised his glass.

"Down the hatch."

"Very good! Down the hatch!" We knocked them back, chased with fresh Pilsner.

"Italy," I said.

"Sorry—?"

"Bogie's character in Key Largo. He was in Italy, so he didn't necessarily kill lots of Germans. He might have killed lots of Italians."

Horst wrinkled his forehead, then rocked his head back and forth a couple of times, acknowledging the possibility that maybe I was right. "It doesn't matter for the story. It matters only that Bogie has stopped believing in the fight against evil and must regain his principles in order to kill the gangsters."

"The reluctant hero." I stubbed out my cigarette, lit another almost immediately. Horst dug out another Camel.

"I've never been to America. Someday I will go." He leaned across the table and picked up the matchbook. "Where dreams come true."

"Don't get your hopes up too high."

"I know quite a lot about it already."

"Yeah, well, you can't believe everything you see in the movies."

He studied me while he sipped his beer, then took a drag off the Camel and blew smoke rings.

"You see, the problem in Germany is that everyone wants to be the same as their neighbor. It's a nation of conformists. Not like America, which is the opposite, a country of freethinkers."

"America has more than its share of followers."

"I don't mean as in the films, with cowboys and gangsters."

"Oh, there are plenty of cowboys and gangsters. But we were talking about freethinkers." A dissatisfied expression crept onto Horst's face, so I suggested we have another schnapps, which brightened him up right away.

It went on like that for a while, Horst reciting the plots to *Shane, High Noon, Rebel Without a Cause,* and *Little Caesar,* to name just a few, in an attempt to help me understand the true nature of the American spirit. I was patriotic enough, and still am, but I've seen the American spirit from top to bottom and nothing is pretty from every angle.

We ended up—I don't know how many hours later—the last two

drunken souls in the place, him trying to convince me that Bogart was the best actor of all time, me championing Henry Fonda, who I'd never given a second thought to until my fifth schnapps. The waitress, a big round lady with a mustache, whose initial good humor had evaporated with the crowd, told us they were about to close, so this would have to be the last round.

Horst saluted her with his drink. "You have served us well! Down the gate!"

"Hatch," I corrected him.

"Yes, hatch!" As he tossed the drink back a strange look came over him—a bizarre smile frozen onto his face. He stood up very slowly, eyes locked onto a nonexistent horizon, placed his hat on his head, bowed to the waitress, and said, "I bid you a good night." One step toward the door and the bottom fell out. He went down hard, breaking the fall with his face.

Feeling a bit light-headed myself, I reacted slowly, pushing away from the table and methodically walking around to where Horst had landed. I steadied myself with hands on my knees and took a good long look at him—he wasn't moving.

"Do you know where he lives?" I asked the waitress.

"Kirchstrasse," came from Horst, still glued to the floor.

I leaned over, asked him if he could move.

"I think not," he responded, one eye opening.

I asked the waitress to call a taxi, but she said none would come at this hour. (Not quick enough for her, anyway.) Behind the bar a big bald guy, who I presumed was her husband, was shaking his head while he wiped out beer glasses. I was on my own.

"Is it far to Kirchstrasse?"

Horst answered again. "Very near. I can show you."

I took a deep breath, pulled Horst up to a sitting position, and hoisted him onto my shoulder, facing backward. He didn't weigh much, but he was all over the place, arms and legs everywhere. The waitress was happy to hold the door open for us and I heard the lock as soon as we stepped onto the street. I regretted leaving her such a large tip.

"I thought you said it was close." After walking for twenty minutes, I was starting to sober up and Horst was getting a lot heavier.

"It is," his voice echoed off the empty pavement. He picked his head up to see where we were—or at least where we'd been, as he was facing backward. "*Very* close."

"Which way?" I turned in a circle so he could see each street in the intersection.

"To the left . . . My left, not yours."

"Are you sure this time?"

"Quite sure!"

I started walking, but the noises coming from above were sounding ominous.

"You all right up there?" I asked.

"I feel somewhat ill," Horst confessed.

"Maybe you should walk now."

"I'm afraid I don't feel my legs. If you are tired perhaps we should stop for a rest."

"If I stop now you sleep in the street."

"It's not far at all. Very close."

We eventually located Horst's building—a nondescript six-story walk-up, the kind that appeared all over Berlin after the war. I leaned against the cold concrete while Horst, still slung over my shoulder, rummaged around in his jacket pockets.

"Can you feel inside my pants, please, Jack?"

"Not on the first date, Horst."

"I seem to have lost my keys. Perhaps they are in the pocket of my pants."

I reluctantly groped Horst's pockets and came up empty. "When was the last time you saw them?" I asked.

"All the time I keep them in the pocket of my jacket. They must have fallen out while I have been on your back."

"Well, sleeping in the gutter isn't as bad as it sounds." I started to unload him.

"Wait—you can ring the bell."

It was something just short of 3 A.M., so whoever Horst was planning to roust was not going to be overly thankful to me for delivering him. But that was his problem. I was just being a good citizen.

"It's the fourth bell from the top," he said. "I think."

I counted four from the top. "Vogel?"

"No!" he sputtered. "Vogel will murder me if I wake him. Perhaps it's the fifth. Turn me around." I did a one-eighty and faced the street while Horst tried to make sense of the doorbells. "Yes, I was right, it's the fifth." He pressed the button, waited ten seconds, then pressed it again.

"I hope that's your mother up there," I remarked.

"Why?"

"Because I don't want to believe that you're dumb enough to do that to your wife."

After a minute I heard footsteps inside followed by a female's muffled voice: "Horst? . . . *Bist du das?*"

"Can you open the door please!" he bellowed.

"Shhh," she whispered as the door creaked open. *"Ihr wecken alle!"* I couldn't see her face, but she had a good voice—rich, like honey, but not too sweet. And positively not his mother's.

"I've lost my keys!" Horst whispered loudly.

She asked if he was injured: *"Bist du verletzt?"*

"I can't feel my legs," he smiled.

"Und wer ist das?"

"This is my good friend Jack Teller, of Pompano Beach, Florida. Turn around, Jack, so you can meet my sister."

She had pale blue eyes—soft and sympathetic, but wary—and silky blond hair, still mussed from her pillow. A white cotton nightshirt, open at the neck, was visible underneath a frayed light blue bathrobe that she pulled tighter when I looked at her. I noticed the long arc of her neck as she cocked her head sideways, trying to figure out if I was to be trusted. She pursed her lips, flattening the lovely curve of her mouth, and said, "Hmm." There was something serene and graceful about her—a quiet, soulful beauty.

"Her name is Hanna," Horst added.

"Sorry about this," I said. "Where would you like me to put your brother?"

"Come in," she answered, with an air of resignation, but also with unexpected warmth.

I navigated the entrance without knocking Horst's head too hard against the frame and found myself facing a flight of narrow stairs.

I looked to Hanna. "Up?"

"The top floor," she confirmed.

I nodded and she followed us up. Horst said, "I feel sick" in German and Hanna responded with, "It serves you right."

The place was small and pretty basic, but neat and clean. The furniture seemed to come from a secondhand shop and the faded wallpaper was peeling away at the edges. I dumped Horst on a worn-out sofa and he stayed where he landed, eyes shut tight. "You must be quite strong to carry me so far," he said.

"You said it was close."

He peeked up at me and smiled like a kid. "It's not *so* far."

Hanna reappeared from the kitchen with a glass of water and two Bayer. She sat Horst up, gave him the tablets, and let him fall back with a groan, pretty much unconscious.

"He's gonna have a tough morning," I said.

"It's morning already." She looked away quickly, moved toward the door.

"I guess it is," I answered.

"He'll have a tough afternoon, but he deserves it." I finally got a half smile. It was nice. "Thank you for seeing him home."

I hesitated at the door, waiting to see if there was anything else to say. There wasn't, so I just said good-bye.

I headed back to the hotel feeling surprisingly good. The sun was up by the time I saw my pillow, so I pulled the drapes and put the "Do Not Disturb" sign outside the door, figuring I would sleep all day.

THREE

The sound shot through my head like a bullet on fire. I came to in the dark and froze, trying to get my bearings. The goddamn buzzer wouldn't quit, scrambling my already decimated brain cells into a lump of confused pain in the center of my skull.

Then it went quiet.

The room started to take shape, but I knew if I tried to move my head it would explode. I managed to locate the bedside light, fumbled around for my watch until I realized it was still on my wrist. I squinted up at it, waited for my eyes to focus. A couple of minutes past five—I'd been asleep roughly an hour. I shut my eyes, went blank right away.

Then the buzzer again. What kind of asshole—!

"Open the goddamned door, Jack!"

An Ivy League asshole. What the hell did Powell want at this hour?

And more buzzing. He obviously wasn't going anywhere, so I scraped myself off the bed and slumped toward the door. Noticing that I was fully clothed, except for bare feet, I tried to recall my last moments of consciousness but drew a blank. It didn't matter, so I let it go.

Powell was standing in the hallway, groomed, pressed, and scrubbed behind the ears, briefcase neatly tucked under his arm. He took one look at me and said, "You look like shit."

"Yeah, well, I feel a lot worse," I croaked. His aftershave wafted across the threshold and made me want to puke. I left the door open and retreated back inside. He followed.

"Big night out?"

I dropped into an armchair and closed my eyes. I could feel him checking the room out.

"How the hell do you rate a place like this?"

"Friends in high places," I mumbled, eyes still shut.

"I'll keep it in mind."

He couldn't get over that they'd put a lowlife like me into a five-star suite at the Kempinski. Even the Berlin station chief didn't rate that kind of treatment. What Powell didn't know, of course—and what I sure as hell wasn't going to tell him—was that I had scammed the room. Nothing elaborate, just a quick call while I was on a layover in Frankfurt airport to the CIA travel office. I'd introduced myself to an overworked young lady as the concierge from the Kempinski, explained that there were no single rooms available for Mr. Teller after all, but the hotel would be happy to accommodate him in a suite, at no extra cost, if that could be authorized. The lady couldn't care less what kind of room I had, and as long as it stayed on budget, nobody else would care, either. So she agreed when I asked her to send a telex to the hotel confirming the conversation. "For our records," I explained in my German accent. When I got to the Kempinski, the reservations desk had the following message from Washington:

Confirm Mr. J. Teller, guest arriving 22 June, authorized for upgrade to suite at hotel cost. End.

There was some question about the phrase *at hotel cost,* but I assured them that it meant at normal hotel rates. If I'd learned anything in my agency days, it was how to sell a story. It doesn't matter how big the lie is—in fact, the bigger the better—as long as it's either: (a) what people want to hear; (b) what they dread to hear; or (c) what they couldn't care less about. In other words, pretty much anytime.

Powell pulled the drapes on the floor-to-ceiling window, flooding the room with unwelcome early-morning light. He took a gilded armchair from behind the Louis XIV writing desk, placed it in middle of the room, on the Persian carpet, sat down, crossed his legs, and stared silently, his lips forming a cocky grin that made him look empty-headed. I felt the crumpled pack of HBs in my pocket, but thought better of it. It wouldn't help the pain that was now migrating to my right temple.

Powell finally broke silence:

"Enjoying Berlin so far?"

"I'm gonna recommend it to all my friends."

"I didn't know you had any friends left."

"One or two," I said.

"In high places."

"That's right."

He paused, kept his eyes locked on me. Powell was the perfect Company man. Urbane, smart, arrogant, ambitious, and a cold-hearted bastard. He'd probably be director one day.

"Don't you want to know why I'm here?" he asked cutely.

"I'll take a wild guess. You got another letter drop from the man with the cane. He's offering another meeting and Washington wants me along even though you tried hard to convince them that I'm a fuckup."

Powell shrugged. "Nothing personal."

It never is with these guys. They'll wire a man's balls up and zap him until he passes out and it's okay, as long as it's not personal. I needed coffee, picked up the phone on the side table. "You want anything?"

"We don't have a lot of time," he said. I ordered the coffee anyway, along with poached eggs and orange juice just to piss him off.

"Why do you think our friend is so interested in you?"

"I'll ask him when I see him."

He stood up, looking like he had a bad case of heartburn, and replaced the chair behind the writing desk. The interview was over.

"What time are we on?" I asked.

"Seven," he said, checking his watch. "Just under two hours." I asked where, but he didn't want to say.

"What are you gonna do, take me there blindfolded?" I forced a laugh, even though I wasn't sure that it was out of the question.

"The market in Kreuzberg. And no fuckups this time."

"I didn't fuck up last time," I said. "I'm gonna get cleaned up. Answer the door if room service rings." He gave me a look as I left the room. Maybe it wasn't personal, but it sure looked like he hated my guts.

My brain started to turn over in the shower. Our mystery man hadn't wasted any time getting back in touch, so whatever he had in mind, he was eager. Maybe there was a time element. That he was a pro was no longer in doubt, not in my mind anyway. He might be out in the cold, looking for a way west. But if he was in trouble, why would he wait for me to fly all the way to Berlin from Florida? He wouldn't. And he wouldn't care if I was alone, either. In fact, he'd feel safer with a crowd. I was intrigued, even on one hour's sleep. I wanted the answer, but I knew that if this guy spotted a crowd—and I was sure he would—he'd be gone before we knew he was there. And there certainly wouldn't be a third chance.

Powell was getting anxious by the time I reappeared in the living room, shaved and dressed. It wasn't six o'clock yet, but we had to get me wired up again and pick up Johnson and Chase at the Berlin Operations Base (BOB) offices on the edge of the city.

I saw that the coffee had arrived.

"Can I see the letter?" I asked Powell as I poured a cup.

"What for?" He seemed genuinely surprised that I would ask.

"Just curious," I answered.

"Don't be."

"He'll know if I'm not alone," I said. "And if he walks this time, you really won't hear from him again."

"Then he'd better not walk. Let's go."

"Why don't we do it his way?"

"What are you talking about?"

"Leave the wire and the honor guard at home. He'll spot them. I'll make contact, see what it's all about, and report back to you." I knew there was no way in hell that Powell was ever going to agree to anything of the sort, but I thought I'd better give it a try before doing what I was thinking of doing.

"I'm not even going to respond to that." He was already at the door, waiting.

"It's your party," I said as I headed out.

"You'd be smart to remember that," he snarled.

I followed him into the hallway, but stopped short. "Damn," I said, reaching into my pocket. "The key . . . Must be in my other pants. I'll get it."

"For Christ's sake," Powell grumbled as I headed back into the bedroom.

I quickly gathered the clothes off the bed, where I'd thrown them before showering, went into the adjoining bathroom, threw them over a towel rack, then covered them with a wet towel. The crumpled pack of HBs fell on the floor and I grabbed them, thinking I might need one after all. I quickly ripped the receiver off the telephone that was next to the toilet and stuck it in my pocket before returning to the bedroom, where I bent over like I was looking under the bed and waited for Powell to appear, which he did pretty quickly.

"Can't find my pants," I shrugged.

"Forget it!" Powell barked. "Get another key from reception!"

"Hey, my wallet, my passport, everything's in there. I thought I left them on the bed before I went into the shower."

"Jesus H. Christ!" he spouted.

"Look in the bathroom, will you?" I said while making a show of pulling the sheets off the bed.

Powell shook his head and took the bait—he headed into the bathroom. I moved quickly across the bedroom, caught a glimpse of him pulling my trousers off the towel rack, grumbling, "Can't even keep track of his own fucking pants and I'm supposed to . . ."

I couldn't hear the rest because I pushed the door shut and locked it from the outside. There was a beat of silence while he registered what was happening, then all hell broke loose.

"WHAT THE FUCK DO YOU THINK YOU'RE DOING, TELLER?! OPEN THIS GODDAMN DOOR RIGHT NOW, YOU PIECE OF SHIT!"

"Sorry, Chief, but I think it'll work out better this way in the long run," I called through the door.

"You *are* fucking crazy," he said, with surprising composure.

"Could be," I agreed. "But look, your boys'll come looking for you in an hour or so. Why don't you get in the bath in the meantime? It's got jet sprays."

"You are in very deep shit, Teller. Very, *very* deep shit."

There was no doubt about that. I wondered why I was doing it. Why should I care what this East German bozo wanted with me? I could go home to Florida and . . . Well, maybe that was it. What the hell would I do when I got back to my beach? Sit there and wonder what the mystery man with a cane wanted to tell me, that's what. And if Powell and his crew were tagging along I'd never know. Anyway, I was used to deep shit. I seemed to feel pretty comfortable in the stuff.

"Come on, Jack." He sounded pitiful now. "Open the door and we'll forget all about it. Hey, we can work together on this, can't we?" Then I realized—I might be in deep shit, but Powell wasn't going to come out smelling too good, either. Not the kind of report you want to send to Washington. "Sorry, guys, I couldn't get your defector because I was locked in the bathroom" wouldn't go over too well. I started to feel better about the situation. . . .

"Don't worry, Chief," I called out as I exited. "If you're a good boy, I might bring you back a spy and we can be heroes together."

His screams faded away as I closed the bedroom door behind me. No one could possibly hear him through the solid oak outer door, which I double-locked. I noticed that the "Do Not Disturb" sign was still on display over the doorknob from the previous night.

Funny enough, as I left the hotel I felt pretty good, as if I'd had a full night's sleep.

The taxi dropped me outside the Markthalle a few minutes before seven. I glanced around the square, wondered who might be watching. It was a pretty safe bet that once Johnson and Chase realized something was up, they'd head for the Kempinski before coming here, which gave me at least an hour. If I didn't have contact by then, I'd go straight to Templehof, get the first flight out to anywhere. Goldilocks didn't fancy the idea of spending the afternoon with the Three Bears.

It was a bright, clear Sunday morning and the place was already lively with delivery trucks and vendors setting out their stalls. The market was housed in a huge nineteenth-century cast-iron building opening onto Marheinekeplatz in the Kreuzberg district. The area seemed to be a haven for a wide variety of fringe dwellers—beatniks, anarchists, pseudointellectuals, revolutionary squatters, that sort of thing. Most came from comfortable middle-class homes and were playing out some romantic notion of bohemian life at the same time they did penance for not being born poor and desperate. A majority of them would end up in the family business.

Heading toward the market, I passed a man washing down the sidewalk in front of his shop. Something about the biting scent of the soap he was using brought back a vague but unmistakable sense of the distant past. Funny how a smell can trigger a sudden remembrance of a place without connecting it to a specific moment or event. It was an unexpected, but somehow comforting sensation, in spite of the sting it delivered to my eyes and nose.

Not knowing where the meeting was supposed to take place, I figured I'd wander, make myself visible. He'd find me when he wanted to. After two years as a beach bum, it felt good to be back in the game. I hadn't forgotten all the reasons I'd gotten out, and it's not like I wanted back in, even if I could (which I couldn't), but I had to admit that I enjoyed the feeling of being out on a limb again.

It was almost exactly a decade earlier, in April 1953, that an encounter at a jazz club on Forty-seventh Street had brought me into the fold. I was doing time behind the bar of the Three Deuces, waiting for something better to come along, when Sam Clay strode in with an Ava Gardner look-alike on his arm. Sam was not your typical ladies' man—short and squat—but he had charisma and back then he even had hair, so he never went lonely. At the time I tagged him as just another overpaid, undersexed executive on a recreational night out and ignored him except to note that the maître d' led him to a prime table, front and center, on reserve for VIPs. The girl started going through Dom Pérignon like it was water, and after a while I noticed that she was getting more and more agitated about something, while Sam sat back, puffing on a Havana, staring straight ahead like she wasn't even there. The girl got louder and louder until eventually everyone in the place was looking over at them.

That went on for a while until, finally, Sam stood up slowly, faced the room, and said: "Ladies and gentlemen . . . As you can see, I'm in the company of a very beautiful woman here. . . . Top-drawer. Unfortunately, she's also a very large pain in the ass. Therefore, if any man here thinks she's such a knockout that she's worth a large pain in your ass, you have my blessing. I hope the two of you will be very happy together."

There was dead silence. After a beat Sam turned to his date and said, "Sorry, honey, no takers." The girl got up, gave him a voodoo look, and marched out the door without a word. The musicians took the cue and launched into "Bye, Bye, Baby" and Sam got a round of applause, at least from the male half of the room. You had to admire the guy for style, even though I thought it was a touch on the cruel side. I sent a thirty-year-old whiskey over to his table anyway, on the house, and he ended up at the bar, where he finished off the bottle and closed the place down with me.

I liked him from the start—a no-bullshit kind of guy who knew the world from the bottom up. I guess he liked me, too, because three days later I got my first late-night phone call from him, offering me a job with an oil consortium he was involved in. "The money's not great," he said, "but you'll see the world and I guarantee you it won't be boring." I told him I might be interested and that was enough for him—a ticket to Teheran arrived the next morning, with a note saying he'd meet me there in a few days to show me the ropes.

It didn't take long to figure out that I wasn't working for any oil company, and Sam confirmed the obvious when he finally turned up, two weeks late. He threw his feet up onto his desk, blew smoke at the ceiling fan, and poked the air with his cigar. "I want you to know two things, Jack," he began. "One, I don't invite just anybody onto my team. I invited you because I think you'll be a good player and I believe I can rely on you. Two, if you don't want to get involved, you can go back to New York right now. Because once you get involved, you don't get uninvolved. . . . Ever."

"You decided to come alone today."

I'd been aware for some time that I was being shadowed, so I'd headed for a dark corner of the market where an old lady was selling an unimpressive array of homegrown fruit. I knew that if he was ever gonna break the ice, this would be his moment.

"Blind dates are hard enough without a chaperon," I answered without turning around, continuing my inspection of little green apples.

"Your people are clumsy," he said flatly. "If they had come today, I would have given up on you."

I gave the old lady a coin for an apple then turned toward the voice. He was younger than I had expected. Mid- to late forties, although the grim expression etched into his face made him seem older. He studied me with a clinical detachment, blue gray eyes peering guardedly out from behind round wire-frame lenses. His features seemed to be set in stone, and I noticed that the cane had been discarded.

"I was about to give up on you," I said.

He nodded, pulled a pack of nonfilters out of his jacket, and offered me one. I turned it down, although I was tempted. He lit up, took a long drag.

"Shall we go somewhere private?" I suggested.

"We'll walk," he said coolly. "I prefer the open air to a stuffy room full of microphones."

We seemed to go forever, first through busy streets and then empty alleyways, without a word being said. He was chain-smoking foul-smelling cigarettes, and combined with sleep deprivation, it was getting to me. I needed something to eat, pulled the apple out of my pocket, and started munching on it. It was delicious and I wished I'd bought more.

We walked through a small park where a couple of young mothers supervised small children playing on swings.

"Do you know Berlin?" he began.

"I got here yesterday," I answered.

"It's quite a place. Perhaps you'll get a chance to become acquainted."

"I don't plan to stay long."

He nodded, tossed his butt aside, and opened a new pack. He offered me one again, and I remembered the HBs that were in my pocket. "I've got my own." I dug into the crumpled pack.

"Suit yourself." He had a deep, raspy voice, a result of the smokes, no doubt. His English was heavily accented but good. It was time to get down to business. I lit one of the HBs off his lighter and went fishing.

"You a diplomat?"

"In the Foreign Office I hold the position of Director for North American Political Studies. In fact, I'm an officer in the Ministry for State Security. I hold the rank of colonel."

It was a stunning piece of news that was said in such a matter-of-fact way that I had to replay it in my head. A colonel in the Ministry for State Security—the infamous STASI—doesn't generally blow his own cover, especially not to a member of the opposition, which is how I assumed he saw me. If he was planning to defect . . . I tried not to jump the gun. He was controlling the meeting.

"And how do I know that you are who you say you are?" I asked.

"I haven't said who I am. I've said what my job is."

"Would you like to tell me your name?"

A corner of the Colonel's mouth showed a trace of a grin. "No, I wouldn't care to do that."

"You know mine," I said, hoping it might draw him on the big question that was still bouncing around my head—why me?

"Then I have the advantage." He stopped, watched a young boy climb up the slide. "But only for the moment." He stubbed out another cigarette, but didn't light another this time. I had a feeling he was about to walk away.

"So . . . Here we are, alone at last." I sat down on a park bench, hoping he'd follow. "What do you wanna talk about?"

He remained standing, watching me and the surroundings at the same time. "I may decide to provide you with some information."

"That could be arranged—"

"I want to be clear," he interrupted, showing the first sign of emotion. "I have no intention of defecting or becoming a double agent."

"Fair enough," I said, wondering where he was heading then. I decided I had nothing to lose by being direct. "Why did you ask for me?"

The Colonel paused to think about his answer. "Does it matter?"

"I came a long way," I said. "It'd be nice to know why."

He nodded slowly, then offered his hand. "It was a pleasure to meet you."

"Is that it?" I blurted out as I stood up. I wished I hadn't pushed him, but it was too late to take it back.

"Thank you for coming," he added, pressing his palm into mine. "I hope you enjoy your stay in Berlin."

As he turned and walked briskly away I realized there was a small scrap of paper in my hand. I slipped it into my pocket and looked around. One of the young mothers had come over to help her son down from the slide, and I thought she turned away too quickly when I looked over at her. I looked back toward the Colonel, but he was gone.

For the first time I realized just how far out on a limb I was.

FOUR

It was midday by the time I found my way back to the Kempinski. I knew the odds were pretty good that I'd find one or more of the Three Bears waiting for me, but I needed a bed and I was low on options because after all that crap I'd given Powell about losing my wallet, I'd actually left it at the hotel. Anyway, I figured it was worth a shot. After all, they'd have to think I was pretty feebleminded to return to the scene of my crime.

I spotted Chase first, which was no big surprise. He was parked half a block up, in a government-issue Chrysler, pretending to be invisible behind a pair of "Made in Saigon" mirrored lenses. He was what he looked like—a dickhead—but he was a dangerous dickhead. One of the "new breed" that was turning up more and more often, changing the face and the rules of the game.

Oddly enough, evolutionary throwbacks like Chase were in fashion as a direct result of the space race. Forget all that stuff about the final frontier and mankind's heroic spirit of exploration. It might be true, but it don't pay the bills. And no one—not us or the Soviets—was sending those rockets up just to go where no man had gone before, no more than Ferdinand and Isabella bankrolled Columbus because they wanted to see if the earth might be round. The only thing the good king and queen believed in was a shitload of gold, and like them, the Company saw gold in them there rockets. Intelligence gold. By the late fifties, they were loading their spy-in-the-sky satellites onto NASA rockets as fast as Howard Hughes could build them (subsidizing the sideshow of blasting a few of America's finest into shallow orbit so they could say on TV what a beautiful view it was). By 1962, there were forty-five satellites buzzing around the planet and forty of them were loaded with Kodak cameras, and I don't mean Brownies.

Of course it didn't take long for the Langley Boys Club to realize what it all meant. Christ, if they could spot a golf ball on the green from eighteen miles up, why the hell did they need a caddie on the payroll? Human intelligence gathering was no longer the thing. Cloak was out, which left only the dagger. So guys like Chase started showing up. Contract cowboys who get a hard-on looking at pictures in *Soldier of Fortune.*

I doubled back and came at the hotel from the other side of Kurfürstendamm, West Berlin's main spending drag. A wide boulevard lined with expensive boutiques, it was a haven for well-heeled foreigners dropping the pounds, francs, and dollars that were the city's lifeblood. The sidewalk was busy enough at this hour, but feeling vulnerable out in the open, I ducked into a small florist's shop with a view onto the front of the hotel.

A woman in her early fifties—jet black hair, bright red suit, and lipstick, covered in gold jewelry—sat behind the counter, surrounded by floral arrangements. She looked over her reading glasses as I entered, gave me an anemic smile, then went back to her newspaper. I pretended to be interested in the window display while I checked out the scene across the street. It didn't take long to locate Powell sitting at an outside table at Café Kempinski, ordering a nice Bordeaux to go with lunch. Baby Bear wasn't in sight, but he wouldn't be far away. It occurred to me that if America's top spy in Berlin had nothing better to do than bag me, then either the world was in a lot better shape than it seemed or a lot worse. Either way, things didn't look overly promising for me.

The smart move would've been to slip out quietly and get lost, but the smart move has never been my specialty. I approached the lady in red, who seemed a bit annoyed that I was going to need her attention.

"Guten tag," I smiled, trying to make friends.

"How can I help you?"

Strictly business, so I dropped the charm.

"I'd like to send some flowers."

"Of course." She opened her order book. "Please give me the address."

I told her they were for a gentleman sitting across the street and pointed him out. She shrugged one of her eyebrows and asked, "How much would you like to spend?"

"The maximum." I smiled, looking her in the eye. She returned the smile, a bit wary, but definitely warmer this time.

"The maximum could be—"

"It doesn't matter." I waved her off impatiently, thinking she'd like that. "As long as it's very big and very showy. I want it noticed. Can you manage that?"

"Of course, yes, I can make something quite conspicuous." She was being very helpful now. "Would you like a card to go with it?"

"Yes, I would, with this message " I dictated as she wrote: " 'To Mama Bear . . . Don't stay mad. I'll be in touch soon. . . . Love, Goldilocks.' " I had to spell *Goldilocks* for her.

"Fine. I will deliver it myself," she promised.

"Thank you," I said. Then, before she could ask: "You can put it on my bill at the Kempinski. Mr. Teller, in Suite 702."

She looked dubious.

"It's all right," I assured her. "Here's my room key. . . . If it's a problem we can phone the concierge—"

"No, of course that won't be necessary, Mr. . . . ?"

"Teller," I reiterated. "Suite 702."

"I'm sure it will be no problem."

"Good," I smiled. She'd check it out, but the hotel would be more than happy to put it on the bill and add a hefty surcharge for the courtesy. The Company would be settling the bill, so it was no skin off my nose.

"Do you have a back exit?" I asked, explaining that it would spoil the moment if my friend saw me before the flowers arrived.

"Yes, of course," she went along. "There is a door through there." She indicated a velvet curtain. "But—"

I pulled the curtain back and heard the end of her sentence at the same moment I saw a mouth full of fangs sink into my calf.

"—watch out for Bruno" was what she said.

Bruno was a big boy, a Doberman with a bad attitude. His mistress was able to call him off before he did any serious damage, but he managed to get a piece of my pants and a chunk of flesh to go with it before unclamping his jaw. She explained that he was usually very friendly, that I'd taken him by surprise. Meaning, I guess, that it was my fault. She asked if I wanted a doctor and reluctantly offered to pay for my trousers, but Bruno looked a little too pleased with himself to worry about any of that. I thought I should get out before he decided on a second course.

The door opened onto a narrow alleyway. I leaned against a garbage can, rolled my pant leg up, and checked my wound. The beast had put two neat holes in my lower leg, like a fucking vampire dog. It hurt like hell, too. I'd have to get it cleaned up, but first I had to figure out what my next move was.

It was 12:40. The Colonel's note, which I'd burned as soon as I'd looked at it, had given me the time and place for our second meeting:

Berlinerstr. 347, 9 pm

Eight hours and twenty minutes to kill with no food, no money, no sleep, and my goddamned leg starting to throb like a son of a bitch. What the hell was I doing here, anyway? I was supposed to be floating on the smooth coral sea with my hook in the water.

Horst looked worse than I felt, which was pretty damned bad. His face was like chalk, his hair was standing on end, and he could hardly open his bloodshot eyes. He squinted out from behind the door and pulled his sister's bathrobe tighter around his waist. It took a minute, but he finally recognized me. I thought he'd be more surprised.

"My goodness," he said in a surprisingly chirpy way. "What is the time?"

"About two."

"I see you've wakened earlier than me," he grinned. "Come in. . . . Please."

He led the way up to the apartment. "I feel as though my head has a hammer on the inside of it," he said merrily. "We have really tied one up last night."

"We sure did," I agreed.

He didn't even ask why I was there, just explained that his sister was at work and excused himself. "I must have a bath. Please sit down, feel yourself at home. . . . Would you like something to drink?"

"As long as it's not schnapps," I answered.

"Not even I would like one of these now," he winced. He got me a Coke and disappeared into the bathroom.

I was so beat I could hardly think anymore. The sofa was tempting, but I knew if I lay down that would be the end. There was a telephone across the room and I thought it might be an idea to touch base with Powell. I didn't want him to put out a shoot-to-kill order, if he hadn't already done so, that is. After that, I'd have to deal with the leg, which was starting to swell up.

The operator connected me to BOB's main number and I finally got through to Powell's office. His secretary put him on the line right away.

"Can you imagine how deep in the shit you are, Teller? I'll tell you. It's creeping up around your ears and you're about to suffocate in it."

"Did you like the flowers?" I asked, forming a picture of that vein in his temple starting to quiver.

"Where the hell are you?"

"I had a nice meeting with our friend." Silence while he thought about it.

"You had contact?"

"Yeah, we spent the whole morning together. . . . And guess what. He's a big fish."

"How big?"

"Somewhere between a tuna and a great white."

"What?"

"Big enough that Washington is gonna be very proud of you."

"You'd better come in, Jack. No shitting, this isn't fun and games anymore."

"Remind me which part *was* fun and games."

"You know it's not just me anymore, Jack," he purred. "You're fucking with everything now, and you know how that goes. They'll crucify you."

"Yeah, and you'll be happy to provide the nails."

"If you get your ass in here, I can help."

"I can't."

"Can't or won't?"

"You choose." I was too tired for word games.

He sighed into the phone, then went silent again. I waited.

"Who is he?"

"I didn't get a name."

"What did he want?"

"I can't say yet."

"What do you mean, you can't say?! Who the fuck do you think you're talking to!"

"I need another day."

"You can't have another day! You can't have another fucking minute!" He tried to get hold of himself. "Look, just come in for a debriefing. . . . If you're worried about this morning, it's forgotten. Just come in and let's figure this out together."

"When does Sam get in?" I asked.

"Tomorrow morning. He's flying in early, but—"

"I'll see you then." I replaced the receiver before he could say anything else. Clearly the call hadn't done much to ease the situation, but at least I could say I'd checked in.

Horst was standing on the other side of the room rubbing his head with a towel. "I hope you don't mind," I said, pointing to the phone.

"Not at all," he answered. I wondered how long he'd been standing there.

"Your leg is bleeding," he added nonchalantly.

I told him about Bruno, leaving out the details, and he led me to the kitchen, made me sit while he rummaged through various cabinets and drawers. "I really have no idea where Hanna puts things," he apologized. Finally pulling a wooden box out from behind some pots and pans, he opened it and found a bottle of iodine.

"Perhaps you should remove your trousers," he suggested.

"I'll just roll the leg up if you don't mind," I replied.

"I don't wish to ruin them."

"I think they're pretty well shot already, Horst," I pointed out, poking my finger through one of the holes that Bruno's fangs had created.

"It can be repaired," he assured me.

It wasn't worth arguing, so I took my pants off and sat back down.

"You'd better prepare yourself," he said. "I think it must hurt a little bit."

I'm not sure if you can ever really prepare yourself for someone pouring a corrosive poison directly onto an open wound, but I sure as hell hadn't. I screamed like a banshee, flew out of my chair, and hopped around the room peppering the air with arbitrary obscenities that I won't try to re-create.

"My goodness," was Horst's reaction.

"What the hell are you doing?" I turned on him, grabbed the bottle of iodine out of his hand. "You don't just pour it on! You use some of that cotton and gently DAB it on!"

He shrugged and pouted. "Perhaps it's a good idea that you get an injection for rabies. . . ."

"It's a terrible idea, Horst! The worst fucking idea I've heard in a very long time! Jesus Christ, do you know how painful this is?!" It was stinging like a bastard.

"Perhaps you've changed your mind and want that schnapps now."

I didn't want a schnapps or anything else. I just wanted to lie down and shut my eyes. He started unwinding a roll of bandages.

"What are you doing?"

"It's best to wrap your wound."

"Forget it."

"It won't hurt."

"You're goddamn right it won't because you're not coming anywhere near it," I said, being as clear as I could.

"I think it's best—"

"It's best to leave it open to the air."

Her voice took us both by surprise. We swung around simultaneously and saw Hanna standing in the kitchen door frame, holding two paper bags full of groceries. She wore a thin cloth coat and a slightly faded blue dress with a creamy floral pattern and pale buttons up the front. A silk kerchief was tied loosely around her neck and her hair was pulled back behind her ear on one side while the other side fell softly across her cheek. She tilted her head and looked across at me.

"Hello again," she smiled, her lips pursed in a gentle smirk. I guess I was a sight all right, standing there pantless with red dye running down my leg.

"Hello," I smiled back.

"Jack has been attacked by a vicious dog," Horst explained.

"Oh, dear," she sighed in mock horror, placing the bags on the counter, then removing her coat. "How lucky then that you've found my brother. As you can see, he is a highly trained professional in these medical matters."

"She takes the piss from me all the time," Horst moaned. "I really don't deserve it."

"What do you deserve?" she scoffed.

He stepped forward and kissed her forehead, then turned to me. "You see, the problem is that my sister believes she is my mother."

"The problem is that my brother is twenty-eight years old and still needs a mother."

"Then you'll cook a meal for us?" he grinned.

"I'm not sure you deserve *that,*" she muttered as she started putting groceries away.

"I suppose I should get dressed," Horst allowed.

"Why not? The workday's almost over."

Horst winked at me and disappeared.

I grabbed my pants, started to pull them on, being as nonchalant about it as I could, which wasn't very. She was arranging soup cans, trying not to notice.

"Leave them off," she said, without looking over.

"Excuse me?"

"I'll sew them for you."

"You don't have to do that."

"I know."

Then she gave me a long, hard look.

"What brings you to Berlin?"

"Business."

"Ah." She went back to the cans. She must have had a very complicated system for organizing them because she kept shuffling them around the cabinet, stepping back, then making one last adjustment that apparently upset the whole arrangement, causing her to start all over again. She was a woman you wouldn't give a second glance on the street. Attractive enough, but not a head turner. There was something about her, though, something I couldn't really put my finger on. Compassion, but without weakness, is the best I can do.

"He's a good kid," I said, just to break the silence.

"He's not really a kid," she smiled. "He just acts like one."

"There are worse things to act like."

She closed the cupboard door and looked at me again. She had this way of looking directly at you that was a little disquieting. Like she was trying to get behind your eyes. Then she'd look away, do something like fold the grocery bags and place them in a drawer.

"My brother is fascinated with your country."

"I noticed that."

"He thinks everything about America must be good."

"He's never been there," I shrugged.

She nodded her agreement, then said, "You seem very American."

"What's 'very American'?"

"You are," she laughed.

"Is that a bad thing?"

"Horst doesn't seem to think so."

"What do you think?"

She hesitated, looked at me again in that intense way. "I think you look very tired."

We weren't close but we were looking directly into each other's eyes. Maybe it wasn't so tough to see that I was exhausted, but she'd hit something else, too. It wasn't just lack of sleep she was talking about.

"You're right," I said. "I am tired."

"Then you must have a nap!" Horst boomed out as he entered the room. "The sofa is quite comfortable, I sleep there every night."

"He can sleep in my bed," Hanna said, her eyes reaching across the room, sending me an unambiguous message. "I'll get it ready for you."

She skittered past Horst and he gave me a look of undisguised astonishment. "This is not like my sister," he said.

Normally, I would've lay there in her bed thinking about her, but I fell asleep the moment I hit the fragrant, soft pillow.

"Lieutenant! . . ." The voice called to me from a million miles away. "Can you hear me, Lieutenant?" it shouted. I couldn't answer, lost in the depths, unable to find my way to the surface, not even sure I wanted to. "Come on, Lieutenant! You have to open your eyes!" I realized he was right. I would have to try. . . .

I came to in the darkness, only half-awake, and realized I'd had the dream again. Damn. I hated that dream. It hadn't been around for ages, why was it showing up now? I replayed it in my head, hoping if I moved it into consciousness, it would leave my subconscious alone. It was the same every time.

I'm separated from my unit, lost and cold, wandering through the snowy woods. The enemy's all around us, confusion everywhere. Suddenly I find myself standing in front of a house—a three-story brick house with a gabled roof. It doesn't belong in the middle of the Belgian forest, but there it is, standing in a clearing, untouched by the devastation that's all around it. It seems impossible. I approach, wondering if it's a trap, if the enemy put it there to lure me inside. But as I get closer I realize—I know this building. I've been inside it many times, know every room and every item in the rooms. But I can't figure out how I know it. Have I been here before? I move to the front entrance, try to open the door, but it's locked. I'm about to shoot the dead bolt off when I realize I must have the key. I find it in my jacket pocket, slip it into the lock, and push the door open. But when I step inside I see that the building's facade was some kind of illusion. Inside, the walls are falling down, the roof has caved in, the windows are shot out. And then I see them. The house is full of bodies—the bodies of every one of the guys I'd lost since Normandy, all seventeen of them, each one lying exactly in the position that I'd last seen him in. I need to bury them, I think, but before I can move, something hits me from behind. . . . A sledgehammer coming down on my neck, then a burning agony shooting down my back. My legs go and I hit the ground. Then there's darkness for a while and the voice comes in.

"Lieutenant! . . . Can you hear me, Lieutenant?!"

And that's when I wake up.

It wouldn't take Sigmund Freud to figure it out, but I wasn't interested in that. I just wanted the damn thing to quit.

Then it hit me—what the hell time was it! I leapt off the bed and found a wall switch. A warm, dim light came on over Hanna's bed. My watch confirmed what I already knew—9:22. Fuck me! I was supposed to meet the Colonel at nine!

Horst was lying on the sofa watching a news report about Kennedy's arrival in Bonn. "Ah! The dead have risen!" he announced as I entered. I could hear Hanna moving around in the kitchen and saw my pants neatly folded on a side table. I quickly pulled them on and stepped into my shoes.

Horst hauled himself up and turned the volume down on the set. "You've slept well," he grinned, checking his watch. "More than six hours. And we have waited dinner for you," he chided.

"I'm sorry, Horst, but I'm late for a very important meeting." I asked where I could find a taxi and was halfway out the door before Hanna came into the room. But there was no time to say anything.

As the taxi pulled up I realized that I was still broke. The driver didn't look like the kind of guy I could intimidate and the last thing I needed was a loud argument with a fat man, so I gave him my four-hundred-dollar Rolex to cover the six-dollar fare. He was happy enough with that.

It was dark, almost pitch-black after the car drove off. The nearest working streetlight was a block away and I could barely make out the silhouette of the gloomy structure that was supposed to be our meeting place. If anyone was in there, it sure as hell wasn't obvious.

I found an old iron gate that took me up an overgrown path toward the front of the building. Once I got closer I could see the place was an even worse mess than it looked from the road. A large town house that had probably been deserted since the end of the war; the windows were broken, the brickwork was crumbling, and it didn't look like there was much left of the roof. In better days it could've passed for the Addams Family home, including a medieval-style turret that rose out of the middle of the property.

A short flight of steps led to a gabled porch dominated by a massive weather-beaten hardwood door. I gave it a push and it moved, but not much. When I put my shoulder to it I was able to slip inside.

Even with the door ajar I couldn't make out my own two feet. I could feel that the floor was covered with debris, probably pieces of plaster from the ceiling and walls, some broken roof tiles, who knows what else. Glass crunched under my feet when I took a few steps into the void. The place was goddamned eerie and I had no intention of going on a blind sightseeing tour, so I stayed put. If the Colonel was still there he'd know where to find me.

I waited. Maybe ten minutes, probably not that long. There was a scratching sound a few feet in front of me. Rats. More than one. And the stench was getting to me.

"DID SOMEBODY ORDER A PIZZA . . . ?!"

My voice bounced off the walls, carried up through the building, and came back to me. I must've been standing in a huge entrance hall. I waited another minute. Nothing but me and the rats. The Colonel was long gone and Powell was going to nail my ass to the wall.

"FUCK YOU, THEN, I'M GOING HOME!"

And I meant all the way home, to my beach house, where I'd pack my fishhooks and my typewriter, get in my boat, and get really lost this time. Maybe the Gulf Coast. Or Mexico. As long as it was warm and there were no spooks, I didn't give a damn.

I was about to take my first step in that direction when I heard a Zippo flip open a few feet in front of me, followed by a spark and a flame illuminating his face. The fire went out, leaving the Colonel's features bathed in the red glow of cigarette ash.

"How long have you been standing there?" I asked.

"Since you came in."

"I mistook you for a rat."

He smiled stiffly and turned a small flashlight on the floor. We were standing in the middle of a rat convention. Hundreds of them. They didn't seem to worry about us, but why would they?

"You're among friends," I said.

"Lucky for you I'm still here."

"Yeah, I'm catching all the breaks." He turned the flashlight off so all I could see was the lit end of his cigarette moving around. "Very dramatic," I noted. "Did you go to the Boris Karloff School of Espionage?"

He brushed by me and pushed the big door shut. "How did you get here?"

"Three taxis, four trains, and a couple of mules," I replied. He didn't think it was funny, and I guess it wasn't. "Nobody followed me," I assured him.

"Why were you late? Did you have trouble?"

"I overslept." I could feel him looking at me from behind, through the darkness, like he had bat eyes. "Look," I insisted. "I was exhausted and I overslept. Everything's fine." I turned to face him, but all I got was a shadow.

He was silent for a moment while he took a long draw of smoke, making up, I guess, for the nicotine-free minutes he had endured while standing across from me in the dark, making some kind of pointless point. He finally threw the butt on the floor, immediately lit another.

"What I have to tell you is extremely sensitive," he rasped. "It must not be compromised."

"If you don't want it to be compromised, don't tell me."

"I'd like to believe I can trust you," he said almost sincerely. Up until now he hadn't treated me like a jerk. If I didn't set him straight, it would only get worse.

"Let's skip the bullshit, Colonel," I said sharply. "If you really are a colonel, that is."

Hostile silence, so I kept going.

"I'm sorry to be blunt, but if you think there's any way you can trust me, then you're not what you claim to be. Now I've got some fairly heavy people very pissed off with me because, so far anyway, I've played this thing by your rules. And the only way I get out of it with my head still attached to the rest of me is for you to give me something so juicy that these guys can't carve me up and ship me off to the four corners of the earth, which is what they really want to do. But you know all that, you set it up that way, so you must also know there's no way in hell I'm not going to use what you give me to save my ass. . . . And that's why I say let's skip the bullshit."

He grunted, possibly a STASI version of a laugh. Then he took a deep breath and exhaled. A sigh almost.

"The information was uncovered quite by accident, in the course of our normal intelligence activities," he began. "However, we are unable to take appropriate action, which is why you have been called upon. Unfortunately, you won't have much time to act."

"Act? I don't think you have the right idea about me, Colonel. I don't act."

"Perhaps you will feel compelled to when you hear what I have to say."

"I'm all ears," I said.

He took a moment, then spit it out without any frills.

"There's a plan to assassinate your president."

Of all the crazy, unlikely stories I had prepared myself to hear, this sure wasn't one of them. It was *too* crazy. I mean, there were always assassination threats, the Secret Service dealt with them all day long, but here was a fucking colonel in the goddamned East German secret police threatening the president. . . . Or was he threatening? What the hell *was* he doing?

"Tell me about it," I managed.

"It's planned to take place here, in Berlin."

I waited for more, but it didn't come. I laughed reflexively, even though I knew he wasn't joking. "Come on, Colonel," I said. "Even you guys aren't that crazy."

"It's not our operation," he answered coolly.

"Who then?"

"You'll have to find out."

He didn't move, just kept looking at me through the darkness and puffing on his weed.

"That's it?" I asked incredulously. "Somebody has a plan to knock off the president of the United States while he's in Berlin. You have no other information—no clues, no leads, no hints—nothing except there's a plan out here, somewhere."

"That's correct," he replied.

I was feeling claustrophobic, had to get some air. I turned to where I thought the door was, but couldn't find it. "Give me some fucking light," I demanded, and he obliged, shining the flashlight into my eyes.

"I don't have to tell you what the consequences might be should this happen. If you choose to leave now, there's nothing more I can do." He moved the light from my face onto the door. "There is your exit," he said.

I pulled the door open and stepped onto the porch. I knew I wasn't going anywhere and the Colonel probably did, too. After a couple of minutes, he stepped out and offered me one of his cigarettes. I accepted. It seemed bright outside after the blackness on the other side.

"Look, if you want me to buy this, you're going to have to give me more." I could see his face now, but it wasn't going to reveal anything.

"I don't have more to give."

"How did you come across it?"

"As I said, in the course of our normal intelligence activities . . ."

"Come on, Colonel. . . ."

He shrugged, like he agreed but could do nothing about it.

"Is it KGB?"

"No," he said quickly.

"There are a hundred threats a week on the president's life," I said. "Thanks for the heads-up, but it's not exactly gonna make headlines." The cigarette tasted worse than it smelled, but I smoked it anyway.

The Colonel looked up into the sky, searching as if there was something to see. "This threat comes from inside your government," he said softly.

"What . . . ?"

"They'll try to make it look like it was our side. . . . But it will be your side." He looked at me, ready to gauge my reaction. I drew a breath, took in too much smoke, and choked.

"For Christ's sake," I coughed. "You expect me to believe—"

"No," he interrupted. "I don't expect you to believe. I expect you to find out." I didn't know what to say to that, so I said nothing. He tossed his cigarette onto the ground, crushed it with his foot, and walked away, leaving me standing speechless, alone in the dark.

FIVE

I met John F. Kennedy once, the result of another one of Sam Clay's surprise phone calls. I was spending Christmas Day of 1962 laid out on my backyard lounger, soaking up sun and tequila, trying to ignore the Season of Joy (it'd been a long time since I believed in Santa Claus), when the telephone started ringing and wouldn't quit. I was able to ignore it for a while, but curiosity finally got the better of me and I staggered inside.

"I hope you're having as shit of a day as I am," Sam's voice cheerfully greeted me.

I told him I was having the time of my life and he spent a few minutes grumbling about his ex-wife, how he had to spend every Christmas at her place in order to keep peace with the kids and grandkids. "It's a goddamned misery," he concluded. "I'd rather spend the holiday with Attila the Hun."

"You've got the same gripe every year," I reminded him.

"I get the same shit every year."

"So stop going."

"What the hell else am I supposed to do on Christmas?" he bristled.

"Come down here, we'll go fishing."

"Yeah, maybe next year," he brushed me off. "Anyway, that's kind of why I'm calling. I'm headed down your way in a couple of days." I didn't have to ask why because it'd been all over the papers for a week.

"Should be quite a show," I said.

"Wanna come along?"

"Me?"

"That's who I'm talking to, isn't it?" He took a sip of something on the rocks, probably good scotch, and waited for my answer.

Going down there hadn't even crossed my mind, probably because I didn't think there was a snowball's chance in hell that I'd be invited. There were plenty of reasons to stay away, that's for sure, but my calendar wasn't exactly jammed with social engagements. It would get me out of my T-shirt and cutoffs, anyway.

"Make up your mind, Jack, because I've got a very large turkey waiting for me in the other room."

"Right. Give my regards to the old girl," I quipped, getting a modest chuckle out of Sam. I told him I wouldn't miss it for the world and we arranged to meet at the stadium and have a drink together afterward. Then Sam went off to carve up his bird.

The event was a kind of welcome-home party for Brigade 2506, the 1,189 Cubans who'd spent the last twenty months in a Havana prison thanks to the Bay of Pigs fiasco. The Bay of Pigs was nothing more than an obscure beach on the deserted south coast of Cuba until it became world famous in April 1961 as the site of the CIA's first public humiliation. In an attempt to overthrow the Cuban government without obvious U.S. involvement, the agency had trained and supplied 1,400 anti-Castro exiles to hit the beach, move inland, and liberate the country. The beach was as far as they got. The brigade was cut to shreds. A few managed to swim off the island, where they were picked up by U.S. Navy vessels, but most weren't that lucky. One hundred and fourteen were killed, the rest were captured.

Kennedy managed, after eighteen months, to buy their freedom with $53 million in food, medicine, farm equipment, and other goodies prohibited by the new trade embargo. A State Department spokesman described it as "a goodwill gesture to the people of Cuba" and Castro called it "war reparations." If anybody had asked me I'd have said it was a good old-fashioned shakedown, but nobody asked.

Anyway, Kennedy had invited all the Cubans in Miami to the Orange Bowl one afternoon a few days after Christmas so he could take credit and try to make peace. You had to give him points for guts because he wouldn't be facing a particularly affectionate crowd down there—the Cuban exile community had expected to have Havana's roulette wheels spinning again by now and the fact that Castro was still taunting them with four-hour speeches didn't really endear the young president to them. And it was a fair bet that the returning vets themselves had less than warm and fuzzy feelings for him. In their minds the U.S. government—and the White House in particular—had pretty thoroughly fucked them over.

In truth, it was hard to disagree with them. Of course, "truth" when it came to Cuba was like light through a prism—it depended entirely on your angle, and there were a hell of lot of angles in that island gem. But I understood more than most why the Cubans felt betrayed. I was there when they were handed "The Big Lie."

I'd been pretty heavily involved in the Cuba Project during the buildup to the invasion, running a disinformation campaign and launching special ops out of Happy Valley, the World War II airfield on the coast of Nicaragua that was being used as the main staging area. But it wasn't until the second week of April 1961—a few days before the attack was scheduled—that I got my first look at the Cubans who were going to hit the beach. They were flown in from Guatemala, where they'd spent the last eighteen months in the jungle, being trained by agency-run Green Berets. As I watched them file off the C-54 transport planes I thought they looked young, intense, and, it seemed to me, pretty anxious. Of course, they had reason to be. Castro had a whole army waiting for them.

The commanding officer at Happy Valley was a Marine colonel named Robert "Rip" Harkin, a hulking six-foot-four-inch former All-American quarterback from Oklahoma who'd been one of the soldiers to plant the original Stars and Stripes at Iwo Jima, two days before it was re-created for the famous photo. But he was just on loan from the Pentagon. The guy actually running the show was Henry E. Fisher.

Henry was credited with conceiving the plan that overthrew the Guatemalan government in 1953. Not that it was much of a plan—a couple of dozen lightly armed farm boys were sent to shoot up a couple of villages while Henry and his crew broadcast radio reports that an army of thousands was on its way to the capital. They buzzed the presidential palace a couple of times with an unarmed warplane and the entire government fled the country. It gave Henry a lot of credibility at Langley, and after a stint as chief of station in Uruguay, he was made top field agent in the Cuba Task Force.

A tall, lanky New Englander in his early forties, he had a receding hairline, a bulbous nose, thin lips that seemed incapable of an honest smile, and a serious disposition that you could mistake for dignity if you didn't know better. He was known as a clever, resourceful operative, but I had my doubts. Castro wasn't gonna surrender based on radio reports.

On the day before the landing, Colonel Harkin summoned the brigade commanders to a final briefing. I went along uninvited and took a place at the front table beside Henry. The Cubans sat facing us in several rows of vintage school desks, eyes glued to Harkin, who stood at a blackboard running down the logistics of the invasion. He went into great detail about landings, communication, resupply, everything they needed to hear. Then, after about thirty minutes, he stopped, shifted gears, and told them what they *wanted* to hear.

"Let me add this final note," he began, narrowing his eyes and honing in on the audience. "I've seen more than a few fighting forces in my time and I can tell you in all honesty that I have never seen a group of soldiers more motivated, better trained, or more vigorous than the men you will lead onto Cuban soil at dawn. You are well organized, well equipped, and well disciplined. And you are ready for battle." He let that sink in for a moment, taking time to look every one of the young officers in the eye before hitting them with the news they'd been waiting for.

"And so are we," he said solemnly.

The room went dead quiet, waiting for more. After a dramatic pause, Harkin gave it to them, playing it for all it was worth.

"I can report to you that at this hour there is an armada of U.S. Navy destroyers sitting twenty miles off the Cuban coast. On board those ships is a contingent of United States Marines. . . . And let me assure you that they are ready and eager to follow you into battle."

I couldn't believe what I was hearing! And he wasn't finished yet!

"Once you've held that beachhead for seventy-two hours," he continued, "I promise you that we will be beside you for the next step." He straightened his back, furrowed his brow, and came to the emotional climax.

"Gentlemen . . . God and the United States of America are with you all the way. What more could you ask for? . . . I wish you every success in your mission." I thought he was going to start crying. Instead, he turned and walked out of the room to a spontaneous round of heartfelt applause.

I was stunned. There was no way in hell those Marines were going anywhere near Cuba. No way! Kennedy, the joint chiefs, the national security adviser, they'd all made that abundantly clear at every turn. And Harkin's own telex to the White House the day before had confirmed it: *The Brigade Officers do not expect help from the U.S. Armed Forces,* it had said. So what the hell was this?!

I turned to Fisher, who was clapping his hands and nodding his head enthusiastically. "Why did he say that?" I whispered.

"Say what?"

"That we're gonna send in the Marines."

"I didn't hear that, Jack." He stopped clapping, turned toward me. "And neither did you." He stood up and starting shaking hands with the euphoric Cubans and I had no choice but to do the same. They crowded around, slapping us on the back and saying things like "God bless America" and "Kennedy is a man who means business." Harkin had told them the one thing they needed to hear—the one thing that would ensure they'd have no second thoughts about stepping onto that beach. It was a brutal deception.

Don't get me wrong. I'd been involved in plenty of deceitful behavior in my time with the Company—it was part of the game and I'd never been squeamish about it. But these men weren't playing in our game; at least they didn't think they were. They were soldiers, men we'd recruited, trained, and equipped to fight a battle that we couldn't be seen to be fighting. Sure, it was their cause, too, but if they were willing to put their lives on the line, they should know what the deal was. At least that's what was going through my mind while the Cubans slapped us on the back and told us how wonderful we were.

Fisher evaded me for the rest of the night, so at around midnight, after a few rum and Cokes, I barged into his quarters. He was spread out on his cot in a T-shirt and Jockey shorts, reading a dog-eared copy of *Peyton Place.*

"Don't bother knocking," he said, laying the book facedown on the bed.

"If I didn't know better, Henry, I'd think you've been avoiding me." I invited myself in.

"It's kind of late, Jack. . . ."

"Yeah, and I can see you're busy," I said, picking up the paperback and leafing through it. "Seen the movie?"

"About three years ago," he moaned, snatching it back.

"I guess I'm a little behind the times." I smiled and straddled a desk chair across from the bed. I think I just stared at him for a minute or two.

"What's on you mind?" he asked painfully.

"I was wondering why we told those men that the cavalry's gonna ride in and save the day when we know it ain't gonna happen."

"Like I told you before, it was never said."

"Henry," I scolded him, "You and I both know there's no fucking way Kennedy's gonna send in those Marines."

"Look, Jack." He swung his long legs around and sat on the edge of the cot. "You're not in the loop on this one, so just forget about it."

"What loop?"

"Really. Forget it."

"What happens when the Cubans realize they've been set up?" I persisted.

"What makes you think they're being set up?" He pulled himself up and headed for the john.

"The White House dispatch yesterday said—"

"I know what the dispatch said," he said calmly, taking aim and releasing. "I wrote the fucking thing."

"It says the brigade doesn't expect help from U.S. forces."

"That was true yesterday."

"You gonna send a new dispatch?"

"I can't get into this with you." He flushed.

"Are we lying to the president of the United States?"

He gave me a long hard look and shook his head. "I hope you're not gonna cause trouble, Jack."

He stood there waiting for me to reassure him, but I just stared back at him. I guess he took my silence to mean that I might cause trouble, although I'm not sure what I would've done. Anyway, he must've figured I'd be less of a risk if I was in on it. He adjusted his Jockey shorts and poured himself a glass of water.

"You didn't hear what you're about to hear. . . . Right?"

I nodded and he went on.

"We're not just blowing smoke up the Cubans' ass. We have reason to believe that the president will change his mind and send in the troops . . . once the situation on the ground becomes clear."

"What situation?" I asked.

"I shouldn't be telling you this," he stalled.

"What situation?" I repeated.

"We expect an attack on Guantánamo." He gulped the water, watched my reaction though the bottom of the glass. He was talking about Guantánamo Bay, the U.S. naval base located on the southeastern tip of Cuba. It had been in American hands for sixty years, since Teddy Roosevelt leased the land from the government of the day.

"Castro isn't stupid enough to attack Guantánamo—" I stopped short as the realization hit me. "Castro isn't going to attack, is he?"

Something that almost passed for a smile started to form on Fisher's lips. "Not unless he's suicidal."

"We are," I completed the thought, hoping Fisher would laugh in my face. He didn't.

"Not us, per se." He dropped onto the bed and stretched out, arms crossed behind his head. He was eager to talk now, so I let him.

"We've been training a group of Cubans up in Louisiana for about six months. Deep-cover stuff. They're in the Gulf now, headed for Cuba southeast, and Fidel himself would take them for Cuban army regulars, down to the buckles on their boots. All we do is point 'em at Guantánamo twelve hours after the brigade hits the beach, Kennedy gets word that Castro's forces have attacked the base, and presto chango, here come the Marines. Neat idea, huh?"

Neat was an understatement. It was inspired. Also dangerous, misguided, insane, and probably treasonous.

"What about casualties?" I asked, trying to stay cool.

"Sometimes you have to look at the big picture," he shrugged.

I didn't know what to say, so I let out a low whistle, which made Fisher a bit uneasy.

"This doesn't leave the room, Jack. We are clear on that, aren't we?" I ignored him, absentmindedly went to the window, and peeked through one of the wooden slats at the pitch-black world outside. "I hope you're not gonna make me sorry I brought you in on this," he said.

"Well . . ." I took a deep breath, trying to keep the lid on, then turned to face him. "I do think it's kind of problematic."

"I'm sorry you feel that way," he said slowly. "I really am, but, well, it's tough shit really. The ship has sailed, literally."

"Let me be sure I've got it straight. You've ordered an attack on an American base . . . ?"

"That's right," he said flatly.

"Sending trained mercenaries in to kill American boys . . ."

He shrugged.

"And you don't see any problem with that?"

"Would you rather those Cubans get massacred and have Castro go to the United Nations and gloat? Because that's what's gonna happen if the Marines don't land. We wouldn't have a fucking chance."

"Jesus Christ . . ." was all I could say. They had set up a suicide mission so they could scam the president into launching a U.S. invasion of a Soviet client state.

"This just isn't right, Henry."

Fisher narrowed his eyes and looked across the room with growing apprehension. "What do you mean by that, Jack?" he asked. "*Not right* in what sense?"

You couldn't really blame the guy for not being sure. It just wasn't a phrase that you heard very often in our business. In fact, I couldn't recall one instance in eight years when I'd heard someone bring up the question of right or wrong in the sense of moral or immoral. There was effective or ineffective, productive or nonproductive, safe or unsafe, and a hundred other risk assessments, but never right or wrong in that sense. Of course, I'd never come across an operation where foreign nationals had been trained to kill Americans soldiers in order to con the president into starting a war. It was new territory for me.

"You know, Henry"—I tried to sound matter-of-fact about it—"to some people this would look a hell of a lot like an act of treason."

"Treason?" He chuckled uncomfortably. "For Christ's sake, do you think I'm running this on my own? This has support from the top."

"But not the president . . ."

"That chickenshit Irish bastard fucked this operation before it started!" He sat up sharply. "Did you know he canceled the second air strike? Castro's still got half his air force intact and our ball-less president won't even provide air cover! It's a damn good thing we have a contingency plan because that cute Kennedy bullshit smile ain't gonna win this one for us." He reached into the drawer of his bedside table, took out a handgun, and removed the safety. I thought it would be best to ignore it. "For Christ's sake," he concluded, "Khrushchev will have him for breakfast!"

He pointed the weapon at my chest.

"You gonna shoot me?" I forced a laugh.

"I ought to fucking shoot you," he said. "But I'm just gonna arrest you for a while."

"Arrest me? For what?"

"We're in Nicaragua, Jack. I don't need a fucking reason."

I spent the next three nights on a moldy cot, sharing an eight-foot-square cell with a variety of lizards, spiders, and large, dive-bombing mosquitoes. I devoted the first night to thinking up ways I could maim, cripple, dismember, and disembowel Henry E. Fisher. After exhausting all the possibilities, I slept for a couple of hours, waking at sunrise. I realized that the brigade would be hitting the beach about then and wondered if the Marines would be following and what might go down after that. I lay there all day, listening to the jungle, thinking how this was the perfect scenario for the suicidal end of an insane world.

A group of anti-Castro Cubans posing as pro-Castro Cubans are sent in by American spooks to kill American soldiers, forcing an unsuspecting president to order an all-out invasion. The Soviet Union takes exception, so, unable to save Cuba, their tanks roll into West Berlin. Street battles ensue and NATO forces are quickly overwhelmed by superior forces. Now Washington is faced with a choice: surrender Europe or go nuclear. No prizes for guessing which option wins the day. We launch, they launch, and within twenty minutes the insanity is over. All because some guys playing war had a "neat idea." If it didn't happen this time, it would the next, or the time after that. And it wasn't just our guys—the boys on the other side were playing with the same box of matches.

I remembered Sam's advice when I'd told him I was being assigned to the Cuba Project. "Get out of it," he'd said bluntly. "Storming the beaches ain't part of our job description."

I didn't get it then, now I did.

At some point I realized that it was over for me. I was out of the game now—not a decision as much as a realization. The agency was no place for moral dilemmas. I guess I didn't mind that much really. My doubts had been building for a while and I'd always kept an image of me, a beach, a boat, and a typewriter tucked away for this eventuality. I just didn't expect to face it for a few more years.

Fisher reappeared on the afternoon of the third day. He unlocked the cell and stepped inside, looking like hell. "The Guantánamo team got cold feet," he explained. "They never got off the boat."

"What about the brigade?" I asked.

"They made some progress at first, then got pinned down by a few militia. Nothing really, small-arms fire, that's all. But they couldn't break out and it gave Castro time to get his forces into place. He drove them back onto the beach, cut 'em to shreds." What he didn't say, and didn't have to, was that the brigade hadn't tried to break out because they expected the Marines to be landing any minute. I found out later that the last radio message from the men stranded on the beach was, "Heading for the swamp! Can't wait for you!"

Fisher leaned against the damp concrete wall. He clearly hadn't slept in three days. "So what about us, Jack?" he asked. "Do we have a problem?"

"Let me ask you something." I stood up to face him. "If the Guantánamo thing was approved at the top, why did you feel you had to lock me up? What did you think I was gonna do?"

He gave me a look, narrowing his eyes while he considered the question. "You were talking like you might go outside the command structure."

"You mean outside the Company?"

"Yeah. Outside the Company."

"You were right," I nodded. "I might have. Or I might not have."

"And now?"

"I haven't decided yet." I shuffled toward the door.

"That would be ill-advised, Jack."

"Yeah, well, thanks for your concern," I said as I walked out, leaving Fisher in the cell, leaning up against the wall.

As it turned out, Kennedy got a smoother ride in Miami than anyone had expected. Forty thousand Cuban exiles—men, women, and children—rose to cheer as he and Jackie walked across the field to the fifty-yard line. The first lady was the warm-up act, not that they needed warming up, but she pushed them over the edge. She spoke in fluent Spanish, breathlessly saying how much she admired the members of the brigade and how she hoped that her young son would grow up to be half as courageous as those brave combatants for freedom. She laid it on pretty thick and they lapped it up like she really meant it.

I was standing on the sidelines with Sam when I spotted Fisher on the opposite side of the field, behind the president. He was with a half dozen of the returning prisoners, men I recognized from the briefing at Happy Valley, though their faces showed the transformation of optimistic young officers into solemn men who had learned a hard lesson in reality. They watched expressionless as Jackie wrapped it up and, accompanied by thunderous applause, returned to her husband's side. I thought Fisher spotted me, too, but he pretended not to.

I leaned into Sam's ear. "What's he up to these days?"

"He was working with Harvey King's group."

Harvey was a legendary character at the agency. A fat egomaniac addicted to booze, hookers, and guns, he was the master of "black ops"—actions that were better kept outside normal channels. In his midfifties, he was as reclusive as he was infamous, a shadowy figure who operated on the edges with few restraints.

"Why 'was'?" I asked.

"Harvey's out," Sam said with a hint of a smile. "Although he doesn't know it yet."

"Harvey King out?" I said, more than a little shocked. It was like Disney letting Mickey Mouse go. "What the hell happened?"

"Kennedy fired him," Sam grinned.

"No shit." I shook my head. "What for?"

"Bobby found out he was putting Mafia hit men onto Castro."

"Since when do the Kennedys object to doing business with the mob?"

"When it's not their idea," he said, in a way that meant the discussion was over.

Kennedy stepped up to the podium, ready to give his prepared speech, but he was cut off by one of the brigade officers, another face I remembered from Happy Valley. The president seemed taken aback, unsure what was going on, until the Cuban offered him a folded brigade flag. Kennedy unfurled it for the stadium and got a huge cheer. He put his notes away and turned to the microphone.

"Commander," he said, sounding genuinely moved, "I want to express my great appreciation to you for making the United States the custodian of this flag." Then, his voice rising with emotion, he declared, "I can assure you that it will be returned to this brigade in a free Havana!"

The place went wild. I turned to Sam and had to shout above the din. "I thought they hated him!"

"He had a meeting with the leaders yesterday," he yelled back. "Made a lot of promises that he can't keep!"

I looked over at Fisher, who was leaning into the ear of one of the exile leaders. It was hard to believe that the Cubans still trusted this guy, but who knows what crap he was feeding them. I thought about how they'd react when they heard Harvey was being dumped. It would be like a second betrayal, and I wondered if the Kennedy boys knew what they were playing with.

The president stepped away from the podium and walked to the sideline, where he started shaking hands with the returning prisoners. Everyone moved in on him, and suddenly we were in the crowd and Kennedy was standing right in front of us. He leaned in and spoke into Sam's ear.

"Looks like I'm a hit!" He flashed his famous teeth and brushed his hair back.

"Yes, sir, it certainly does," Sam agreed. Kennedy glanced over at me, and Sam pulled me forward. "This is Jack Teller, Mr. President. He used to work with us, now he just goes fishing."

Kennedy smiled and leaned over. "The spy business didn't agree with you?"

"Let's just say we didn't always see eye to eye, Mr. President."

"I know the feeling!" he said, and moved on.

The crowd started stomping their feet and shouting, *"Guerra! Guerra!"* War, they demanded passionately, but they would once again be disappointed by Kennedy.

SIX

Powell had been giving me the cold shoulder since picking me up to go out to the airport, so we just stood there on the tarmac, not saying a word. He was pissed off that I was holding out on him about the Colonel, which I could understand, but he was acting like a wronged woman about it. I was glad Sam was coming in to save me.

After leaving the house on Berlinerstrasse, I'd walked back to the Kempinski, where I knew either Johnson or Chase would be ready to take me "into custody." I was relieved to find it was the young Texan laid out on the king-size mattress, eyes closed, hands folded across his chest, like a corpse waiting for a funeral. He was fully dressed except for his eyeglasses and shoes, which were sitting beside the bed, military style, at a precise ninety-degree angle to the wall.

"You know," he said without moving a muscle, "I never woulda believed a bed could be as comfortable as this one is. It's like floating on air."

"Yeah, well, don't let me disturb you," I said, grabbing my wallet off the dresser top.

He lay there a beat, reluctant to end his transcendental experience, then smoothly swung his legs around and sat on the edge of the mahogany bed. He removed a handkerchief from his pants pocket and gave his eyeglasses a quick polish before fitting them onto his face.

"You're in a mess of trouble," he said almost sympathetically.

"Really?" I started counting the bills in the wallet, first the marks then the dollars. It didn't make a whole lot of sense since I had no idea how much had been in there to begin with, but Johnson didn't know that. He watched patiently until I'd finished and put the billfold away.

"I'll hang on to your passport," he informed me as he pulled his shoes on and laced them up. "I guess it wasn't the smartest thing you ever did to leave that stuff behind."

"I'll take that as a compliment," I replied.

He stood up and smoothed the bed out, carefully eliminating any trace of his presence. "I'd better let the chief know I've located you," he said, reaching for the phone. I pointed out that I was the one who'd located him, but he wasn't interested in the nuance. He dialed out and waited.

"Shame to bother him at this hour," I said. "He's probably asleep."

"Oh, he'll want to see you right away," he assured me with a smile. "No doubt about that."

BOB—Berlin Operations Base—was located on the grounds of U.S. Army headquarters in the southwest corner of the city. The huge gated complex of two-story stone buildings on Clayallee was built for the Luftwaffe in 1938 and was home to Hermann Göring for much of the war. In '45, the U.S. Army confiscated the facility, which hadn't suffered too much damage in Allied bombing, and the military government, headed by Eisenhower, established itself there. Ten years later, the relatively new Central Intelligence Agency needed offices for its expanding Berlin operations and was allocated a building in the compound. The Company and the military had maintained a cordial but mutually mistrustful relationship since then.

Powell was waiting in a windowless interrogation room on the second floor, feet up on a long table, flipping through a copy of *Life* magazine with an elfish Shirley MacLaine on the cover. His checkered shirt and casual slacks made him look almost normal, but that impression was quickly rectified when he fixed me with a cold, hard stare as I was escorted in.

"Thanks, Andy," he said, eyes locked on me. "Go home and get some sleep."

"Feel free to use the suite," I tossed out as he exited. "I don't think I'll be needing it tonight." Johnson glanced back with a hint of a smile, which I took to mean he might just take me up on it. The kid was okay. We'd talked on the way over and I found out that he was the youngest of seven boys, joined the Marines at seventeen, made the Green Berets, and was recruited by the agency out of Laos. He'd spent some time in Guatemala on the Cuba Project, but I skirted the subject and he didn't press me, which I appreciated.

I took a seat across from Powell, who showed signs of rigor mortis. That was fine with me—he could give me the evil eye all night and I'd be very happy. There was a pack of Kents on the table, so I reached across and helped myself. I noticed that the magazine, which he'd set aside, was open to a photo spread of a Buddhist monk who'd committed suicide in Saigon by dousing his body with gasoline then setting himself ablaze. The picture was making all the papers and getting Vietnam a lot of unwelcome attention, from our perspective anyway. The monk was protesting against the regime of President Diem, a Catholic who by all accounts treated the Buddhists pretty badly—his troops had recently fired into a street demonstration and killed nine monks. All this made things awkward for us since we had about sixteen thousand military "advisors" supporting Diem's fight against Ho Chi Minh. But the way I heard it, Diem was more concerned about the Buddhists than he was about the Communists and there were rumors that he might even be talking peace with the North. If that was true, his days were numbered, and it wouldn't be a very high number.

Powell coolly watched me smoke his cigarette down to the filter before he spoke up.

"It's true what they say, then."

"Okay," I smiled gamely. "I'll bite. What do they say?"

"That you're such a dumb asshole you don't even know when you're being well and truly fucked."

"You're just upset because I made you look like a jerk." I crushed the butt in a tinfoil ashtray. "By the way, what did you put in your report? I mean, you couldn't really say that you got locked in the bathroom, could you? Stuff like that tends to stick."

He smiled, but not out of amusement. "You'd better have a damned good story for me."

"I don't know about the story"—I shrugged—"but I've got a hell of a storyteller."

"Go on," he said. "Make me happy."

"Would a STASI colonel do it for you?"

It stopped him cold. He pulled his feet off the table, leaned forward, and extracted one of the Kents from the pack. "How do you know that?"

"He told me," I answered.

"Maybe he's lying."

"No, he's for real," I said flatly. "I'm sure of that." Powell gave me a dubious look, but he believed me.

"Name?"

"He wouldn't go that far," I said. "But you've probably got him on file." I was hoping to get stuck on the question of identity and avoid talk of assassination plots until the morning, when Sam arrived. I could look at photos all night.

"Does he want to come over?"

I shook my head. "No. That was the first thing out of his mouth."

"Can we get him to double?"

"I didn't get that impression."

He paused to light up and think. "So? What does he want?"

"Well . . ." I shifted in my seat, tried to look like I was considering it. "He was kind of elusive. You know, said a lot but didn't give out much."

Powell knew I was stalling. He gave me a look, stood up, and paced the room a couple of times before stubbing out his cigarette and sitting on the edge of the table. Taking the high ground.

"You had two meetings with the guy, correct?"

"Right."

"Why don't you take me through it. Step-by-step."

There was no legitimate reason to hold out on him. After all, he was chief of station and had an absolute right to know everything the Colonel had said to me, word for word. But the guy was cross-examining me in an interrogation room. What an asshole.

"I'd rather wait for Sam," I said.

He went rigid and his face started to turn red. I really thought he was gonna go pop this time.

"Who the hell do you think you're talking to, Teller?" he snarled, low and quiet, from the back of his throat.

"Look, Chief, I don't want to fuck with you," I lied. "It's just that Sam brought me into this and I feel like I should go over it with him before anybody else. It's not personal." I ended with a smile.

That was bullshit, of course, and he knew it. But there was another, more legitimate reason I didn't want to say anything. The idea of a conspiracy within the U.S. government to assassinate the president seemed even more far-fetched now than it did when I'd first heard it. I didn't want to give Powell the pleasure of laughing in my face.

At the moment, of course, he wasn't laughing.

"Okay," he said, standing up. "If that's how you want to play it, that's how we'll play it." He scooped up his magazine and headed for the door. "Sorry we don't have any jet sprays in here for you. Sleep well," and he turned out the lights. I stretched out on the floor and, actually, I didn't sleep too badly.

Sam was the last one off the aircraft, which had flown in from Frankfurt with a motley crew of journalists, Secret Service, and advance men. He finally emerged with the pilot, immersed in deep conversation. They stopped at the bottom of the stairs, Sam talking excitedly and jabbing his finger into the man's chest, the pilot holding his ground. Finally the two men shook hands and parted.

Sam spotted us and sauntered over with a cocky grin on his face. "I just got three-to-one on Clay to take the title from Liston. Dumb bastard. Where's the car?"

"Over there." Powell pointed toward the terminal building where we'd left the driver. Sam took the lead and we fell into step.

"Did you see what the kid did to Cooper in London last week? And Cooper's no pushover."

"I missed it," Powell said with deliberate apathy. "What happened?"

"Your man went down, that's what happened," I said to Sam.

"Ah, he was playing with the guy and got caught off guard. I was there, in the first row, and I've got Cooper's blood on my suit to prove it. It was over in the second round, but the kid was pussyfooting around, waiting to get him in the fifth just because he said he would. You should've seen him," he laughed. "Dancing around, making faces at the poor bastard."

"I heard the poor bastard laid Clay out pretty good," I noted. "If Liston connects like that, they'll have to scrape your guy off the mat."

"You want a piece of the action?" he offered, but I declined. Sam didn't make losing bets.

"Too bad he's got such a loud mouth," Powell threw in, just to stay in the conversation.

The driver, waiting by the car, opened the back door for Sam, who stopped long enough to give Powell a contemptuous look. "This kid's got the best jab in the history of boxing and he's gonna be champ before he's twenty-two years old. Who the fuck cares if he's been to charm school?"

I was starting to feel better already.

Powell sat up front with the driver, I got in back with Sam. We had a few moments of silence, just the hum of the Mercedes while Sam cut a Monte Cristo and fired it up. He looked tired, older than in Miami, which had been just six months earlier. Maybe time was catching up with him, or maybe it was the travel.

"So I hear you boys don't play well together," he grumbled through the cigar. "What's the story?"

Powell turned around so he could look Sam square in the face. "I want him out of my hair. He's dangerous."

Sam turned to me. "Jack?"

"He's right, I am dangerous," I said.

"And still a pain in the ass," he muttered, before turning back to Powell. "So what the hell happened? I told you to get this guy on tape from the git-go."

"You try wiring up a loose cannon," Powell hissed, turning his back on us.

"He's upset because I gave him the slip," I said.

"You gave him the slip?"

"That's right."

"You locked him in your goddamned bathroom! You're lucky he hasn't put a bullet in you. I sure as hell would have!"

I looked at the back of Powell's head, incredulous. "You put the bathroom thing in your report? *What's wrong with you, man?*" He ignored me.

"He's a team player," Sam declared. "Unlike you."

"Okay," I admitted. "I'm not a team player. And if I was, you wouldn't have a STASI colonel on the line."

Sam gave me a look and I detected a hint of a smile. "He's got a point there, Jim."

Powell faced us again. "All we have is what he's told us, which isn't a whole hell of a lot."

Sam nodded and turned to me. "What about it, Jack? Is this guy the real McCoy?"

"Yeah, he's for real," I said.

Sam turned to Powell for confirmation. "Is he?"

"Since he decided to go solo I have no way of knowing, do I?" He was pouting now.

"Did you go through the files?" Sam asked, losing patience.

"Not yet . . ." Powell waffled. "We didn't have time." I gave him a look, but kept quiet. We'd had all night to go through files.

"Well, that's number one," Sam said firmly. "We get an ID on this clown, then Jack makes like a tape recorder and goes into playback mode. End of discussion."

And it was.

The "target room" at BOB was the gathering point for everything we knew about Soviet and East German operations—personnel files, architectural plans, information on safe houses and drop zones. There was even a file with names and numbers for the garbage men at hotels where government officials stayed. The ultimate Cold War reference library. Sam had cleared the room so we could sit at a table and go through the files without anyone looking over our shoulders. It didn't take long for me to find the Colonel and I handed the folder over to Powell.

"Josef Becher," he said. "He's STASI all right. We've had him pegged for a while, although we weren't sure of his rank." He handed the black-and-white photos over to Sam, who put his reading glasses on and leafed through the images. They were taken in various locations around East and West Berlin—on the street, in a restaurant, getting into a car. Becher had the same solemn expression in every shot and I thought he almost seemed aware of the camera. I guess watching his back had become second nature.

I pulled his bio out of the file. It made for interesting reading:

> *There is no information on Becher prior to 1936 when, as a member of the German Communist Party, he fled the Nazi regime to fight with the Loyalists in the Spanish Civil War. Captured by Franco's forces in 1938, he must have escaped because he turned up in Moscow in 1940. Little is known about his activities during the war, but it is likely that he played a role in Soviet military intelligence. It is even possible that he was inserted back into Germany in a covert capacity between 1942 and 1945, although this cannot be confirmed. However, he surfaced in Berlin soon after the war and was assigned to the paramilitary "People's Police," which was the forerunner to the "National People's Army." He was then assigned a position in army intelligence before taking up a political appointment at the Foreign Ministry in 1956. Assessment is that Becher functions in the upper ranks of Section 9 or Section 10 of the HVA, reporting directly to the deputy minister of state security. There is no record of him ever being married or having children.*

"What's the HVA?" I asked.

"Security admin," Sam answered absentmindedly, still studying the photos. "The guys that run the show. Let me see that." He held his hand out for the bio, skimmed it quickly, then removed his glasses and rocked back in his chair. "So it looks like we've got a big fish on the line. How do we reel him in?"

"We could start with a little more information," Powell said pointedly.

"How about it, Jack?" Sam looked to me. "Wanna fill us in?"

"Or would you rather I leave the room?" Powell threw in sarcastically.

"Knock it off, Jim," Sam said sharply. Powell gave him a piercing look, but Sam ignored it. "Let's get beyond the playground. Jack—the floor's yours." I could feel Powell burning a hole in me, but I kept my eyes on Sam and didn't mince words.

"He told me there's a plot to kill the president while he's in Berlin." The statement hung there for a moment while they absorbed it, then Sam leaned forward, started tapping his pen on the table. Powell continued to stare at me.

"Did he give you any details?" Sam finally asked.

"Not really."

"What the hell does that mean?" Powell snapped.

"It means no, he didn't give me any details."

"Did he say anything else?" Powell asked drily. "Like who's behind this supposed plot?"

"Not specifically."

"For Christ's sake," Powell moaned.

"I assume you asked him if it's a Soviet operation?" Sam interjected.

"I did and he said it wasn't."

Sam nodded slowly then continued. "Jack . . ." He scrunched up his face in an expression of pain. "I get the distinct feeling you've got something else to say. So why don't we stop playing twenty questions and you can just spill it."

"He said it was an intelligence operation."

"He said that?" Sam frowned. "In those words?"

"Not exactly," I said. They knew there was more, so I gave it to them. "He said it was being run from our side." There was silence for a long moment, then Powell laughed contemptuously.

"That's ridiculous!"

Sam leaned forward, cocked his head. "Do you realize what you're saying, Jack?"

"I'm not saying anything," I asserted. "He is."

"You're being taken for a ride." Powell started gathering the photos and replacing them in the file.

"I'm just telling you what I was told."

"Come on!" He was getting warmed up now. "The East Germans uncover a plot to kill the president and decide the one person in the world they need to tell is Jack Teller? Please!"

It was a good point.

"Any indication why he asked for you in particular?" Sam asked.

"None," I admitted, realizing that I hadn't even thought about that since the Colonel had sprung his story on me. It was puzzling, to say the least.

"Whatever the reason, you're being played," Powell asserted.

"It does look like you're being romanced," Sam added.

"What for?

"It's usually because someone wants to screw you." Sam turned to Powell. "Section 10."

Powell gave a nod of agreement.

"What's Section 10?" I asked.

"Disinformation," Sam responded. then continued with Powell. "What do you think?"

Now it was Powell who didn't want to talk in front of me. He looked at me sideways. "Don't worry about him," Sam said. "Tell me what you think."

"Iceberg," he replied reluctantly.

"That's what I think, too." Sam stood up, stretched his back. "Look into it."

"Right." Powell closed the Colonel's file and tucked it into his briefcase. He stood up and turned to me. "How did you leave it with Becher?"

"I'm supposed to find out what I can and wait for him to get in touch," I shrugged.

Powell curled his lip. "You seem to take directions from the Commies better than you do from your own side," he said, very pleased with himself.

"If you're on my side, Chief, then I do believe I'm fucked."

"You're fucked any way you look at it," he smiled.

"Yeah, we're all well and truly fucked," Sam said wearily. "Aren't we lucky?"

Powell spun around and headed for the door. I followed with Sam.

"What's Iceberg?" I asked him.

"I'll have a car take you back to the hotel, Jack. Get some rest and pack your things. We'll have you on tomorrow's flight to Miami."

"What about the Colonel?" I asked.

He put his arm around my shoulder and said, "Don't worry about him. We'll take it from here."

SEVEN

They could turn the whole thing over to Daffy Duck for all I cared—what the hell difference was it to me? The Colonel would evaporate, at least until it all blew over, but that didn't matter if they were right about him working a disinformation campaign. It was all just bullshit, then, meant to scare us into keeping Kennedy in a low profile, away from large crowds where he could give rousing speeches that would make the old men in the Kremlin nervous. It was the kind of ridiculous operation that wasted everybody's time, on both sides. I was happy to be out of it. That's what I tried to tell myself, anyway. The truth was that I was hooked.

The Colonel didn't strike me as a time waster, especially now that I knew a bit more about him. I'd been impressed by his bio. He'd joined the German Communist Party when the Nazis were clearly the future and he'd fought on the losing side of the Spanish War. After capture and escape from prison, he could easily have left war-torn Europe by going west into Portugal, then on to anywhere in the world. Instead, he went east, somehow making his way through German-occupied territories in order to volunteer for duty against the fatherland when it looked like he was choosing the losing side yet again. Whatever else he was, the Colonel wasn't an opportunist, and not the kind of man who'd be wasting his time on something as silly as this.

And there was still that nagging question—why me? As Powell had pointed out, even if the East Germans did uncover a conspiracy, it was unlikely that the one person on the planet they'd feel the need to tell would be Jack Teller. But it was just as weird—maybe weirder—that they'd bring me all the way from Florida so they could run a disinformation campaign through me. In fact, it was ridiculous, since they were sure to know that I didn't exactly have the agency's ear anymore. I'd have to make that point to Sam.

On the other hand, my two days in Berlin hadn't exactly been a picnic in the park. Hell, why not go quietly back to my sunny beach, make myself a pitcher of margaritas, and leave the whole sorry world to itself? If the Colonel was on the level, somebody else would have to deal with it. And if they didn't . . . Well, there'd be a big flash of light in the sky and it'd be over before you knew it.

Johnson was right about the bed—it was like floating on air. It was too damn comfortable, in fact.

I got up, went into the living room, and flicked the set on just in time to see Kennedy being treated to a wild ride into Cologne, his second stop in Germany. The route was jammed with fans straining to get a glimpse of that Kennedy magic. They loved the good looks, the boyish charm, the easy intellect. It was easy to love.

Of course, he wasn't what he seemed to be. In fact, he was pretty much the opposite. The devoted family man was actually a sex-crazed maniac who needed to screw every halfway decent-looking female that came along. The tough cold warrior who stood eye to eye with Khrushchev and made him blink was really an egotistical dilettante who let the Soviet leader scare the shit out of him in their first meeting, tempting the premier to place nuclear weapons ninety miles off our shore, bringing us to the brink of war. And the idealistic crusader for justice was, in fact, a cynical cheat who stole the White House with the help of his crooked father and some Chicago gangsters. He was magic all right, but as any good witch doctor will tell you, magic is all based on misdirection.

Don't get me wrong—I liked Kennedy a lot. He had roused the country from a ten-year coma and had excited the world with his energy, his ideas, and his eloquence. He made America look like the future. And, most important, he made me laugh. I was sold when he told an audience on the campaign trail that he'd just received a telegram from his father: " 'Dear Jack,' " he quoted from it, " 'Don't buy a single vote more than necessary. I'll be damned if I'm going to pay for a landslide.' " That comment got him my vote.

So what if he screwed every skirt in sight? If Jackie didn't mind, why should I? And maybe he was a bit green when he first faced Khrushchev in Vienna, but he'd stood up to him when it counted. And as for politicians stealing elections—wake up if you think Nixon wasn't trying to steal the same votes in 1960. Kennedy just did it better. In spite of the fact that he was a complete fraud and an expert con man, I thought the president was a breath of fresh air.

There were plenty of people who would strongly disagree, of course. Walk down Main Street in Montgomery, Alabama, with a JFK button on your lapel and you'd find out. You'd be lucky if you were just tarred, feathered, and run out of town on a rail. Yeah, there were folks out there who despised the president all right, hated him as much as most of the country loved him. But they weren't the people the Colonel was talking about. He was talking about a conspiracy from within the government and, more to the point, inside the Company.

It was no secret that the president and the CIA were not on the best of terms. Hadn't been since the Bay of Pigs. He didn't trust them and they resented him. He'd fired Allen Dulles, who'd been director since 1953, put his own man in, then still ignored agency advice, effectively cutting them out of his administration. Everybody knew he had Bobby running his own half-assed covert operations out of the Justice Department, and it was not appreciated in Langley, to say the least. So I had no illusions about the president's standing with the agency and no doubt that there would be few Company tears shed at his demise. But would they really go that far? The Colonel was talking about a coup d'état by a group within the intelligence service of the United States government. It was enough to send a shiver up your spine.

"Jesus Christ, how the hell did you get this place?" Sam walked into the room unannounced. He didn't have to bother with the doorbell because the clean-cut agent who was stationed in the foyer had let him in. "It's bigger than mine!"

I gave the stock answer. "Friends in high paces."

"Not for long the way you're going. Does it come with scotch?"

I went to the bar, poured two doubles even though it was barely past noon. Sam wandered over and stood in front of the television, which seemed to be providing minute-by-minute coverage of Kennedy's day. He watched the mayhem for a moment then turned it off, without comment.

"How's the trip going so far?" I asked.

"He's a real pain in the ass when Jackie's not along," he replied, flopping into an armchair. "A goddamned bird dog off his leash."

I handed him the drink and sat opposite. "Cheers," he said, the glass already at his lips. He took a couple of good swallows and sighed. "Christ, Jack, I send you out for a little recruitment job and you come back with a plot to kill the president."

"Just lucky, I guess."

"Yeah, lucky," he echoed, examining the color of the whiskey. "Sorry about Powell. The guy desperately needs a proctologist."

"No shit," I agreed.

"Exactly," he chuckled. "No shit."

"And what's with the help?" I said. "Why's he using guys like Johnson and Chase?"

"Because I told him to." He paused, sipped his drink. "They're on temporary assignment, might as well use them."

"What kind of temporary assignment?"

He gave me a look over the rim of his glass. "Johnson's naval intelligence. Nothing to do with me."

"Chase belongs back in the jungle, cutting somebody's throat," I said and Sam shrugged. He didn't say anything for a minute, so I jumped on the lull. "What's Iceberg?"

He looked at me and grinned. "You know, I think I'll take this room after you leave." He held his empty glass out and I took it over to the bar for a refill.

"You really sending me home?" I asked.

"I thought you wanted to go. Catch some more fish or whatever it is you do to pass the time. You know, I take my hat off to you, Jack. I could never sit around waiting for a fish to make my day. It takes a special kind of patience, I guess."

"Go to hell," I said.

"Booked in a long time ago, my son." He took hold of the second scotch.

"What if the Colonel's right?"

"You've been out of it a while, Jack. You don't have the whole picture."

"Wanna put me in it?"

"Love to," he smiled, sipping the whiskey this time. "But it's top-secret stuff. You know—"

"Like Iceberg?"

He shrugged.

"Come on, Sam," I prodded. "You owe me some kind of explanation."

"Do I? . . . Okay, then," he conceded. "Iceberg's the code name for a KGB cell that's been operating in Berlin for the last couple of months. Highly trained and very secret. At least that's what they're saying in Langley."

"What's new about a KGB cell in Berlin?"

"It's part of a political assassination unit." He looked for a response but I didn't give him one. "Iceberg's specialty is damage control," he added.

"What kind of damage control?" I asked.

"Hitting a target's easy," he began.

"Like Castro?"

"Well, relatively easy," he corrected himself. "The hard part is damage control. Public perception. Come on, you haven't been out of it that long. You know what I'm talking about."

"Are you saying the president might be a target?"

"Washington doesn't think so."

"What do you think?"

He stood up and wandered over to the window before answering. "If he is, he's the Russkies' target, not ours."

"Why would the Soviet Union want to assassinate Kennedy?"

"I don't know," he shrugged. "Maybe they're pissed off because the missile thing made them look bad. Maybe they don't like his haircut."

I gave him a look. "It doesn't make sense, Sam. If they wanted to start World War Three they'd just fire off a few thousand warheads."

"Maybe they don't want to start a war. Maybe the idea is to make it look like our side was responsible. Or at least cause enough confusion so nobody's sure."

"Why do it in Berlin, then, where suspicion is going to immediately fall on them? They'd do it in New Orleans or Alabama if they wanted to make it look like us."

"Maybe they want it to look like we were setting them up."

I had to laugh. It was the perfect Company answer. If it looks like a "6" it must be a "9" because the whole goddamned world is upside down.

"Know what I think, Sam? I think you guys have your heads so far up your intelligence ass that you can't find your own tail."

He looked a little insulted. "If they were gonna pull something, this is exactly how they'd operate. Your Colonel plants the idea that there's an element within the U.S. intelligence community that's plotting to assassinate the president. Afterward, the information gets out, along with a few other well-placed 'clues,' and there's enough of a question mark that no one knows for sure."

"Or," I suggested, "the Colonel's telling the truth and someone in the Company—"

"I wouldn't talk like that, Jack. It could get you into real trouble. *Real* trouble. Anyway"—he changed gears—"chances are the East Germans are just running a chaos operation. Trying to get us to keep Kennedy in a low profile."

"I thought about that," I said. "There's only one problem. Why would they insist on getting me all the way over here so they could run the story through me?"

Sam gave me a good long look before he hit me with it: "I was hoping you could shed some light on that, Jack."

I didn't like the implication, especially coming from Sam. It was natural that they'd think in those terms, but I didn't expect it from Sam. It threw me.

"What does Powell think?" I asked coolly.

"He thinks you're part of it."

"Is that why I've got the babysitter?"

"Yes," he said, to the point. "Powell insisted on it. You know, you didn't exactly impress him with your team spirit."

"Did you send me here to impress Powell?"

Sam shrugged, conceding the point.

"If you really thought I was involved you wouldn't be sending me home," I pointed out.

"I never said I thought you were involved." He polished off his drink, set the empty glass on the table. "I'm sending you home because I don't need you anymore."

"Maybe I'll stick around on my own for a while," I said, just to test him.

"Not an option," he said, leaving no room for negotiation. We stood there without saying anything for a few seconds—long enough for it to feel awkward.

"Well," he finally said. "Thanks for the drink."

"Anytime," I answered. He smiled and headed for the door, picking up his hat on the way. He stopped at the entrance and turned back, casually dropping the question that was the real reason for his visit: "By the way . . . How are you supposed to get in touch with Becher? Do you have a signal or have you got a meeting set up already?"

"I thought you said you didn't need me anymore."

"Did I say that? What a tactless son of a bitch I am."

"He said he'd contact me," I said.

"I see," he nodded, then exited with a shrug.

I stepped into the shower, pulled the curtain, and leaned into the tiled wall, letting the hot water clear my head. I was surprised and disappointed with Sam. Surprised that he was cutting me off, disappointed that he had doubts. I would have expected it from the likes of Powell, but Sam and I had history.

It didn't even make sense that I was working the other side. What if they had managed to turn me? They'd want to get me reactivated, sure, but not by dropping a line to the agency that practically said "please send our new double agent, Jack Teller." It was too stupid for words. Sam had to see that. Even Powell had to see it. He was a lot of things, but he wasn't thick, at least not that thick. On the other hand, maybe he was well aware of it and he was just blowing smoke. Maybe Powell had something to hide.

A chilling thought. What if there was a plot and the Berlin chief of station was mixed up in it? It made a kind of uneasy sense. He had dismissed the whole idea before I even got it out of my mouth—no questions, no concerns, no allowance for the possibility that there might be some truth in it. And if he was somehow involved, his next move would be to discredit me. Sam had said that Powell thought I was "part of it" and he made a point of saying the house arrest was Powell's idea. Maybe Sam was trying to tell me something. Maybe he had the same idea but, for obvious reasons, couldn't say anything.

If what I was thinking was true, then it wouldn't be enough for Powell to ship me back to Florida. I'd never make it that far, or if I did, I'd wash up on the beach one morning in the near future and it'd be "poor bastard, what the hell was he doing out there in the middle of the night anyway?" I turned the shower off and laughed at myself. Powell was a topflight asshole, but I was getting carried away.

The phone started ringing in the bedroom. I stepped out of the tub, threw on one of the hotel bathrobes, and picked up.

"Yeah?"

"Mr. Teller?"

"That's right."

"This is room service."

"Room service? I didn't—"

"Do you remember me?" the voice said. "I served you yesterday evening." I recognized the Colonel's smoky voice.

"Yes . . ." I answered. "I do remember you."

"May I confirm your dinner order for tonight?"

"Go ahead," I said.

"The same as yesterday and at the same time?"

I glanced at the clock at the side of the bed. It was twelve forty-five, giving me eight hours, more than enough to figure out how to lose my nursemaid.

"Yes," I said. "That'll be fine. Same as last night."

"For one person, is that correct?"

"Yes, I'll be alone," I confirmed.

"Thank you very much, Mr. Teller," he said, then hung up.

I waited before putting the receiver down, and sure enough, I heard the secondary click of the third party hanging up. I wondered if Sam knew about the tap or if it was off Powell's bat. Either way, it was unlikely they'd tumble—the Colonel had played it well and I hadn't blown it.

Now all I had to do was figure out how to get past the junior James Bond sitting by my door. I could either go through him—not likely since he had at least one gun—or I could go around him. The window was out of the question. It was six stories up and my Spider-Man days were long gone. Anyway, it was broad daylight. My best chance was to finesse him. I thought if I could get him inside I'd figure something out. Maybe I could even lock him in the bathroom.

I went through the living room and opened the door leading into the foyer. My sentry was slumped over a chair by the door reading an old copy of the *Saturday Evening Post*. One of the nameless foot soldiers who were kept around for this kind of duty, he was right off the production line—early thirties, short hair combed back with a dab of grease, and a cocky "don't mess with me" expression on his face. The .38 that was tucked away in his shoulder harness peeped out from under his navy blue jacket.

"How you doing?" I greeted him.

"Just fine," he answered coolly.

"I'm Jack," I said. "Jack Teller."

"Yeah," he acknowledged. "I know."

"You?"

"Smith," he deadpanned.

"Right. Well, Smith"—I smiled, quickly losing confidence in my plan—"I'm ordering room service, so what can I get you? They do a mean sirloin."

He stared blankly at me. "Thanks, anyway."

"Okay," I said. "How about a drink?"

Still nothing.

"Look," I persisted. "There's no point in you sitting out here when I've got a whole suite in there. It's a hell of a lot more comfortable."

"I'm fine right here," he said.

Jerk. He was told to stay and he was gonna stay no matter what I tried. "Suit yourself." I shrugged and went back inside.

I considered a diversionary fire, with lots of smoke and chaos. It had worked for me one time in Caracas when I was in a similar jam, but Smith was the type who'd die of smoke inhalation before he left me. I wandered into the bathroom to take a leak and shave, running various scenarios in my head. I was thinking about the time that I lost an unwanted companion in Mexico City by donning an evening gown and tiara when I saw the answer, right there in the ceiling above me—an access panel.

I threw some clothes on (making sure I had my wallet this time), grabbed one of the Louis XIV chairs from the living room, placed it on top of the toilet, and climbed on. It was a high ceiling, but when I balanced myself on the chair's carved wooden arms, I was able to reach high enough to push the panel aside. I grabbed the inside frame and, with some effort, managed to pull myself up. The chair went flying as I left it, making a hell of a sound as it bounced off the bidet. I waited, ready to pounce on Smith if he came running, but he stayed put.

There was a space between the false ceiling and the insulation above, but it was filled with electrical wires and pipes. Just enough room for me to squeeze through if I lay flat on my belly and pulled myself along the thin support beams that held the ceiling up. I figured I could follow the water pipes, which would feed every room along the length of the hotel, until I came across another access panel.

It was slow progress—dark, hot, and dusty. The insulation was getting up my nose and I was having trouble breathing. I was starting to think I should've stuck with the fire idea when I felt a panel in front of me. It sounded like it was raining below and I realized that someone was in the room taking a shower. There was no way

I was going any farther and I didn't like the idea of waiting there until the room was clear, so I did what I always did in a tight spot—go for it and hope for the best.

I pried the panel open with my room key and was met with a blast of hot steam. When it cleared I lowered my head and looked around. I spotted a woman's robe hanging on the back of the door and then, rotating halfway around the room, a woman's soapy body pressed against a clear plastic shower curtain. She was humming something while she lathered up, maybe "Bali Hai" from *South Pacific.* She had a nice voice. I don't know exactly how long I lingered there, but the blood started rushing to my head, so I pulled myself back into the crawl space in order to plan my drop.

Better a she than a he, I thought—hysterical screams are easier to deal with than physical violence. I untied my shoes, put one in each jacket pocket, then lowered myself down, feetfirst, as far as I could. Then I closed my eyes and let go. It was a soft landing and I thought I'd be okay until she abruptly stopped singing.

"Harold? . . . Is that you?"

I threw myself against a wall and said something along the lines of "Ugh."

"Why don't you come in with me, darling? It feels absolutely divine!" I considered my options and decided a quick exit was the only sane one. I reached across the room, flushed the toilet, and grunted again.

"Don't you want to, sweetheart?"

I took a deep breath and made for the door as quickly as I could. I squeezed the handle and pulled it open a crack, aware that Harold could be lurking anywhere.

"Well, fine, I'm sorry I asked. . . ." She pouted as I shut the door behind me. Luckily, Harold was snoring on the bed. I felt a slight pang of guilt about the silent treatment he'd get when he woke up, but in the end I was sure he'd apologize and all would be forgiven.

I stepped into the hallway and found myself at the door next to my suite. It was all clear, so I headed straight for the elevators, located at the far end of the corridor. There was a phone ringing in one of the rooms and I realized that if it was mine, Smith would wonder why I wasn't answering and check it out. I picked up my pace, called for the elevator, but the damned thing was stopping at every floor on the way up. I wasn't feeling lucky, so I headed for the door marked EMERGENCY EXIT. Good thing I did because just as I got there Smith appeared at the opposite end of the hall, waving his gun in the air.

He took aim and fired.

"Jesus Christ," I yelled, "you almost hit me!" But he was lining me up again, so I didn't stick around to give him any more accuracy reports. I whipped the emergency-exit door open and his second shot tore through the wood a few inches from my head.

"WHAT THE HELL ARE YOU DOING?!" I shouted, even though it was pretty damn clear what he was doing. I pulled the door closed behind me and made a dash down the stairs. I heard his footsteps above me, but if he wanted to shoot me—which by now I was convinced he did—he'd have to catch me because there was no shot from above.

I hit bottom, pushed the door open, and stepped into the lobby, gasping for air. He wouldn't be able to gun me down in front of the concierge, so I walked—briskly—toward the hotel entrance.

Then a voice called out.

"Jack! Hey, Jack! . . . Jack Teller!"

EIGHT

I spun around and saw that Horst was standing at the reception desk, house phone in hand. "I have just phoned to your room!" he exclaimed, replacing the receiver and walking toward me. Over my shoulder I could see Smith step into the lobby, holding the .38 in his jacket pocket.

I grabbed Horst and hustled him toward the door. "How did you get here?"

"What do you mean?"

"Have you got a car?"

"Yes, but—"

"Show me!" I pushed him out the door, glancing back to see Smith picking up his pace.

"What are you doing, Jack?" Horst laughed as he straightened his jacket.

"WHERE'S YOUR GODDAMNED CAR, HORST?!"

"There!" He pointed across the street and my heart sank at the sight of the clapped-out old Volkswagen Beetle convertible. It looked like it might make forty if you got out and pushed.

"It looks not so good, but—"

"Give me the keys," I said.

"But—"

"Give me the damn keys, Horst!"

He took the keys out of his pocket and I grabbed them. Racing across Kürfrstendamm, I glanced over my shoulder to see Smith emerge from the hotel, and managed to just miss going under a bus. Leaping onto the curb, I high-jumped over the car door, slid in behind the wheel, pushed the key into the ignition, and turned it over.

Nothing.

I pulled the choke, tried again, and the Bug sputtered to life. I shoved it into first gear, hit the floor with the pedal, and popped the clutch. . . . The car rattled forward a couple of feet and died.

Smith was negotiating his way through traffic, his piece out in the open now. I was about to make a run for it when Horst casually opened the passenger door and slipped in beside me.

"Place the choke exactly halfway out," he said calmly. "Then give it no throttle until you have reached second gear."

I followed his instructions and we pulled away just as Smith bounded onto the sidewalk. I thought he was gonna start shooting, but he headed for his own car—a big black Chrysler parked up the street. I watched him in the rearview mirror as he got in, revved the engine, and came rocketing after us.

"What are we doing?" Horst inquired, not looking overly concerned.

"Hold on," I said, and took a sharp left into oncoming traffic, forgoing the brakes. A tangle of cars screeched to a stop, piling into each other in a chain reaction of crunching metal as we swerved safely through the intersection. I reached over to grab Horst, who'd come loose and was hanging precariously onto the windshield, pulled him back into his seat.

"My goodness!" was his reaction.

The Chrysler made the same turn and started gaining on us again. "I think you'd better grab hold of something this time!" I yelled.

"Thank you for the advice," he said, bracing himself as I hit the brakes sharply, spinning the car a hundred and eighty degrees until the Chrysler was coming straight at us. I popped the clutch and gave it full throttle, taking Smith head-on, who gave it all he had, more than happy to match the Chrysler against the Beetle.

Horst braced himself as I raced forward. Staying with it until the last possible moment, I whipped the wheel sharply to the right, and the tailpipe went *crunch!* as we bounced over the curb onto the sidewalk. The Chrysler sped past us, came to a screeching stop, tires smoking, a hundred feet down the road. I punched the gas and swerved back onto the street, scrambling through the same intersection, where a dozen irate motorists were still surveying the damage.

Horst banged the dashboard a couple of times and let out a wild yell. "WOOOO-HOOOOO! A car chase!" Then, more calmly, he added, "I've never been in a real car chase."

"Yeah, well, it's my first in a tin can," I replied.

"You're doing quite well," he assured me. "But he comes again!" Sure enough, Smith had managed to get behind us and was coming up fast. He was on us in no time, playing bumper cars, accelerating into the rear end of the VW, then backing off and slamming us again.

"He seems quite persistent," Horst said, his enthusiasm fading with the destruction of his automobile.

"I noticed that," I agreed. The Bug was coming apart beneath us and I was starting to think about alternate escape plans when I spotted an alley halfway up the block. It looked just about wide enough for the Volkswagen, with nothing to spare.

"Hold on!" I yelled, swinging into a ninety-degree right turn.

The back end swerved into a building, taking out the rear fender. I spun the wheel back, managed to get control, pointed the car into the alleyway, and hit the gas. What was left of the Bug bounced back and forth along the walls like a pinball in heat while the Chrysler ended up wedged between the two walls. I had to smile when I thought about the phone call Mr. Smith would be making home.

"I'll pay for the damages," I offered weakly as we surveyed what was left of Horst's car. It wasn't pretty—the right front fender was hanging by a thread, the left rear one was gone, the back end was crushed, and the engine was spewing steam and oil. It had died soon after scraping through the alley and we'd pushed it off the road into an empty construction site, where it sat.

"I'm not so sure it can be repaired," Horst said. I concurred and offered to buy the car from him. "No." He shook his head sadly as he walked around the wreckage. "You can't do that."

"Why not?"

"Because it belongs to Hanna."

"Oh," I said. "I see."

"She was quite fond of it," he said gloomily. "She even gave it a name—Otto. I don't know why Otto." I nodded sympathetically and he stood there, head bowed, for a few minutes, looking over the twisted metal as though it was a fallen friend.

"How much would it take to get her another one?" I finally ventured.

"I don't think there is another like this."

I suggested that she might appreciate something a bit newer, a bit jazzier even. She could call it Otto Jr.

"It could cost quite a bit," Horst suggested quietly.

"How much?" I wondered.

"Three hundred?" He shrugged.

"Marks?" I asked, and he looked askance.

"Dollars."

I nodded, reached for my wallet, and counted three hundred into his palm. It pretty much cleaned me out of dollars, but I had enough deutsche marks to get me through a few days. I figured I could get the Company to cover the cost of the car as a legitimate business expense. If they didn't kill me first, that is.

Horst removed the plates and we left it for others to decide Otto's final resting place. The familiar grin reappeared on Horst's face as he swung his arm around my shoulder.

"So why not a drink? I think our nerves do deserve it."

He knew a little hideaway in the district called Stateside Inn. You could've been walking in off Route 66—license plates hanging from the ceiling, sawdust on the floor, a pool table in the back, and Hank Williams on the jukebox. It was Horst heaven. The only customers at this hour were three off-duty soldiers and a pair of old girls trying to do business with them and not having much luck. Gus the bartender went with the scenery, too, although I found out later he was a retired English teacher from Philadelphia who had never been west of the Mississippi. We sat at the bar and Horst ordered a couple of Buds.

"You live in the beer capital of the world and you drink that piss water?" I smiled.

"You're right." He leaned in and whispered, "It's terrible. But they have no Pilsner here." He shrugged and offered a Camel, which I took. "By the way, how is your dog injury?" he asked.

"Not too bad," I answered, rubbing my calf. "Just a little sore."

"That's good," he said. "Sometimes these things can become quite nasty." The beers came and I asked Horst what the hell he was doing at my hotel.

"I came to see you," he shrugged.

"How did you know where to find me?" I didn't remember telling him where I was staying and it was kind of strange that he'd turn up out of the blue, particularly at that moment.

"I don't understand," he said.

"I never told you I was at the Kempinski. Did someone tell you I was there?"

He gave me a quizzical look. "Who would tell me?"

"Then how did you—"

He displayed the Hotel Kempinski matchbook he'd just used to light our cigarettes. "Don't you remember? You gave me a light with this match on the first night. I said to you all Americans stay at this hotel."

"You're right." I smiled, feeling stupid. "I remember now."

We both took a swig off the beers, then Horst said, "Who was the man that chased us?"

"A guy named Smith," I answered. "It's not important."

"Ah," he nodded, getting the message and changing the subject. "So . . . It's a shame you have left so quickly yesterday evening. Hanna has made quite a good meal for us."

Of course I owed him an apology. And Hanna. I felt like a real heel. "Christ, Horst, I'm sorry. Tell Hanna, I'm sorry too, will you?"

"It's not a problem." He waved it off. He asked if I'd made it in time for my meeting and I told him I had. He suggested that I come to dinner tonight instead, then I could apologize to Hanna myself.

"I'm sorry, Horst, I, ah . . . I have to be somewhere again tonight."

"I see," he nodded earnestly. I didn't want him to think I was avoiding him and I had to admit that the thought of seeing Hanna again was certainly appealing. "I'll tell you what," I suggested. "How about I take you both out to dinner one night? Someplace very expensive."

"I know just the place!" he smiled.

"Good. That's what we'll do, then. Just give me a couple of days to clear up my business."

Horst nodded happily, polished off his beer, and decided he'd better find a taxi since he was supposed to be using Otto to collect Hanna from the factory where she worked. He tried to get me to come along but I begged off, staying at the bar and ordering another Bud. I bought a pack of Marlboros from the machine and asked Gus how he ended up in Berlin. I listened for a while without really hearing, then asked if there was a public phone in the house. He pointed me to the back, next to the men's room.

Sam was in his office, probably waiting for my call.

"That son of a bitch tried to kill me!" I said as soon as he picked up.

"Which son of a bitch?"

"Smith," I said.

"Who the hell is Smith?" He wasn't talking to me, so I assumed Powell was in the room with him. Sam came back after a moment: "He says he fired two warning shots."

"Is Powell with you?" I asked.

"That's right," he confirmed.

"The guy came within six inches of my head."

"He says he came pretty close," he said to Powell; then, after a pause, to me: "The feeling here is that if he'd been trying to hit you, we'd be at the morgue identifying your body right now."

"That's bullshit!" I said.

"Look, Jack," Sam said in his "let's cut the crap" voice. "Maybe the guy got carried away, but that's not exactly the big issue down here at the moment. The big issue is what the hell are you up to?"

"I don't know," I admitted.

"That's great, Jack. Great fucking answer." He paused and I guessed Powell was saying something to him. When he came back on the line he asked, "Who was the guy waiting for you at the hotel?"

"Nobody," I said. "Just a guy in the lobby that I hijacked."

Sam relayed the information then chuckled.

"What's funny?" I asked.

"How'd you manage to pick a guy with such a hot car?"

"Just lucky, I guess," I said, but Sam had stopped laughing.

"Why don't you just tell me where you are so I can send somebody out to bring you in?"

"Somebody like Smith?"

He didn't say anything for a minute and I could tell he was pissed off. "I guess you think I'm part of the conspiracy, huh? Maybe all of us are. Powell, me, Smith . . . Who else? Maybe the whole fucking world's out to get you."

"Let's just say I want to finish what I started."

An unhappy silence greeted me. When he finally spoke, it was in a low-key, cold-blooded voice that I'd heard on Sam before, but never directed at me: "If you fuck with me on this, Jack, I'm gonna have to cut you loose. You'll be on your own out there with nobody to come home to."

It sent a shiver up my spine, which was exactly what it was supposed to do.

"Be smart, for a change," he added.

I was about to spit out some kind of bravado bullshit, but I came up empty, which was unusual but probably just as well. So I just said, "Sorry you feel that way, Sam," and hung up.

I went back to the bar, nursed my beer, and chain-smoked Marlboros while I thought things through. It was disturbing. *If you fuck with me on this . . .* he'd said. *Fuck with him?* That wasn't how Sam and I operated. What the hell was it supposed to mean, anyway? Fuck with him *on what?!* And how did he think I'd respond to that kind of bullshit? Fold? Christ, he knew me better than that. But he meant it, that was for sure. So there was no going back now, even if I wanted to.

It looked like I was going to have to depend on the Colonel. Not the most comforting thought I'd ever had, but for some inexplicable reason I felt he was playing it straight with me. There was no evidence of that and nothing in his dossier to suggest that he was anything other than a callous instrument of the state, but I had a gut feeling—a sense that I could trust him. Of course, that's exactly when you're most vulnerable. I'd try not to forget that.

I considered how to play it. The Colonel couldn't know that I was on my own now; that would make him too comfortable. He'd have to think I could walk out at any time. And I couldn't seem too eager, either. In fact, I had to be the opposite, play it cool, let him think I couldn't care less. If he was on the level, you had to assume he was operating with Moscow's blessing, at the highest levels, and that the idea was to prevent the assassination. If not, why bother telling anyone? So the Colonel would be getting pressure from above. I'd go in like I didn't have a care in the world, say I'd passed the information on and was happy to be heading back to Florida. If he let me go, then I'd know it was all a scam. On the other hand, if he was serious he'd have to give me something to work with.

It was pushing five o'clock and the place was filling up, so I decided to move on. When I hit the street I realized I was a bit woozier than I should've been on two beers. Maybe it was the pack of Marlboros that I'd polished off, or the fact that I hadn't had any real food in two days. I stopped at the first Imbiss I saw—one of the street-corner kiosks that were scattered around the city—and ordered sausages and coffee.

As I stood at the counter I couldn't shake the feeling that I wasn't alone, that someone had been watching me since I left the bar. Just to be sure I'd change cars a couple of times on the way to the meeting.

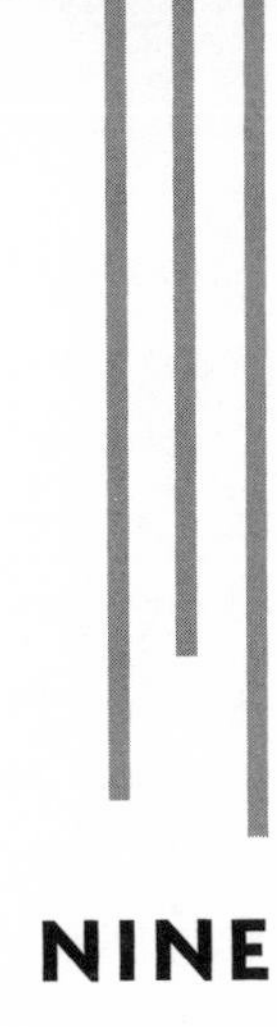

NINE

I arrived forty minutes early and had the taxi pull up a block away from the house on Berlinerstrasse. I wanted to see if I could catch the Colonel off guard, maybe get ahead of the game for a change. The driver, happy enough with the meter ticking over, sank his head into a newspaper while I waited, watching the last rays of sunlight give way to a veil of murky darkness. The night air brought with it a sense of anticipation and I felt a surge of energy.

There was no sign of anything by nine o'clock, so I paid the driver and sent him off. I made my way through the pitch-black toward the house, wondering if the Colonel was already inside or if he was the one who was gonna be late this time. It seemed unlikely that he'd hang around in that rat hole for longer than he had to. I wished I'd thought of buying a flashlight.

The street was eerily quiet and my heart picked up a beat as I approached the gate. Something made me stop there—a noise, maybe thirty yards in front of me. I held my breath and listened. . . .

Suddenly an engine roared to life and I was hit with a blinding white light. The car came off the mark quickly and was there before I could figure out which way to jump. It screeched to a halt in front of me and sat there idling for a moment. Then the Colonel's raspy voice came at me out of the darkness.

"Get in," he ordered.

The door opened and I slid into the backseat of the Mercedes sedan. The Colonel sat there, motionless, his face obscured by shadow. A glass partition separated us from the driver, who eased the car into gear and gently pulled away.

"You certainly have a flair for the theatrical," I said after a moment of dark silence.

"Yes," he said ambiguously, reaching for one of his revolting cigarettes. He lit up without offering me one, which was just as well because I probably would have taken it. "Have you made any progress?"

"I passed your information on," I answered. "It's out of my hands now."

The light caught his face as he turned toward me. He looked edgy, kind of anxious, unlike when I'd seen him before. "Did they tell you that I'm running a disinformation campaign?"

"Something like that," I answered.

"What do you think?"

"I think I'd have a hard time buying your story even if it was in paperback."

He let that stand for a moment, nervously flicking an ash. "Fact can be stranger than fiction," he finally remarked. "That's what they say, isn't it?"

"They say a lot of things and most of them aren't true. Anyway, your story's a bit thin in the plot department."

"I was hoping you would help fill it out."

"You hoped wrong. I'm going home, where the only thing that smells fishy are fish."

"I see." He removed his glasses and pinched the bridge of his nose. It was the first overt sign of strain I'd seen. "Why did you come, then?" he asked.

"I guess I wanted to see if you had anything new to say," I shrugged.

"I can't tell you what I don't know."

"Then why are *you* here?"

He sighed. "What would you like me to say?"

I paused, looked him in the eye. "You could tell me about Iceberg."

He looked at me blankly. "I've never heard of it. What is it?" I shook my head. "You don't believe me," he said.

"Imagine that," I laughed.

"What reason do I have to lie?"

"You guys don't need a reason. It comes naturally."

"Do you include yourself in that?"

"You invited me to this party, Colonel. I'm happy to go home if we're gonna play the same game over and over."

"I see," he said quietly. "Where does that leave us?"

"It leaves us nowhere," I answered bluntly. "So feel free to drop me anywhere."

He returned my stare for a moment, then nodded. "Of course." He tapped the glass and signaled the driver to pull over. There was nothing out there but darkness and trees and more darkness. We were probably in Grunewald Forest, a massive woodland in the southwest corner of the city. It was a long walk to anywhere, even if I had somewhere to go, which I didn't.

He smiled. "Is this all right?"

"Sure," I said, hoping my bluff was better than his. "Perfect."

I opened the door, stepped onto the road, and looked around. If it wasn't a bluff I'd be sleeping under a tree. Bastard.

"Thanks for the ride," I said. "Let's do it again soon." I started to close the door but he stopped me.

"There is one thing," he said. "Something I don't understand."

"What's that?"

"If you're so certain that I'm lying, why did you perform such a dramatic escape in order to meet me?"

"You know about that, huh?" I was busted, so there was no use pretending.

"You weren't very subtle."

"Not my specialty," I agreed. "Did you actually see it?"

"Enough to know that they want to keep you away from me. Why do you think that is?"

"They think you're a bad influence."

He motioned me back into the car. "You have nowhere else to go, so you might as well get in." He was right, so I did and we moved off, saving me from a night with the squirrels.

"It seems that circumstances have forced us into a temporary alliance," he said.

"What's your angle in this?" I asked.

"The same as yours."

"Which is . . . ?"

"To prevent something stupid from happening."

"What else?"

"Isn't that enough?"

"Why did you lie about Iceberg?"

"I wanted to see what you already knew," he shrugged.

"Give me a little credit, Colonel."

"You're right. I apologize." He cleared his throat and continued. "Iceberg is the code name for a unit working under the CIA Executive Action Group known as ZR/RIFLE. Have you heard of it?"

"Not by name," I confessed. I knew the Company had been involved in several political assassinations, directly or indirectly, in recent years, but those operations were held pretty close to the vest. I was surprised the Colonel knew the code name and even more surprised he was telling me he knew.

He went on: "Iceberg is the public-relations unit within the group. They attempt to divert blame by creating false evidence or, at the very least, to cause enough confusion that no one can be certain who is behind the action."

"Plausible deniability," I added.

"Yes."

"Why didn't you tell me about it the first time we met?"

"I wanted to see what, if anything, they would tell you."

"They told me it's KGB, and that you're probably part of it."

"That's what they would say." He put another cigarette between his lips. "It's not true."

"And that's what you would say."

He lit up. "For the moment, you don't have any other choice but to believe me." It was bluntly put, but it was on the money. I hadn't just burned my bridges, I'd incinerated them.

"Okay," I conceded. "Let's say I believe you and there's some kind of internal conspiracy to get Kennedy. What makes you think I can do anything about it? As you pointed out, my stock's not too high at the moment."

"It's possible you have more friends than you think. . . . Sam Clay, for example."

I gave him a look, genuinely surprised. "Is that why you dragged me into this?"

"Not entirely."

"Because if you think I have some kind of special influence over Sam, then you really are wasting your time."

"He recruited you, didn't he? And was always your advocate within the agency."

"*Was* is the key word," I stressed. "You must have a hell of a mole hidden away somewhere."

"Because I know about your relationship with Clay?" He forced a laugh. "That's hardly top secret."

"ZR/RIFLE is. How do you know about that?"

"That's not going to be part of our discussion," he said firmly.

"This isn't a discussion," I said, getting peeved. "It's a goddamned merry-go-round! How am I supposed to do anything if you won't tell me anything? How did you come across this alleged conspiracy?"

"In the course of—"

"—our normal intelligence activities! See what I mean? It's déjà vu all over again. If you can't give me anything to work with, Colonel Becher, what the hell are we doing here?"

He took a long drag off his cigarette. "Bravo, you know my name. Should I be impressed?"

"Believe it or not, impressing you wouldn't give me much of a thrill."

He chuckled, then looked at me cagily. "Shall we come to an agreement?"

"What kind of agreement?"

"Can you give me your word that anything said here remains strictly between us?" It was a strange thing for him to ask. Either he was willing to place an unusual amount of trust in my word, which wasn't likely, or he was going to tell me something that he wanted to get back to Sam.

"You can't trust my answer any more than I can trust your question," I replied.

"You make it sound like a hopeless situation."

"It is what it is," I said.

"What can I do to make you trust me?"

"Tell me something I don't know."

He paused, looked me up and down, then smiled uncomfortably. "All right," he said, his expression dropping back into neutral. "I will."

He hit the glass twice, nodded to the driver, then settled back into his seat. We continued the journey in silence.

I recognized the unique metal profile of the Glienicke Bridge as we approached from the west. The border crossing had been in the headlines the previous winter when it was the scene of the only spy exchange to take place during the Cold War. Francis Gary Powers, the U-2 pilot shot down by the Russians in 1960, and Rudolf Abel, a Soviet agent who'd been caught with his fingers in the nuclear-secrets cookie jar, had walked the length of the bridge on a frigid February morning, passing each other halfway across as they went from captivity into freedom. It wasn't the happy ending that the papers made out, though, at least not for the two men. Both had violated the First Commandment of Spookcraft—Thou Shalt Not Get Caught. Powers was excommunicated by Central Intelligence, reviled for not swallowing the poison pill he'd been provided for just such an occasion. Abel fared no better. Denied the rank of "Hero of the Soviet Union" because his name sounded too Jewish, he was dumped in a two-room apartment in Moscow and forgotten. It made you wonder why they went to the trouble of arranging the exchange in the first place.

I looked over at the Colonel as we pulled up to the floodlit barrier on the American side. "Say nothing," he whispered. An armed guard stepped out from a portable hut that had been plunked down in the middle of the road, jotted down our license-plate number, and approached the car. Our driver lowered his window and handed him three East German passports. It wasn't too big a leap to assume that one of them was mine. The soldier flicked through the documents, opening each one to the photo, then shining a flashlight into the car until he found the corresponding face.

I wondered why the hell I was going along with this. If Powell had been sharp enough to post my picture at the crossings, I'd be up shit's creek without so much as a canoe, let alone a paddle. And what was the Colonel up to? He'd gone to the trouble of having a passport made for me, so he'd obviously been planning to smuggle me across for some time. Why? I could think of a few unpleasant answers, but there was no point playing a guessing game. It was too late to back out and I'd find out soon enough what they had in mind.

The guard handed the papers back to the driver and signaled his colleague inside the station to raise the barrier. We pulled away, and had only to slow down for the East German guards to let us pass. I guess the Colonel was a frequent traveler on the Glienicke. As we left the bridge he said, "Welcome to the German Democratic Republic," and then fell back into silence.

We'd driven through dark countryside for a good thirty minutes when the scenery started to change. At first it was clusters of broken-down old houses, then, as we hit the outskirts of the city, huge concrete structures rising up out of the ground like Stalinist monsters. I assumed they were apartment buildings, although there was no detectable sign of life in them. As the car headed toward the heart of the city, a light rain began to fall. We drove through dark, empty, colorless streets, past bullet-ridden buildings and piles of rubble not touched since the city fell in 1945. East Berlin looked like a ghost town that was stuck in a time warp.

"I'm sorry we've taken such a long route"—the Colonel suddenly came to life—"but it was the safest way."

"What now?" I asked.

"Be patient," he answered. "We're nearly there."

A few minutes later we pulled off the main road and stopped in front of a set of tall black iron gates. The driver got out, unlocked the thick chain that was wrapped around the doors, then pushed the rusted gates open and returned to the car. As we moved through the entrance onto a gravel road, the headlights swept across a worn-out old sign. I felt a jolt in my gut as I read it:

KIEFHOLZ-BRÜCKE FRIEDHOF

I didn't react, still unsure if I was right about what was happening. The car made several twists and turns through the darkness before finally coming to a stop. The Colonel looked to me, then got out of the car without saying a word. I did the same and saw that he was already walking away, the flashlight that he was holding the only way to track him on the moonless night. The light danced around as he stepped over the uneven ground, occasionally illuminating one of the stone crosses or black marble monuments that filled the grounds.

I found a narrow path and followed, stumbling several times and nearly falling. Then, a few yards in front of me, I could see that the light had stopped moving. It was perfectly still, a solitary beam pointed onto the ground in front of where the Colonel stood. I moved closer and stood next to him. There, half-hidden in the overgrown grass and weeds of the forgotten cemetery, he was lighting a headstone. On it were the carved letters that were also etched somewhere deep in the hidden recesses of my memory:

Gertrud Teller

1895–1927

I fought a rising tide of emotion as the full impact of the moment came down on me. I had carried my mother with me since that day in September when I stood on that same spot and watched her being lowered into the ground. She traveled in some secret place inside me, somewhere that even I was unaware of. But now, as I stood over her grave, she was no longer some delicate shadow that could be filed away under "lost childhood" and forgotten. She was warm flesh and soft breath, the tender arms that held me when I was hurt or afraid, the only safe place in the world. I was thirteen again and knew what it felt like to watch her being covered with earth, knowing that I would never have the safety of those arms again.

I didn't cry on the day they buried her, or anytime that I can remember since, but I couldn't stop my eyes filling up now, thirty-six years later. I remembered her laugh, the way it came from deep in her throat, and how her eyes lit up when I came into a room. I thought about how she'd been there, forgotten for all those years, with no one to pull the weeds or put flowers on her grave. She deserved better.

"I used to come here quite often." The Colonel's voice came from behind, jolting me back to the present. I turned my head sharply, and when I looked into his eyes I finally recognized the younger brother I'd left behind all those years ago.

TEN

"Josef . . . ?" I whispered.

"So now you know my name," he said drily, eyes cutting through the darkness and meeting mine head-on.

I stood there, stunned into silence, studying his face, trying to equate it to an eight-year-old boy I hadn't seen in almost forty years. If anything of that child remained in this man's features, it was lost to me. Still, I had no doubt that it was my brother standing in front of me—something more than a face tells you that. And if I did have doubts, they would've been erased by the recollection of a black-and-white photograph that hung on the wall by my mother's bedside, an image of a smiling soldier. The Colonel was the spitting image of our father.

Josef turned away, looking toward the stone that marked her

grave. "I haven't been here in some time," he said quietly. "I came several times after the war, but then . . ." He trailed off. "It wasn't a conscious decision, I just stopped coming."

We stood silently over her resting place, thinking about what came next. A thousand questions flew through my mind, but this wasn't the place for them.

"Come," he finally said, placing a hand on my shoulder. "We'd better have a drink or two before we leap blindly into the past."

A mist hung in the air as the driver pulled over to the side of a dark road and killed the engine. The dank smell of crumbling bricks mixed with the unmistakable scent of cat piss wafted into the backseat as he opened the door and approached what looked like a deserted building across the street. It was a desolate area, even by East Berlin standards. The shell of a house stood precariously on the corner of the block, rising out of the debris of its own wreckage. It was as though the bombs had fallen yesterday, not twenty years earlier.

The driver rang the bell several times until the lights on the ground floor finally came up. A man appeared in one of the windows, pulling a lace curtain aside and peering warily out into the night. Once he spotted the car, he hurried to the entrance, where we were enthusiastically beckoned inside.

It was a small rectangular room with faded gray walls. A plain wooden counter ran along its length, behind which shelves were stocked with copious amounts, if not a wide selection, of alcohol. Half a dozen round tables were lined up on the opposite side of the bar, chairs turned up on them so the cracked tiles on the floor could be washed down. The only decorations were three faded prints depicting turn-of-the-century Berlin and some sad-looking red Christmas tinsel taped precariously to the ceiling.

The proprietor, a short middle-aged man with several gaps in his nervous smile and a mop of dirty brown hair, nodded respectfully to Josef as he removed the chairs from atop a table in the back. I got the impression that this was not the first time my brother had called on our host in the off-hours and that the barman obliged with equal measures of pride and fear.

We sat down with a bottle of schnapps and two good-size glasses between us. Josef poured two healthy shots, we saluted each other and tossed the drinks back. He dug a pack of smokes out of his pocket and placed them on the table while I refilled our glasses.

"Why did you change your name?" I began.

"Becher is the name of the man that married our aunt," he said impassively. "It was a few years after you left. Four or five." I nodded, left him space to say more if he wanted to. He extracted a cigarette from the pack and gestured for me to help myself, but I decided to hold off for the moment.

"He was the postman," Josef continued, a cloud of smoke forming between us as he lit up. "At first she wanted nothing to do with him, but he persisted. Each morning he knocked on our door and refused to leave until he put the letters directly into her hand. At first she humored him, but every day he stayed a little longer until one day he didn't leave at all."

I wanted to ask what had happened to our aunt—she would've been in her late sixties now—but I said something innocuous like I was glad she'd found somebody and I hoped they'd been happy together.

"He treated her well enough," Josef shrugged. "And he paid for my education. But in the end, he was a Fascist."

"There was a lot of that going around," I said, trying to be sensitive for a change, but Josef threw me a look that I took for disdain. My brother was a realist who saw the world as a bitter pill and he wasn't interested in the sugarcoating.

"I came to hate him," he said matter-of-factly. "He poisoned her mind. She—" He stopped himself, concentrated on flicking an ash onto the floor. "She was better than that."

"Do you remember our mother?" I asked. He shifted in his chair and frowned. I wondered if I'd been too abrupt.

"I was young," he said. "And you? Do you have a clear memory of her?"

I wanted to be able to give him something, maybe a moment that might spark his memory, something he could take away with him. But all I could come up with was: "I don't go into the past very often."

There was a beat of uncomfortable silence. I think we both knew that whatever was going to happen, this would be our one night to rake through the past, and we were trying to find a way into it. It was difficult, almost painful. Not so much the memories themselves, but getting at them after they'd been tucked away for so many years.

Josef finally broke the silence. "We lived not too far from here," he said. "Just a few blocks."

I shook my head in disbelief. The drink was starting to kick in and I was feeling softer. "What happened to the house?"

"Gone. Part of the rubble." He tossed his cigarette onto the floor and crushed it with his foot.

"That's a shame," I said weakly. "I'm sorry."

He shook his head and waved it off. I wondered if that answered my question about our aunt's fate, but I was still reluctant to ask. In a funny way, it felt like it was none of my business, like it was nothing to do with me. The proprietor approached the table with an ashtray, but beat a hasty retreat when Josef looked up at him. I don't think he meant to scare the man off—it just came naturally.

"Do you remember the toy soldiers?" I asked, getting a blank look. "The ones I bribed you with?"

"Ah, yes," he finally said. "They bought my silence. I wonder what happened to them."

"Lost in the past," I said as I poured us each another schnapps. "Like so much else."

I thought about the cold December day when our mother took me to the toy shop and how I fell in love with those painted soldiers. I remembered my feeling of misery as we left the shop, knowing she would never allow war toys into the house, and my delight when I found a package under the Christmas tree that contained two infantrymen, one blue and one red. I thought about telling Josef the story, but there was no point. I raised my glass.

"To my younger brother, the STASI colonel," I toasted. "I don't know whether to be proud of you or to shoot you."

He laughed—I think it was the first unguarded moment I'd seen in him—and we downed our drinks. He lowered his glass to the table, narrowed his eyes, and leaned forward. "Why did you quit?" he asked, his eyes searching mine. "Did you lose your faith?"

I laughed. "I don't know too many spooks who are motivated by faith."

"I disagree," he said, leaning back. "It's essential to have faith in our business. How else can we justify the things we do? We do them in the name of a future we believe in, to bring about a greater good." He paused for my reaction, but I didn't have one, so I avoided his look and bowed to the inevitable by helping myself to one of his cigarettes. I knew about the "greater good" theory, I just didn't buy it anymore.

He offered me a light. "I still believe that I'm on the right side of history. Do you?"

I took a long, sickening drag off the cigarette. "I'm not on anybody's side."

"You used to be," he persisted. I wanted to get off the subject, poured us a third schnapps.

"How long have you known about me?" I asked.

"Since Teheran."

"Ten years," I said, and he shrugged. "Were you saving me for a rainy day?"

He shook his head slowly. "I didn't expect we would ever meet." He paused, wanting to expand on the answer. "I thought it best that neither side became aware of our relationship, so I kept it to myself. They would have tried to use it."

"Like now?"

"I wouldn't have involved you if there had been another way," he said, sounding almost sincere enough to believe. I felt my brother was playing me.

"I hope you don't think that because we're brothers, you can trust me," I said.

"I trust only that our interests have converged at this particular moment," he said, then paused and smiled caustically. "I must confess, though, that I was curious . . . curious to see who you had become. . . . Did you never wonder about your brother?"

I would have liked to give him an honest answer, but, in truth, I hadn't wondered about him in a very long time. "Sure," I said, "I've wondered. . . . But—"

Nothing came.

"Perhaps you presumed I was dead," he said. "It wouldn't have been an unreasonable supposition."

Maybe he was right. Maybe somewhere along the line I had given him up for dead. Or maybe it'd just been easier to pack him away into that dark vault of childhood memories that was buried in some obscure corner of my brain. Whatever the case, I felt it was better to get off the subject.

"You really want to know why I quit?" I asked.

"Yes, I do."

"One of the reasons was that I was tired of hearing people justify the evil shit they do by saying it's for the greater good and it's okay because they're on the right side of history." I stubbed my cigarette out. "Everybody thinks they're on the right side of history."

"Not everybody can be wrong. One side or the other will win."

"Or we could all lose," I said. "The truth is that you guys need each other more than anybody else needs you. You justify what you do by saying the other guy's doing it, too. It's a vicious circle and it's got nothing to do with the 'greater good.' "

"What's the other reason?"

"What?"

"You implied there was another reason you quit. What is it?"

"Why do you care?"

"Curiosity," he said with half a smile. "That's all."

"Okay," I said, leaning forward. "The other reason I quit is because I believe that one sunny day I'm gonna look up into a clear blue sky and I'm gonna see a big flash of light. The one we've all been waiting for. And in the few seconds I'll have before the wall of fire hits, I'm gonna be pretty damn sure that it was some spook's demented notion of 'a good idea' that took us down. I quit so I'll be able to say to myself in that final moment, 'Hey, it wasn't me.' "

Josef stared at me and shifted uneasily in his seat. "That would make you feel better?"

"Maybe," I smiled. "Although I admit it wouldn't last for very long."

He shook his head incredulously. "Why don't you save the world instead?"

"It's been tried. Never works out."

Josef glanced over his shoulder, leaned in, and whispered across the table. "What do you think would happen if the world believed the president of the United States had been assassinated by a Soviet agent while visiting Berlin?"

"Are you saying—"

"I'm not saying he *would* be assassinated by a Soviet agent, I'm saying what if it *looked* that way to the world? What would be the reaction under those circumstances?"

I didn't have to think about it.

"It would be seen as an act of war. . . . There'd be demands for retaliation—air strikes on military targets, possibly an invasion of Cuba. The Soviets would respond by rolling into West Berlin, things would spin out of control . . . Europe at war . . . the missiles fly. . . ."

He gave me a long serious look. "Yes," he said, locking his hands together. "I think you are right."

"And if I am," I said defiantly, "what the hell am I supposed to do about it?"

He leaned back in his chair, lit another cigarette, and eyed me cagily for a long moment, a slow smile creeping across his face.

" 'I'm doomed,' cried the mouse!" Josef sprang to life. " 'There is a wall to the left of me and a wall to the right, but if I go forward I'll run into the trap!' . . . 'But you have only to turn around and run in the other direction,' said the cat that was chasing him."

"Inspiring," I said. "Is there a point?"

"The point is that it's better to be the cat."

"I guess that makes me the mouse."

He cocked his head thoughtfully and exhaled smoke through his nose. "No. Not at all. You, my good brother . . . you are the trap."

ELEVEN

Hotel Europa was three and a half blocks from my five-star suite at the Kempinski, but it might as well have been on the dark side of the moon. Josef had delivered me back into the American sector and dropped me at the flea-bitten dump, the kind of place that rents by the hour, assuring me that I'd be safe there. I needed a spot to lie low since I was pretty sure that by now Powell and Company would've trumped up some phony charges and enlisted the local police to help uncover me. Since the management of the Europa didn't worry themselves too much about details like identity papers, I could disappear for a couple of days, which was all I needed.

I had to laugh when I opened the door, even though the joke was on me. I'd managed to go from the lap of luxury to abject poverty in one easy night. It was a closet-size room with no window and—judging by the smell of stale cigarettes and I hated to think what else—no ventilation. The amenities consisted of a dented double bed, a cold-water sink, and a flimsy wardrobe that held a week's supply of faded towels. The only lamp provided a dim pinkish light that you might assume was a sorry attempt at atmosphere but whose real purpose was to save you from getting a good look at the person you were screwing, a blessing for anyone who'd sunk low enough to have sex in this hole.

I was too wound up to sleep anyway, even if the sheets hadn't looked a bit crusty, so I headed back downstairs, past the dozing desk clerk, and out into the fresh night air. It was after one o'clock, and other than the so-called girls hanging around the hotel, the streets were dead. I started walking, in no particular direction, eventually drawn toward the bright lights and shop windows along Kurfürstendamm. It was a welcome relief after the bleakness of the other side.

Seeing my brother had stirred something up. I felt anxious, unsettled somehow, like there was some distant alarm bell going off, but just out of reach. There was no shortage of reasons to feel edgy, of course, what with my brother, the enemy agent, giving me thirty-six hours to save mankind. But believe it or not, that's not what was getting to me at that moment.

Josef looked exactly like the photo of our father. That's what was occupying my thoughts. It was no surprise that I hadn't noticed it before—my father probably hadn't entered my mind in years. I tried to conjure up a memory of him, but it was elusive, like a cluster of faint stars that disappears when you try to look directly at it. I was only four when he was killed, in the last month of the Great War.

It was a sunny morning in October, one of the last warm days before a long cold winter set in, when my mother entered my room and suggested we walk in the park before lunch. It was something we did as often as the weather allowed and I always enjoyed getting out of the house, seeing what the world was up to. I must have sensed that something was wrong because she would usually chat away about the trees, the flowers, people, birds, whatever crossed our path, but on that morning she was quiet and I wondered why.

She sat on a bench while I chased pigeons and threw rocks into the pond. I don't know how long we stayed, but I remember thinking that it was unusual not to be hurried along. She would usually say, "Come now, Jakob, let's see what's waiting for us around the corner!" or something to that effect. When I finally returned to the bench, wondering about lunch, I could see that she'd been crying. An attempted smile didn't fool me.

"Why are you crying, Mama?" I asked plainly.

She pulled me toward her, holding me to her breast while she steeled herself for what she had to say. After a moment she pulled back, but kept hold of my arm, probably unaware of how tight her grip was on me. She looked directly into my eyes as she spoke.

"Papa has been killed," she said softly, with no prologue. Her lip quivered slightly, betraying her resolve, but only for a moment. "He died bravely," she said. "And we must be very proud of him."

I knew what it meant, even at that tender age. There were boys and girls in my school and in our neighborhood whose fathers and uncles wouldn't return from the war, either. But I never for an instant imagined that it could happen to my father. It didn't seem possible. He was too strong, too smart, too spirited to fall to the enemy.

"How did it happen?" I asked.

"I don't know, my darling," she said. "He was killed in a battle."

"By who?"

"I don't know. . . ." She struggled with it. "The enemy."

"I'll get a gun and kill the enemy when I grow up," I said defiantly, tears welling up inside me.

She grabbed my arm tighter and pulled me closer. "No, Jakob," she said firmly. "There will be no more wars after this. Papa has died so that you will never have to fight."

I realized that I was crying. It was a strange sensation, something I wasn't used to, and it took me by surprise. I'd left the lights of Kurfürstendamm behind and was standing on some dark bridge over a fast-running river, with no idea where I was, how I got there, or how long I'd been walking. Thankfully, I was alone and could wipe the tears away without feeling foolish. But I felt foolish anyway. So many years had passed since that morning in the park. Could I really feel his loss so poignantly after all that time?

Then, out of nowhere, a lost moment came to me and I could see him as clearly as if it had been yesterday. He was in uniform. A bright, pristine uniform with polished boots and a wide belt that smelled of new leather. He towered over me, arms held aloft, as if he expected me to jump into them. Then his voice came through, clear and distinct, like he was standing next to me on the bridge.

"Are you too big to kiss your papa good-bye?"

He laughed and leaned over to scoop me up in his arms. "You have to be strong now, little man," he whispered in my ear. "You take care of everything."

What would a small boy feel at that moment? Could he know that the man who had thrown him over his shoulder and chased him around the house until he collapsed in helpless laughter had strapped a gun on in order to fight, kill, and maybe die for his country? How would a child comprehend any of that? But I must have understood something about the significance of the moment to have stored it away for so long. I thought I felt my father's presence, there beside me, and tears started to come again.

For Christ's sake, get a hold of yourself, I thought. Not a good time for a breakdown. I tried to regain control, but some barrier had been broken and there was no holding back the tide of memories that rose from somewhere deep in my subconscious. I took a shaky breath and crossed the bridge, feeling better once I was moving, invigorated even. It was as if, now that the wall had burst, I'd been released from the burden of supporting it. I picked up my pace and let the images wash over me.

I thought about the day I left home, the last time I'd seen Josef. I'd looked back just once, and saw his face in the window of the attic room we shared. Neither of us made any gesture to mark my departure, but I thought I saw a smile on his face, probably the result of the newly acquired armies he held under his arm. Then, when I turned away, I left it all behind. My parents, who I loved dearly, were both gone, but I felt no overpowering grief or sadness—just an unrelenting emptiness that I interpreted as resolve. The world would never betray me like that again.

I thought about the disparate paths Josef and I had taken since that day and wondered what he had been like as a young man. He would've been just fourteen when Hitler came to power, the same year that the Nazis fed "Marxist" books to a bonfire at Berlin University. He could have easily joined the mob, like most of his generation, but he chose instead to read the books. When he was fifteen the first Jews were shipped off to concentration camps, along with forty-five thousand socialists. Perhaps he had already joined the Communist Party by then and had to hide from the police, or maybe his sympathies were still forming. He had fallen out with his adopted father over his beliefs. Had the Fascist postman betrayed him, maybe even reported him to the authorities? Life in Nazi Germany in the late thirties would have been hell for a young Marxist. He must have been thrilled to arrive in Spain and find an international brigade of young idealists like himself, ready to change the world. They probably thought they could do it, too.

Life went a little differently for me. I arrived in New York in February 1928 after working my way over on a Norwegian freighter that I'd picked up in Hamburg. Things were pretty tough that first frozen winter, but I got my bearings, learned the ropes, and changed my name to Jack. By midsummer I had settled in, delivering groceries for tips in the Bowery, sleeping rough in Washington Square. It wasn't bad, unless it rained. I got to know a few guys my age who were competing for the same benches and we formed the "Brotherhood of Greenwich Village Nights." We weren't doing anything too illegal, at least nothing we got caught for, and we looked out for each other. When warm summer evenings gave way to cold autumn nights, we pooled our resources and four of us shared a room on Delancey Street. It was a good time.

We soon went our separate ways, but the brotherhood came through a couple of years later when I was on the edge of desperate. I ran into Tommy LaPorta, who told me he'd been making good money driving a cab and thought he could get me in. When I said I'd heard you could make up to twenty a week hacking it around Manhattan, Tommy couldn't stop laughing. These weren't just any cabs, he informed me, producing a fat roll of twenties out of his pocket and peeling one off for me. These were Johnny Kaye cabs.

Johnny Kaye was a gangster straight off the silver screen. A flashy dresser with a smart-ass personality, he was the top bootlegger in Manhattan and he ran the biggest, loudest, wildest speakeasies in the Broadway district. He got into the business by accident in 1920 when, driving a taxi himself, he'd picked up a fare on Seventh Avenue who wanted to be driven to Montreal. The fare ended up being over sixty dollars, but when Johnny arrived in Canada he realized that there was even better money to be made on the return trip. A case of whiskey that cost ten bucks north of the border could easily sell for ninety back home. By 1930, when I started driving, there were a dozen cabs making the trip twice a week, carrying twenty cases per load. I was pulling in a very cool eight hundred a month and getting a lesson in how capitalism worked.

It wasn't long before I was moving up in the world. Kaye liked me, thought that I was wasted behind the wheel, and put me in charge of the Kit Kat Klub on West Forty-third. Aside from running the usual functions of a nightclub—food, drink, entertainment, and security—my duties included taking care of graft, bribery, and extortion. Mostly it was making sure the weekly deliveries of fat envelopes got to the right people, but occasionally a judge or a politician would try to put the squeeze on us and I'd have to arrange for a night out, which would invariably end with a photograph of the greedy party in a compromising position. Resolution of the dispute was usually achieved in the early hours of the following morning. It was a valuable lesson in human psychology and came in handy when I went to work for the Company. In fact, there were quite a few similarities in the way the two organizations operated.

Things went downhill for Johnny Kaye after the repeal of the Volstead Act in 1933. Kaye's delusions of grandeur got the better of him and he decided to become a Broadway producer, dropping a load on a turkey starring his girlfriend, who was devoid of any talent that you could put on a respectable stage. But Johnny's ego was too big to quit. He started pouring more money into a worse play, which came crashing down on opening night when he finally figured out his girlfriend was fucking the director. He pumped four .38s into the poor bastard and decided to pin it on me. I decided it was time to lower the curtain on New York.

I spent the next two years drifting west, keeping a low profile. I'd blown most of what I'd made in the rackets, so I was soon riding the rails, scrounging for whatever work I could get. I sold Bibles door-to-door for a while and did a short stint in St. Louis as a professional boxer, making some pretty good money taking dives until I realized that life as a punching bag didn't offer much in the way of long-term prospects. In 1937, the same year that Josef signed up to fight fascism in Spain, I hit Hollywood. I managed to land a job as a stuntman and was living it up, being shot off horses with pretend bullets, while my brother was trying to stay alive dodging real ones.

I reached the pinnacle of my movie career in 1939, in a scene with Randolph Scott. The picture was *Frontier Marshal*. Scott played Wyatt Earp and I was Curly Bill's Man. My first and last spoken line on celluloid went like this:

```
INT. SALOON—DAY
Earp enters and looks around the place. He
spots three of Curly Bill's boys at the bar. At
first they don't notice the Marshal, but then
one of them sees Earp standing at the door,
staring them down. The bad guy makes a slow
move for his six-shooter.

                  WYATT EARP
You best place that Colt on the bar, friend.
                Nice and easy.

                CURLY BILL'S MAN
        Why don't you try and make me, Earp!

The outlaw draws, but he's no match for the
fast-drawing Marshal, who gets him clean
through the heart. He tumbles onto the floor,
clutching his chest.
```

I thought it was the highlight of the picture, but, sadly, it marked the end of my acting career. My Hollywood days came to an end soon afterward, having to do with a certain unbalanced studio executive and his gorgeously sexy wife. But that's another story.

My mother had been wrong, of course. Our father hadn't given his life so there would be no more wars for his sons to fight. In one of those ironic twists that history seems to love, Josef and I ended up fighting against the same army that our father had died for, though we fought from opposite ends of the field, in different uniforms.

I didn't know when I joined up that Josef had deserted Germany, too. I thought about the prospect of facing him across a battlefield, but decided pretty quickly that I'd have to put that out of my mind. If I was going to wonder whether it was my younger brother lined up in my sights every time I took aim at a German soldier, I knew I would leave the war in a body bag. So I forgot about it. Forgot about Josef and forgot about my childhood and anything that connected me to Germany. Berlin became nothing more than a military objective.

It was the right thing to do, too. By the time we hit Omaha Beach, I'd been given a platoon of young men to command and there was no room for second thoughts. It's possible that somewhere in the far reaches of my mind I made a deal with myself that if I made it to Berlin, I'd try to find Josef, but I was stopped by a bullet in the Ardennes and spent the rest of the war in an army hospital in Sussex. I never considered returning to Germany after that. I guess I had let my past go and didn't see any reason to go chasing after it.

Of course, I wouldn't have found Josef even if I had tried. He was already well underground in the Soviet sector, preparing the way for a new tyranny, though he wouldn't have seen it that way. He had kept faith with the system he'd fought for, though I couldn't imagine how. How could he be so blind to the obvious? My brother's "comrades" were a different breed of oppressors, but not so different from the Fascists he had started out hating. I guess that's why the words *blind* and *faith* go so well together.

The CIA had their religion, too. The agency might've been packed with a misguided bunch of lunatic psychopaths, but they were true believers, worshipers at the altar of Capitalism, which they referred to as democracy and freedom. There was no doubt in their collective mind about the righteousness of the cause, either.

We were the good guys and they were the bad guys, plain and simple. For Christ's sake, we had Coca-Cola and Ford Mustangs and Sinatra and the goddamned Green Bay Packers! What the hell did they have?!

As I lay in that hospital in Sussex I consoled myself with a lie. I didn't know it was a lie at the time, any more than my mother did when she said my father had died in a cause that would put an end to war. I told myself the same lie: This time there really would be peace. It sounds naive now, maybe it was then, too, but after what the world had been through, it seemed impossible that we could contemplate going through that horror again, at least not in our lifetimes.

But here we were, less than twenty years later, at it again. Sure, it was a quiet, dirty war, and the lie this time was that it was being fought to prevent yet another war—one that really would be "The War to End All Wars" because if we let this one loose there wouldn't be anybody left to fight in the next one. I bought it for a while, and to be honest, it was fun playing cloak-and-dagger. But Josef was right: I had lost faith. Not in the system we were fighting for, but in the men who had been enlisted to fight for it. Guys like Henry E. Fisher—an intelligent man whose logic had become so twisted that he believed it was a patriotic act to train a bunch of Cubans to attack American soldiers. For the greater fucking good.

Sure, somebody had to do it, and yes, it was a dirty business, but how dirty were these guys willing to get? How far would they go? *Would they murder their own leader?*

The assassination of heads of state was nothing new to the CIA. If it was decided that killing a foreign president or a prime minister served the national interest, the Company was not only sanctioned to carry it out, it was expected to carry it out. It was called "Executive Action," giving it that boardroom sound that the Company loved so much.

But in the tangled minds of spooks and spies, how hard would it be to turn their crusade inward in the same way Fisher had in

Cuba? What if the congregation of true believers decided the president was detrimental to the cause? What would they do when they determined that *he* was the risk to national security, a stooge who was being played for a sucker by the international Communist conspiracy? In their minds, they would have an obligation—no, a *sacred duty*—to do the sordid job.

They would have to kill the president in order to save democracy from its own gullible electorate.

TWELVE

I looked up and saw that I'd taken myself to the doorstep of Horst's building. Not intentionally, but not by accident, either. My subconscious seemed to be running the show that night.

I decided to turn around and go back the way I came, but found myself stepping into the doorway instead. It was one of those times when every bone in your body knows that you're about to do something stupid but it doesn't matter a damn because you're gonna do it anyway. That kind of behavior is usually a by-product of alcohol-bloated brain cells, but I was perfectly sober as I stood there pretending I could decide whether to stay or go.

I rang the bell.

A wave of regret hit me as soon as I did, but it was too late. The door opened and Hanna appeared, dressed in her bathrobe, though it didn't look like she'd been sleeping.

"I hope I didn't disturb you," I said as casually as I could.

She looked at me sideways and narrowed her eyes, looking more curious than angry. "Horst isn't here," she said warily.

"Right," I said, faking disappointment. "Out on the town?"

"I suppose so." She smiled politely, holding the door tightly, ready to push it shut. I hesitated, decided I'd better spit it out.

"I don't think I came to see Horst," I said.

She gave me a long ambiguous look. "You're not sure?" She cocked her head to one side and I thought maybe she was flirting, but I wasn't convinced.

"One of those nights," I said, with no idea what that was supposed to mean.

"It's very late," she frowned.

"I'll go," I said, knowing I had just one more shot at it. "But you have to tell me to."

She stood there for a moment, looking out from behind the door, trying to decide what to do with me.

"Wait here. I'll get my coat."

I walked around in a circle for a few minutes, asking myself what the hell I was doing, not getting any answers. I would've given a lot of money for a Marlboro.

Hanna finally reappeared wearing a raincoat over her nightgown and a scarf tied over her head. She looked down at the road as we walked, hands shoved into her pockets. I stole a glance at her as she brushed a strand of hair off her face when a gentle breeze lifted it from under the scarf. She looked lovely in the pale light.

"I don't want you to get the wrong idea," I said, breaking the silence.

"What idea do you think I have?" she said, sounding slightly bemused.

"Well, ringing your bell in the middle of the night, you might wonder what I had in mind."

"What did you have in mind?"

"Nothing. I . . ."

"Nothing?"

"Well, not nothing. I guess I thought it would be nice to see you. You know, I enjoyed talking to you the other day, and—"

"Oh, yes . . . How was your business meeting?"

"Business meeting?"

"Isn't that why you left so suddenly? That's what Horst told me."

"Oh, right, yes, the business meeting," I waffled. "I'm sorry about that."

"Sorry about what?"

"Well, that I had to leave . . . so suddenly. I was late for this meeting and—"

"Did you make it in time?"

"No," I lied. "He'd already left."

"Too bad," she said. We continued on in silence while I tried to think of a way to start over.

"I'm sorry about Otto," is what I came up with.

"Otto?"

"Your car," I said, getting a blank look. "The Volkswagen . . . convertible?" She didn't know what I was talking about. "Horst said you called it Otto. . . ."

"If I had a car, I wouldn't call it Otto," she laughed. "But I don't have a car. . . . Not even a driving permit."

"Oh," I said, forcing a smile. "I guess I got it wrong."

She let it go at that, but I wondered whose car I had wrecked and why Horst had told me it was Hanna's. It could've been stolen, of course, but that didn't seem like Horst. Then again, maybe I was underestimating him.

"Do you have any more apologies?" She smiled up at me.

"I think that's it," I smiled back. "For now, anyway."

"Good. Then what would you like to talk about?"

"Well . . ." My mind went completely blank.

"Has it been a successful trip for you?" she asked, saving me only after letting me twist in the wind for a moment. "In spite of missing your meeting."

"Too early to tell," I said. "But it's certainly been interesting."

"Berlin is an interesting city."

"Yes, it is," I agreed, then surprised myself by adding, "I was born here."

"Really?" She looked genuinely surprised. "I wouldn't have guessed it. You seem such an American."

"I left when I was thirteen," I explained.

"Ah."

"It's a different city than the one I remember," I said.

She thought about that for a moment then looked at me. "The past is hidden in Berlin," she said. "Buried inside the people."

I realized then why I'd come looking for Hanna. I wanted to tell her everything. Why, I don't know. Something in the way she looked at me maybe. Something that made me feel safe. Whatever it was, I opened up—about the memories, the ghosts, the feelings that had been engulfing me that night. I even told her how I'd seen my brother again after all those years, although I said he was a factory worker and that I had searched him out. She listened intently as I described the memory of my father's departure and how I'd felt his presence on the bridge.

"It was his spirit," she smiled.

"You think they stick around this long?"

"They never leave," she said softly, almost to herself. She let a few moments pass, just the sound of our steps on the pavement, before speaking again. "My father was killed at Stalingrad. I don't remember much about him." She looked up and smiled unexpectedly. "I think his spirit never came home."

She took a deep breath and continued. "Horst and I had an older sister. Her name was Katharina. . . ." Her voice fell away and she gently cleared her throat. "She was fourteen when the Russian soldiers came in Berlin." She hesitated, looked to me again. "You know what they did."

I nodded.

"I was too young, just ten, but Katharina—" She stopped, but not because she couldn't go on. I don't think she had ever told the story before and she wanted to tell it correctly.

"We were hiding in the basement when the soldiers came. One of them who spoke a kind of rough German told my mother to go upstairs with Katharina. She begged them to leave her with me and Horst, but they didn't care. First they laughed, then they threatened to kill us all if Mama didn't do as they said. . . ."

I would have stopped her, but I sensed that she wanted to finish.

"I stayed with Horst, telling him everything was all right, but really I thought the soldiers would—" She hesitated. "I thought they would just kill them and then come back for us. It was hours before Mama and Katharina returned. It seemed forever. But I didn't cry until I saw them, because then I could see into my sister's eyes and I knew she would never be the same again. How could she be?"

Hanna didn't expect me to say anything, but I said I was sorry. She looked at me with compassion, knowing that I wished there was something better to say.

"Katharina killed herself two weeks later. Mama found her in the basement, where she had hung herself, in the same place that Horst and I had waited for their nightmare to end. But of course, it never ended. Mama tried, for us I think, but she died two years later."

Hanna stopped walking and raised her eyes toward the road ahead of us. "Look," she said. "We're blocked."

I saw that the street came to an abrupt end, interrupted by a twenty-five-foot-high concrete barrier. I had seen the wall from a distance, but its impact was different from this perspective. It seemed to tower over us, more imposing than its size, an ominous reminder of the dangers that still inhabited our insane world.

"I hate it," Hanna said quietly.

"It's just bricks and barbed wire," I said. "You should hate the men that put it there."

"I don't know the men," she said. "I know only the wall."

She reached into her pocket, removed a small black-and-white photograph from her wallet, and handed it to me. She watched my face closely as I turned it toward the light of a nearby street lamp and studied the picture. Hanna and a young man sat on a blanket laid out on the grass of some park, the remains of a picnic lunch scattered around them. They were sitting close to each other, but didn't touch except for their hands, which overlapped inconspicuously on the ground between them. There was something relaxed and contented about the two of them. They looked happy.

"His name is Alfred Mann," she said. "He's a teacher, of mathematics. We were to be married last year, but now he's behind this wall. Perhaps he's found a wife already."

"Not if he's smart," I said, handing the photo back to her.

She looked up and smiled at me. I'm not sure if she was crying or if it was the mist hanging in the air between us that made her eyes flash the way they did. Whatever it was, they cut through the darkness and nailed me.

"It's not easy to leave the past behind," she whispered.

I moved toward her, until I was close enough to feel her warmth. She held my look without flinching and I reached out to touch her cheek. She responded, closing her eyes and turning her head into my hand so that her mouth brushed against my palm. I wasn't prepared for the shiver that ran up my arm and through my body.

I woke in the early hours as the predawn light filtered through the worn curtain that was pulled across the window of her bedroom. I was on my back, naked, and she lay on top of me, head nestled in my arm, more or less the way we'd finished. I felt the delicious softness of her breasts pressing against my chest and I thought I could easily wake her and start all over again, but I didn't move.

Having my brother turn up out of the blue had thrown me into a tailspin. He knew what he was doing, too, had gone out of his way to throw me off balance, setting me up and stringing me along, then hitting me with it at the cemetery. It had been calculated for maximum impact. That didn't matter, though. I knew where we stood now.

"History has put us on opposing sides," he had said, breaking a twenty-minute silence as we reentered the Western sector. His eyes were closed, head pressed into the back of the soft leather seat. Light from the street lamps flashed on and off inside the car as we passed under them, creating a slow strobelike effect on his face. "There's nothing we can do about that. But for the moment, even if our motivations are different, we share the same goal." He turned his head and looked straight at me, underlining his point: "Kennedy must not be assassinated in Berlin."

"I don't know if anyone in Washington would be so concerned if the KGB was trying to knock off Khrushchev."

"We'd do it quietly and call it a heart attack." It was a good point.

"I need a starting place," I said.

He sat there for a moment, very practiced, then leaned slowly forward and reached into the seat pocket in front of him. He removed a manila envelope and held it on his lap. "You're not supposed to see this," he said.

"I guess contempt for authority runs in the family," I responded, not believing a word of it.

He sighed, removed an eight-by-ten glossy from the envelope and passed it to me. It was a black-and-white shot of a man standing in front of a white wall with a large Soviet flag pinned to it, the familiar hammer and sickle against a red background. The man held a rifle, a Russian-made Tokarev with a telescopic sight. A sniper's weapon. He grasped it military style, with both hands, and wore a sidearm over combat fatigues. The guy himself was small, dark and kind of bony. Frail-looking. And deadly serious.

"He goes by the name Aleks Kovinski," Josef explained. "A Polish national living in West Berlin. He's been used by KGB in the past."

"I don't think much of his cover," I said.

"He also works for your side."

"Whatever side that is."

"The Central Intelligence Agency," Josef said drily.

"Is that my side?" I deadpanned. "I'm getting very confused."

"You know," he said, stone-faced, "I don't find you nearly as amusing as you seem to find yourself."

"Don't worry," I assured him. "Nobody does."

"Kovinski was recruited by CIA," he continued. "About eighteen months ago. We found it useful to let him think we didn't know. He was fed false information about our assets in the West, hoping to create some confusion. We obtained some information about how they handle their double agents. None of it was very important. He's insignificant, really."

"Then why are we talking about him?"

"After the assassination, this photograph will surface. It will be one of the pieces of evidence that will convict him in the court of public opinion. Posthumously, of course. He is, as you would say in Hollywood, the fall guy."

"Where'd you get the photo?"

He hesitated. "A reliable source."

"Look, Colonel, brother, whoever you are—if you're serious about this, we don't have a lot of time. I need to know what you know. Everything, no fucking around. Whoever gave you this photo knows something."

"I can't say anything about that."

If he was right about the conspiracy, it had to be someone inside the Company. "Someone in Berlin?" I asked.

Josef was quiet.

"Washington?"

"No," he said, a little too quickly. There had been speculation for some time that there was a double agent operating out of Company headquarters. Counterintelligence, run by the enigmatic spy catcher James Jesus Angleton, had set up a unit specifically to hunt for the theoretical traitor.

"The Langley mole," I said. "You got this from him." The Colonel's look was confirmation enough.

"How high?" I asked.

"I didn't say anything about a mole," he said, looking pretty uncomfortable. If that was Josef's "reliable source" it was no wonder he couldn't tell me about it. The implication suddenly hit me.

"You're on your own in this, aren't you?" I said.

He didn't answer, just looked out the window. Christ, I thought, he is alone. He'd been telling the truth about going against orders when he showed me the photo. The Soviets would rather let Kennedy be assassinated and take the blame for it, risking a world war, than compromise an asset operating at the highest levels of the CIA. It fit. Why would the Soviet Union assign a colonel in the East German secret police to enlist his long-lost, burnt-out brother of a spook to save the world? The answer was easy—they wouldn't. The Kremlin knew about the conspiracy and knew they'd be blamed for it, but they chose to risk the extinction of the human race over compromising their most valuable asset. We were all as fucked up as each other. And Josef was as far out on a limb as I was.

"Speaking hypothetically," I said softly, "if there was an individual, someone near the top, who provided this photograph to you . . . It means that the plot to get Kennedy—if it's real—goes to the highest levels of the U.S. government."

Josef nodded slightly, acknowledging what he already knew. "It might even be that—hypothetically—this highly placed individual was recruited into the conspiracy." I knew where Josef and I stood now, anyway. He was for real. Not that it made me feel any better, because if he was for real then so was the conspiracy.

"Is Kovinski being run by Iceberg?" I asked.

"Probably, but he wouldn't realize it."

"Do you know who handles him?"

"No," he answered. "But his code name is Lamb."

"As in sacrificial . . ." I studied the face in the picture. It was defiant, unflinching, maybe even hostile. "There's one thing I don't understand," I said.

"Only one thing?"

I smiled. My brother had made his first joke.

"Why would he pose for a photograph like this?"

"You can ask him when you find him."

"I don't suppose you happen to have an address?"

"He won't be hard to locate," Josef promised. "It's the following stage that will be difficult."

We pulled up in front of Hotel Europa. It was every bit as glorious on the outside as it was on the inside. A woman in a platinum-blond wig and fishnets came out of the shadows and eased toward the car. At least I thought it was a woman until she got closer, then I was stumped. I gave her a warning look through the window and she backed off, waited by the hotel entrance, ready to pounce.

"Okay if I keep this?" I said to Josef, meaning the photo.

He nodded, but I knew he would've preferred not to let it go. If it got into the wrong hands and was traced back to him, his future wouldn't be too bright. But I needed one more piece of information.

"What's the name of Kovinski's KGB handler?" Josef gave me a look. "I know it's asking a lot," I said, ". . . but look where I'm sleeping tonight."

"Kovinski knows him as 'Sasha,' " he said. "But that's all I can give you. You're on your own now. I'm sorry. I wish it could be otherwise."

"So do I," I said, opening the door and sliding out of my seat.

He leaned over and held out his palm. "I'm glad we met."

"Me, too," I said, and we clasped hands. As soon as the car pulled away it occurred to me that the last time Josef and I had held hands was on the night our mother died.

I heard what sounded like whispering coming from outside the door. It was faint, so I couldn't be sure if the voice was in the living room or if it was coming through the wall from the next apartment. I looked down at Hanna, who was still asleep, her chest moving rhythmically up and down with each breath. I gently lifted my arm out from under her, replaced it with a pillow, then eased myself to the edge of the bed. She stirred when I sat up, burrowed her nose into the pillow, and turned over.

Our clothes were strewn across the floor in a trail from the door to the bed. I slipped into my boxer shorts, followed by socks and T-shirt. I was stepping into my pants when I saw that she was watching me.

"Are you leaving?" she asked in a sleepy voice.

"There's something I have to do."

"Another meeting?"

"Something like that," I said, moving toward her and sitting on the bed. I stroked her cheek with the back of my hand and she felt every bit as good as the first time I'd touched her.

"Listen," I said. "I'll—"

"Shhh." She touched my lip with the tips of her fingers. "Don't say anything. . . . It's all right. I don't regret anything." I leaned over and kissed her forehead, then left without looking back.

Horst was stretched out on the sofa, fully clothed and wide-awake, sipping a cup of coffee. "I see you and Hanna have become better acquainted," he smiled, a bit too effortlessly. "Please don't feel embarrassed. It's quite natural."

"I'm not embarrassed," I said. "Are you?"

"No," he answered with a shrug. "Would you like a coffee?"

I said sure and looked around the room while he went off to the kitchen. I noticed that the telephone had been moved to a table beside the sofa where Horst had been sitting. It could have been the whispering I'd heard, but maybe I was just being paranoid.

Even if he had been on the phone, he could've been talking to some girlfriend—or a fellow car thief, for that matter.

I picked up my shoes, which were right inside the door, sat down to put them on, but stopped cold when I spotted my jacket. It lay in a crumpled pile on the floor behind the sofa, the manila envelope protruding halfway out of the inside pocket. Had it been removed and hastily put back? Possibly, but I couldn't be sure. I tried to recall where the jacket had fallen the previous night, but it wasn't something I'd been particularly aware of as Hanna was undressing me.

"I hope it's not too sweet," Horst said, balancing an overfilled cup as he entered the room. "I didn't know how many sugars you like."

"Actually, I'll have to take a rain check," I said, "I didn't realize what time it was." I scooped the jacket off the floor, allowing the envelope to fall out, and headed for the door.

"You've forgotten something," he called after me. I turned around and he handed me the envelope. "It might be important."

"Not really," I said, but I was pretty sure by the way he avoided looking at it that he'd already seen its contents. Maybe it was just innocent thievery and he was disappointed that it hadn't been filled with hundred-dollar bills.

Then again, maybe not.

THIRTEEN

My brother was right, Kovinski wasn't hard to find. In fact, he turned out to be a listed spy. I came across a public phone a couple of blocks from where Horst and Hanna lived, decided to start there, see if I got lucky. And there he was—"Kovinski, A," sandwiched between "Kosche, G" and "Krause, H." I tore the page out, stuffed it in my pocket, and jumped into a taxi.

In the ride over, I took the photo out and studied his face, thought about how I should handle him. He was a weasel, the kind of clown who thinks he's playing all the angles when in fact they're playing him. He'd act tough at first, but fold under pressure. I had an idea about how to play him, but I wasn't gonna fuck around if he didn't go for it. There wasn't time and I wasn't in the mood.

Kovinski lived in a low-rent neighborhood, in a cluster of concrete high-rises built in the Josef Stalin style of architecture. The buildings were grouped around a sad-looking common that was probably planned as an urban oasis, where residents could get away from their drab, airless apartments, but ended up as an empty patch of dust and overgrown weeds. There wasn't a soul in sight.

I paid Melik, my Turkish cabby, double the meter and told him to keep it running. A young immigrant with a twinkle in his eye and passable English, he nodded squarely when I told him to follow at a discreet distance if I went anywhere. I found my way to Kovinski's building and rang the bell for apartment 5C.

"Wer ist es?" came a voice over the speaker.

"I'm looking for Aleks Kovinski," I said. There was a beat of silence before he responded, this time in heavily accented English.

"Who is asking?"

"I'm looking for a lost lamb," I said, knowing that would cut through a lot of bullshit. An even longer pause followed.

"I come down," he finally said.

It was turning out to be a perfect June day, sunny and bright, but the stillness of the area was kind of spooky. I felt like I was being watched, but shook it off. Pregame jitters, I told myself. When Kovinski appeared he didn't hang around, flew out the door and right past me. I caught up after a few yards.

"Who are you?" he asked, glancing over without slowing his pace.

"A friend." He gave me a contemptuous look, with good reason.

"Do you have a name?"

"Not one you need to know."

"Some friend," he scoffed.

"Maybe the only one you have."

"What do you want?"

"To talk."

"Go ahead," he said. "Talk."

"Can we slow down a little?"

He eased up a bit, looked me over more thoroughly. He was

pretty much what I'd expected, only more so. I hadn't even said "boo" yet and he was ready to panic.

"No one is suppose come here," he said. "They don't tell you?"

"Who are 'they'?"

He stopped walking, looked at me, and frowned. He had said too much and realized it. "Who do you work for?" he demanded.

"Same as you," I smiled.

"You make mistake," he sputtered, taking a step back. "Maybe you look for someone else."

"You're 'lamb,' aren't you?"

"You find wrong person." He turned around and started back toward his building.

"That's a shame," I called after him. "Because the Aleks Kovinski I'm looking for needs help."

"Go to hell!" he yelled back.

"Ever had your picture in the paper?" He kept walking. I took the envelope out of my pocket, waved it in the air. "Because I thought you might wanna see the one that's gonna go with your obituary! . . . You know what obituary means?" Apparently he did, because he stopped walking and turned around. I took the photograph out of the envelope and held it out to him.

"Take a look," I said. "Should make tomorrow's evening edition." He hesitated, not sure what to make of it. "Because if you don't talk to me now, tomorrow's the day you die."

"Show me," he demanded, edging nearer. I complied, without handing it over. His whole body seemed to tense up when he saw himself standing in front of the flag with the rifle in his hands.

"It's not the most flattering angle," I said breezily. "But it makes a statement. The sidearm's a nice touch."

"Where you get this?" he said, voice shaking.

"Somebody you know gave it to me," I said, and he looked at me sideways.

"Who?"

"How about I buy you a cup of coffee?"

He led us to a bar around the corner, where we ordered coffee and sat at a wobbly wooden table in the back, away from the window. The place wasn't doing much business, just an old man and his lame dog who looked like they were settling in for the day. Kovinski pulled out a pack of nonfilters and started puffing away nervously. Bumming one was out of the question, so I convinced myself I wasn't interested.

"Is not me," he said.

"What's not you?"

"This picture . . . Is not me." His leg was bouncing up and down like a Mexican jumping bean.

"You're a bit high-strung for this business, aren't you?" I said.

"What business?"

"The playing-both-sides-of-the-fence business. You don't exactly have nerves of steel."

"Go to hell," he said, leaning back in his chair and blowing smoke rings, proving that he was as cool as a cucumber.

"Yeah, you said that before."

"I dunno this picture. Is not me."

"You said that, too."

"Is truth," he shrugged. I pulled the photo out again, made a big show of looking back and forth between it and his face.

"It sure as hell looks like you," I said.

"Is fake," he said, trying to look bored. "My head maybe, not the rest." He glanced nervously toward the old man and his dog. He was looking everywhere except in my eye.

I took another look at the photo. It looked real enough to me, but what did I know? If it was a fake, it was a damned good one. It did strike me that Kovinski's shock when he saw it had been genuine. Then again, Kovinski was a natural-born liar. In the end, it didn't make much difference. Bogus or not, its purpose was the same.

"You're being set up, Aleks," I said. "If the picture's really a phony, it should be all the more obvious to you."

"I dunno nothing."

"I can help you, if you cooperate."

He blew smoke in my face, which was stupid beyond belief. It was hard to believe the guy could have survived this long in the game he was playing. Of course, his future prospects weren't looking too bright.

"If I get out of this chair, you're dead tomorrow," I said. "Tell me what you want me to do."

"This is bullshit," he said, stubbing out his cigarette, leg still going a mile a minute.

"You saw the picture."

"So what? A picture! Maybe you make it!"

"Come on, Aleks, I hope you're smarter than that. You already know who made it. Shall I tell you *why* they made it?"

He tipped his head back and looked at me out of the bottom of his eyes. I waited. "Okay . . ." he finally said. "You tell."

"The CIA is planning the assassination of a senior official in the West German government," I said. "It will take place tomorrow, while Kennedy is in Berlin. The picture's part of a plan to frame you. It looks like you're being set up to take the fall."

He froze. Even his leg stopped moving. He leaned forward. "American CIA to kill *West* German official?"

"That's right," I said. It was out of the question to tell him that the target was Kennedy, so I'd come up with this story in the taxi on the way over. And if he already had an inkling that he was being set up for something, it would ring true.

"I don't believe. . . ." Kovinski shook his head. "Why they do this? CIA is ally with West Germany."

"The Americans think the West Germans are getting a little too cozy with the Russians. The idea is to make it look like the official was hit by a KGB agent. And you're it."

"Bullshit," he said, leaning forward.

"How much do you wanna bet that you're holding the murder weapon in that picture?"

"I never saw this gun!"

"Sure, I believe you, but you won't be around to clear that up after tomorrow. Killed while trying to get away, probably by some cop who's working with them."

The poor jerk sat there with a look of bewilderment on his face. He was trying to fit the pieces together, but his head was spinning. I leaned in and landed the knockout punch.

"Sasha knows you double-crossed us," I whispered. "He knows you've been working for the Americans." Kovinski went chalk white.

"But you—? How do you—?" He looked helpless, truly lost.

"I work for him," I said, sipping black coffee.

"Sasha sent you?" he said, almost breathless. "What does he think—?"

"He doesn't think, Aleks. He *knows.* How do you suppose I got your CIA code name? Sasha has people everywhere, you ought to know that. I'm one of them."

"I never told anything important. . . . I swear! Never!" He said it with desperate sincerity. Watching him squirm was turning my stomach, so I put an end to his misery.

"Sasha is willing to give you a second chance," I said. "A chance to clean the slate."

"Anything . . ." he said, suddenly eager to please. "You tell me what and I do!"

At this point, of course, I could have told him to give me the name of his CIA controller. Chances are, though, he would've bullshitted or stalled me, even as frightened as he was. It was his nature. Even if he had played it straight, he wouldn't have the guy's real name, so I had to take a chance.

"I want you to make contact," I said. "Arrange a meeting as soon as possible. This morning. Say it's an emergency. Can you do that?"

"I think so. Yes."

"Tell him your cover is blown, that the Russians are on to you but they're giving you one last chance. Say you've been sent back to get information about an assassination plot, that the KGB knows someone's gonna be hit—they don't know who or when, but they're sure it's somebody important. Don't say anything about me or the photograph. Tell them if you don't get some information to bring back, you'll be killed. Have you got that?"

He nodded.

"Tell me."

"Sasha found out I'm double agent, but he gives another chance if I get information . . . about plot to kill important man, but he don't know who."

"What about the photograph?"

"I say nothing."

"And what happens if you don't come back with some information?"

"I get killed."

"That's right, very good."

He swallowed hard.

"They'll probably send you back with some bullshit," I said, knowing it was just as likely that they'd bump him off and find another patsy, but he didn't need to hear that. Maybe he knew it already and was trying to figure out which side he stood a better chance with, not realizing that whatever he did, he was finished. It was just a question of how long he could delay the inevitable.

"We'll meet back here today, at four o'clock," I said. "Okay?"

"Yes. Four o'clock," he repeated.

"Good." I stood up. "That's it, then." He grabbed my sleeve as I turned to leave.

"Tell Sasha I do good work for him," he said pitifully. I gave him a look and he let go.

Melik was parked down the street. I got in and gave him a pat on the back. "Nice going," I said. We didn't have to wait long because Kovinski was out like a shot and scurrying like a rat up the sidewalk toward the car. I scrunched down in the back until he passed.

"We follow?" said Melik.

"We follow," I confirmed, and he pulled the car around, nice and slow, easing it up the street, staying well behind our man. I wondered if all taxi drivers in Berlin were as practiced in the art of surveillance.

Kovinski didn't disappoint me, went straight for a phone. My only concern had been that I'd overcooked him and he'd run scared. I'd counted on him being smart enough to know that he didn't have anywhere to run and I seemed to be right. It had worked out well, I thought. Kovinski's story would shake things up, maybe even cause a misstep. At the very least, he would lead me into the circle. What I'd do after that, I had no idea. Play it by ear, like always, I guess. I had to admit, though, I was enjoying my comeback.

About an hour later we pulled up in front of a small "art cinema" strangely situated in the middle of a leafy residential block of what would otherwise be a typical middle-class neighborhood. There was no marquee, just some steps leading down from the sidewalk, where a discreet billboard listed the feature attraction as *Schmutziger Engel* (rough translation: "Smutty Angels"). It was a perfect meeting spot for the clandestinely inclined—the picture played around the clock and the customers would be intent on their own business, so to speak. Kovinski had taken three buses to get there and, as far as I could tell, hadn't spotted us. He looked at his watch, hurried down the steps, and disappeared inside.

I sat in the taxi with a dilemma. Whatever the public demand for a film about angels having sex, the place was bound to be empty at this hour, so there was a good chance that if I went in I'd be made, which would blow everything. On the other hand, anyone with half a brain would realize that Kovinski was a security risk and arrange an alternate exit in case someone like me had followed him and was watching the door. If I hung around I might lose him out the rear exit and be back to square one.

"Have you got a hat?" I asked Melik, and he produced a black fisherman's cap, which would have to do. I took it and told him to wait, even though I knew he wouldn't be going anywhere with the meter pushing seventy marks.

I went down the steps and inside the building. The lobby, if you could call it that, was dark, the only significant light coming from the ticket counter, which was a converted cloakroom inhabited by a young lady with bright pink fingernails who was reading a copy of *Der Spiegel* under a bronze table lamp in the shape of a reclining nude.

"Zwei Mark fünfzig," she said, looking up without moving her head. I gave her the money and she pushed a ticket across. I noticed the magazine was open to a story on the election of a new pope, following John XXIII's death earlier in the month. I remembered reading at the time that Kennedy's European tour, which included a stop in Rome for an audience with the Holy Father, had been delayed by his untimely demise. The president, unwilling to miss out on the chance to be blessed by—and photographed with—His Holiness, simply rescheduled the trip for the following week and announced to the world that he would look forward to meeting the new pontiff, putting a fair amount of pressure on the College of Cardinals to make a quick decision. It looked from the article like they'd come through, sending up the white smoke in a record-shattering two days.

The girl misinterpreted my interest, gave me a "don't even think of talking to me" look, and turned the page. She wasn't much older than sixteen, I thought. Back in the States, she'd be listening to Ricky Nelson records and dreaming about the junior prom.

I made my way into the basement screening room. It was small—maybe a dozen rows, ten seats across, with an aisle down the middle. I pulled the cap down over my forehead, slipped into a seat close to the door, and glanced around. I had underestimated the film's drawing power. There were twenty or so avid angel fans scattered around the room, in various states of consciousness. At least one of them was snoring. At least I hoped it was snoring.

Kovinski and his controller weren't hard to spot, the only twosome in a room full of solos. They were tucked away against the wall about halfway down the opposite side, Kovinski leaning over, talking animatedly to the guy, blocking my view of him.

I turned my attention to the screen. It was night, lit by moonlight, in black and white, very grainy. Two blondes with cardboard wings strapped to their backs were stretched out in the garden of some stately home performing heavenly acts on each other. Every once in a while the picture would cut to a reaction shot of the various marble statues overlooking the scene, which I guess allowed everyone to pretend they were watching art.

Kovinski was getting loud. I couldn't make out what he was saying, but it didn't sound good. He was agitated, making demands. He'd probably blown it, talked about the photograph. I thought he might, and even though I wished he hadn't, I knew it was worse for him than it was for me. In fact, it might work out fine for me. There was no way this guy, whoever he was, would let Kovinski walk away after he mentioned the photo. He'd have to put him on ice and it would be interesting to see where.

They started to attract attention. A guy in front kept looking over and finally shushed Kovinski. I pushed myself down into the seat, kept my eyes fixed on the moaning angels. I could sense Kovinski's companion getting agitated, looking around the theater, checking things out. Out of the corner of my eye, I saw him lean over and whisper something, presumably along the lines of "Let's get the hell out of here." As the two men got up and headed for the exit, I got my first look at the control agent's face—my old friend Baby Bear Andy Johnson, the Green Beret from West Texas, was heading up the aisle behind Kovinski.

He'd walk right by me, just inches away. Damn! Why the hell hadn't I waited outside? And why had I taken an aisle seat? The angels seemed to be reaching a climax and I prayed that the scene wouldn't end with them going up in a blaze of orgasmic light. I needed dark right now.

I tilted my head down slightly so the cap would cover most of my face. If I was too obvious I'd just draw attention, but my heart was pounding away so loudly that I thought they might hear it. I couldn't be sure, but I thought Kovinski spotted me then quickly looked away. He was such a klutz I was afraid Johnson might pick it up, but nothing came. They walked right by and out the door. I exhaled, counted to thirty, pulled myself out of the chair, and followed.

The lobby was empty except for the girl.

"The two men . . ." I said urgently. "Where did they go!"

"Out," she said, with studied boredom.

"Which way!" She lifted her head and showed me a smirk that shouldn't have been in her repertoire yet.

"Is there a back door?" I said urgently, realizing if Johnson had parked a car out there I was screwed. I hadn't thought it through, was playing it a bit too much by ear.

"The back door isn't allowed for the public," she shrugged lethargically.

I dug into my pocket, pulled out a few crumpled bills, threw them on the counter. She looked at them, then at me, wanting more.

"I think you'd better tell me," I said, taking a step toward her. She smiled, a little nervously, and pointed at a velvet curtain hanging on the opposite wall.

"There," she said, stuffing my money into her bra. "It's open."

I pulled the curtain aside, pushed the door open, and stepped into a narrow alleyway between two buildings.

Then the world went dark.

FOURTEEN

I woke up on a hard bed in a strange room, emerging from my black hole with the faint realization that I was still alive, a fact that became less gratifying as the pain hammering away at the base of my skull worked its way into my consciousness. I made an ill-advised attempt to lift my head, realized the mistake, and let it fall back onto the pillow. I think I groaned.

"He's comin' 'round," somebody said.

My eyes opened without warning and I recognized Andy Johnson—a little fuzzy around the edges—standing beside an open door. I started to pick up the thread of where I left off, wondered how much time had elapsed since he'd karate-chopped me into oblivion.

"I guess that's two I owe you," I croaked, lifting myself onto one elbow and feeling for a lump. It was pretty tender and I winced when I found the spot.

"Three strikes an' you're out," he drawled as Sam waltzed in, followed by Powell.

"How's the head?" Sam inquired.

"Sore," I grunted.

"Bruised ego, no doubt," Powell snorted, the sound of his irony-laden voice adding nausea to my growing list of complaints. I noticed he had my envelope in his hand.

"Fuck you all," I said, swinging my legs around to sit on the edge of the bare mattress, feeling slightly less vulnerable in an upright position. It was a bare room—four walls, the bed, a table, two armchairs, and a hidden microphone.

"Where are we?" I asked.

"One of our safe houses," Sam answered.

"Funny," I said, rubbing my neck, "I don't feel that safe."

Johnson slipped out the door, closing it behind him. Powell took up his place in one of the armchairs, leaning back with a self-satisfied grin on his face, while Sam paced back and forth at the foot of the bed. He took a few laps before opening the show.

"What the hell, Jack?"

"Am I supposed to answer that?"

"You're working the wrong side of the fence. They're the bad guys, goddammit!"

"Bad guys come in all shapes and sizes," I said, glancing at Powell.

"What about the Colonel?"

"What about him?"

"Last time I checked, he was the enemy."

"Look, Sam," I said, aware that I was wasting my breath as long as Powell was in the room, but knowing I had to say something, "The Colonel thinks there's a play on Kennedy. I don't know who, how, or why, but I don't think he's jerking us around. He's got good reason—"

"You mean this?" He stuck his hand out and Powell put the Kovinski photo into it.

"That's part of it."

Sam paused, gave me an unhappy look. He turned away, pulled a Havana out of his pocket, and took some time lighting it up. We waited for him.

"You got something else, Jack, you better spit it out," he finally said.

"Nothing solid," I said, knowing I couldn't say anything about the source of the photo, the Langley mole. I might later, but not while the information could be traced back to Josef and certainly not in front of Powell.

"What's this picture supposed to prove?" Sam said through a cloud of smoke.

"Doesn't it strike you as a bit odd that a guy who works for the KGB would pose for a shot like that?"

"Kovinski claims it's a fake," Powell interjected.

"And what does that tell you?" I shot back.

"I'm afraid you're the one who's answering the questions," he simpered.

"What should it tell us, Jack?" Sam demanded.

"That somebody went to a fair amount of trouble to make Kovinski into a crazed Commie killer."

"Kovinski thinks the Russians are setting him up," Powell piped in again.

"You think the KGB faked the picture in order to implicate themselves?"

"Kovinski says—"

"Kovinski will say whatever he thinks you want to hear," I interrupted, losing patience. I looked to Sam for help, but Powell had taken over. Sam stepped back, leaned against the wall, smoked his cigar, and listened.

"Why would the KGB set Kovinski up?" I persisted.

"Because they found out he works for us."

"Then why go to the trouble of making him look like one of their own, with the flag and the rifle? It's stupid." Powell's expression tightened. He was about to erupt when Sam answered the question.

"Maybe they plan to expose the photo as a fake after the fact. To show we were behind it."

"Come on, Sam," I said. "If the KGB wanted to assassinate the president—"

"Sam's not talking about the president," Powell interrupted. "You're the only one who buys into that fairy tale."

I turned to Sam. "What are you talking about, then?"

"Kovinski says the KGB are planning to hit a West German official and he's being set up to take the rap."

I drew a breath and laughed.

"That's funny?" Sam said.

"Forget the West German official." I shook my head. "Nobody's going after a West German official. I fed that to Kovinski and he spit it back at you. Anyway, I told him *you* were planning to whack the guy, not the Russians."

Sam looked to Powell, who lost the smirk.

"Why would we want to knock off a West German official?"

"As far as I know, you wouldn't," I answered.

"Then why would you tell Kovinski that?" he chafed.

"Because I didn't want to tell him the truth."

"The truth being that the Soviets are planning it."

I looked at him, incredulous. "I just told you—I made it up!"

"I'm afraid your word doesn't go very far around here at the moment." Powell smiled and leaned back in his chair, case closed as far as he was concerned.

"You fucked up, Jack," Sam shrugged. "But there's one angle I'm not totally clear on." He turned to Powell. "What do the Russkies get out of it?"

Powell hesitated, put on his professor's voice. "Look at it from their perspective. What would the Soviets most love to accomplish?"

"World domination?" Sam said with a sly smile. Powell ignored him and continued his lecture.

"To drive a wedge between us and NATO, that's what. Imagine the reaction in Western Europe if the Soviets could pin the murder of a European leader on us. What do you think de Gaulle would say about it? And what about the West Germans themselves? NATO's crippled, maybe forever, and they're toasting each other in Moscow."

"Good scenario," Sam admitted. "What about the Kennedy stuff?"

"The only source we have on that is Teller."

Sam nodded his head sagely, turned to me. "Jack?"

"It's a wonderful theory," I said. "The only problem is that no one is planning to hit a West German official. . . . *I made the fucking thing up!*"

"What else have you made up?" Powell grinned.

"Fuck you," I answered.

"What about Sasha?"

"What . . . ?"

He smiled. "You know the name Sasha, don't you?"

"In what context?" I said, feeling the noose tighten.

"You told Kovinski that you work for a KGB agent named Sasha," he purred. "Is that right?"

"Are you kidding me?"

"You can be sure I'm not kidding you. Did you or did you not say that you worked for a KGB agent named Sasha?"

I looked to Sam again.

"Answer the question, Jack," he said. I could see that he was getting no joy from this. He'd told me that I was on my own and I was finding out how much he meant it.

"Yes," I said. "I told Kovinski I worked for Sasha, but it was bullshit. I've never met the guy."

"How did you know Sasha was Kovinski's KGB controller?"

"The Colonel told me."

"A STASI colonel gave you information about a KGB control agent?"

"That's right," I said.

"That's Colonel Josef Becher, who you've been having unauthorized contact with?"

"Yeah, the one that you guys brought me all this way to see."

"After he insisted that he would see only you . . . Colonel Becher must have a great deal of trust in you to reveal sensitive information like the name of a KGB controller."

An answer to that question seemed a bit pointless, so I didn't bother.

"Where did you get the Kovinski photo?" Powell was in high gear now, playing to the microphone and enjoying every minute.

"The Colonel gave it to me."

"Did he tell you where he got it?"

I said no, but they both picked up my hesitation. Powell replaced the photo in the envelope and stood up.

"To sum up," he said, "you obtained a falsified photograph showing Aleks Kovinski, a CIA asset, holding a Soviet weapon in front of a Soviet flag. This photograph was given to you by a colonel in the East German security service with whom you've had several unauthorized contacts. When you showed Kovinski the photograph you indicated that you were working for a KGB agent whose code name is Sasha and there was a plan to assassinate an official of the West German government. You told Kovinski that the photograph would be given to the newspapers in order to implicate him in the assassination. We believe it would then be revealed as a fake and other evidence would surface to implicate Central Intelligence in the assassination. You instructed Kovinski to arrange a meeting with his CIA contact in order to obtain certain information, which he was to pass back to you in a meeting you arranged for later today. Presumably you would then forward that information to Sasha through Colonel Becher and it would be used as part of the evidence to connect Kovinski to the agency. . . . Other than empty denials, is there anything you'd like to offer now that can refute the preceding facts?"

It didn't matter what I answered because I knew the transcript, which would be in the next Washington dispatch, would conclude with the words *SUBJECT OFFERED NO RESPONSE/END INTERVIEW.*

For the record, my response was: "Shall I applaud now or should I just throw peanuts?"

The pain in my head was subsiding, leaving just the steady drumbeat of my throbbing brain to deal with. I lay back on the bed, eyes shut, and considered my situation. I probably should've been more worried about Powell's indictment, but I couldn't believe anyone would take it seriously. Anyway, it was more important at the moment to figure a way out of there.

I came up empty.

It was disappointing about Powell. When I'd seen that Johnson was Kovinski's contact, I was sure that it meant the station chief was involved, too, but his thickheaded need to avenge the bathroom incident had more or less proved his innocence. He was a jackass, all right, but he wasn't stupid enough to go on tape the day before the president was hit and call the plot a "fairy tale" if he knew anything. On reflection, he wasn't the type, anyway. Powell was a political animal, working his way up the Company ladder, doing what was necessary to get ahead. Oh, he'd approve the assassination of his grandmother if it helped his career, but he was too calculating to lay it all on the line unless it was a sure thing. If they got the president, he'd happily join the club and submit his résumé. At that point, the high priests of Langley would gather around and make all the awkward tapes and documents magically disappear, including today's laughable interrogation. They'd vanish into the agency's black files, never to be seen again. And so would I, which was an excellent reason to get back to the question of how I was gonna get the hell out of there.

I drew a blank again.

My mind turned to Andy Johnson. What about Baby Bear? Kovinski's contact, there was no doubt that he was involved. But he was naval intelligence out of special ops, a former Green Beret. Those guys have a religious devotion to the chain of command. They specialize in taking orders. So if Powell wasn't running him, who was? I wondered how long he had been assigned to Berlin and who had put him there.

I heard Sam's voice in the next room, talking in hushed tones. Where did my old friend fit in? He seemed strangely disengaged, unlike I'd ever seen him. Powell had been running the debriefing, if you could call it that, but Sam was going along. Why? He couldn't buy any of that crap about me working for Sasha or a hit on a West German official. So why was he letting me twist in the wind? Sure, the stakes were high, but up until now Sam had always come through for me.

The door opened and he walked in, alone this time. He looked preöccupied, unusually restrained.

"Come to get your knife out of my back?" I said, folding my hands behind my head, trying to look relaxed.

"I love you like a son, Jack, but I'm not about to put my ass on the line for you." He shoved his hands into his pockets and frowned. "For Christ's sake, you set *yourself* up! Didn't you know Kovinski would fuck you over?"

"I thought he'd be too scared," I shrugged.

"Yeah, he's so damned scared he never wants to see you again. The son of a bitch is demanding political asylum."

"Since when do guys like Kovinski get to make demands?"

"Personally, I don't give a shit."

"That your new motto?"

He looked at me, stung. I felt bad at first, but got over it. "A lot's changed in eighteen months, Jack," he said. "McCone doesn't have a clue and everyone's running around saying the sky's gonna fall after the election."

John McCone had been appointed DCI—Director of Central Intelligence—by Kennedy after the Bay of Pigs went pear-shaped and Allen Dulles, the quintessential Company man, was removed, along with several of his top lieutenants. But McCone was an outsider, a civilian, and if JFK thought he could get a handle on the agency that way, he was whistling Dixie. Everyone saw McCone as a caretaker, put in to hold the fort until Kennedy could "splinter the CIA into a thousand pieces and scatter it to the winds," like he'd promised in '61. The word was that once he got the second term under his belt, he'd fold the agency into Justice, where Bobby could run things.

"Where's Kovinski now?" I asked Sam.

"How in God's name could the whereabouts of that pissant be the most important thing on your mind right now?"

"You're pretty good at history, aren't you, Sam?" He shrugged, but I knew he was. "You know the name Gavrilo Princip?"

"The guy who shot the Archduke Ferdinand," he answered without hesitation. "What's he got to do with the price of eggs in China?"

"He was the pissant that got the First World War under way."

Sam pulled on his earlobe and made a face. "Do you really believe all this crap, Jack? You think there are guys in the agency who'd go that far?"

"Ever hear of the Black Hand?"

"Should I have?"

"No, the whole point is that you shouldn't have. The Black Hand was a secret society made up of Serbian army and intelligence officers. They planned and executed the assassination of Ferdinand because he was on a peace mission and they thought peace was another word for surrender. They wanted war and victory, so they arranged for the pissant named Gavrilo Princip to pull the trigger on the duke. It's just possible that if he never got the chance to take the shot that day, the Great War wouldn't have happened. So that's why I'm interested in where Kovinski is."

"I don't know where he is." Sam shook his head. "But there are plenty of pissants around. If you stop this one, there'll be another one in his place next week."

"So we have to get the Black Hand," I said. Sam gave me a long look and sighed. "Or maybe I should just go home and throw a beach party."

"Christ, Jack."

"What?"

"You're under arrest for treason."

I tried not to look concerned. "So unarrest me, Sam."

"No can do," he said. "Powell telexed a transcript of our chat to Langley and they want you detained in a military cell over at Clay-allee. I'm sorry."

"You gonna go along with this?"

"I just arranged the transport," he shrugged. At least he looked me in the eye when he said it.

Johnson put me in cuffs and walked me down to the street, where Chase, decked out in his trademark black turtleneck and leather jacket, was waiting in the Chrysler. The safe house stood on a tree-lined avenue of unexceptional homes whose unexceptional residents could be counted on to mind their own unexceptional business. No one was around to watch Johnson guide me into the front seat then slide into the back, positioning himself directly behind me. Like the mob does when they take you for a ride.

Chase put the car in gear and we moved off.

I thought about various options, but they all ended in disaster. My only hope, a small one, was to catch them off guard. I was still a bit disoriented, unsure how long I'd been unconscious, so I asked the boys what the time was.

"Quarter to twelve," Johnson replied.

"Tuesday?" I said, just to be sure.

"Tuesday," Johnson confirmed.

"I want you guys to know that I don't hold this against you," I said. "I realize that you're just doing your job."

Chase allowed himself a little chuckle. "That's a real load off my mind, Teller."

I rattled my chains: "Well, Alcatraz here I come."

"They closed it," Johnson said. I twisted around, ostensibly to make eye contact, but actually I wanted to see exactly where he was sitting.

"Closed the Rock?" I said, incredulous. In fact, I'd read about it in the *Miami Herald*. It was too old and too expensive to run, or so the board of governors said anyway.

"Couple of months ago."

"Is nothing sacred?" I said, facing front again. If I went for Chase, you could count in milliseconds how long it would take Johnson to have me dead or unconscious. And there was no doubting his credentials.

"Too bad," Chase said. "You woulda fit in nicely."

"I guess they'll find me someplace just as nasty. I don't mind, as long as it's not in West Texas."

"Up yours, man," Johnson said with a chuckle. Even after he'd attacked my larynx and bruised my skull, I still kind of liked the kid. At least he had a sense of humor, which was more than I could say for his partner.

"How about you? What rock did you crawl out from under?" I said to Chase, and got back his standard murderous look.

I saw that my door wasn't locked. I wondered if I could open the door, roll out onto the street, and make a run for it. Chase was moving along, though, doing fifty or better. My best bet was a traffic light along the way. I'd pray for red and hope for the best. They'd probably shoot me down before I made ten steps, but it was better than nothing.

"I don't know about you, but I won't miss this city," I said, hoping to strike a chord, keep them relaxed. "It's a real armpit."

"You can say that again," Chase mumbled.

"How the hell'd you get stuck here anyway? You seem like a guy who likes a bit more action."

He kept his eyes straight ahead like he was going to ignore it, but then he said, "I'll be back in Saigon by Friday. Southeast Asia, man, that's where it's at."

"I've heard that," I said, and I wasn't lying. Word was they had an army of killers out there and were going through the population one by one. "So how'd they get you to come over here?" I said, pushing my luck as always. "You're a contract guy, right?" This time Chase saw through it and offered up a real "fuck you" look.

"Don't you know when to quit, Teller?" Johnson said from the back.

I was about to say something clever when . . . *wham!* Out of nowhere, we hit something hard. The car lurched sharply to the right and came to a crashing halt, accompanied by the sound of screeching tires and crunching metal. I was thrown forward and bounced my head off the windshield.

I was conscious but knocked silly. I lifted my hands, still cuffed together, and touched my forehead. There was blood but I couldn't tell how much. Everything was in slow motion and muted, like we were underwater. My second concussion of the day and it wasn't even noon yet.

"Jesus Fucking Christ!" Johnson was saying. "Don't do that!" I looked over and saw that Chase had a big Colt Anaconda pistol in his hand.

"Put it away!" Johnson said. "It's just a taxi. . . . You drove into a goddamned taxi!"

Chase turned on Johnson, eyes flashing. "The prick pulled in front of me!" You could see he wanted to kill somebody.

"Stow the goddamn weapon, man!" Johnson ordered, and after a brief standoff, Chase returned it to the shoulder holster under his jacket.

I noticed there was a fair amount of blood on my shirt. Johnson leaned forward and put a hand on my shoulder. "You all right, Teller?" I said something, I'm not sure what, but it sounded like somebody else had said it.

"The driver's coming over," Chase said with an edge in his voice.

"Get rid of him," Johnson said. "Give him some money if you have to."

"Like hell," Chase growled. "The prick cut me off!"

This is it, I thought, my moment. Get the fuck out! But I was paralyzed, so punch-drunk that I couldn't even raise my arm to open the door. I dropped my head onto the back of the seat and turned my eyes toward the window. That's when I saw Melik walking toward us.

FIFTEEN

"Ist alles okay?" Melik leaned into the driver's-side window and looked around the interior of the car. Chase didn't say a word, just glared at him.

"Everybody's fine," Johnson answered from the back.

"He is not look so fine," Melik said, glancing at me.

"It's just a scratch," Johnson assured him.

"He is need doctor."

"He's fine." Johnson smiled. "So if you could just move your vehicle, we'll be on our way." Melik paused, took a second look at me.

"I take to doctor. . . . Come." He gestured to me but I stayed put for the moment.

"I'm a doctor," Johnson said. "So there's nothing to worry about.

Here, let me give you some money for the damage and we'll be on our way. How about that?" He reached for his wallet.

"Put the money away," Chase said quietly. Johnson tried to hand Melik a fistful of bills, but Chase blocked him. "He's not getting any goddamned money," he said, then turned to Melik. "Get the fuck outta here, you piece of shit."

I was trying to hold back the flow of blood with my palm, waiting for my moment.

"Give him the money and let's get the hell out of here," Johnson said firmly.

"He fucking cut me off!" Chase hissed. "You're not getting any handouts, Ahab, so fuck off home and take a bath. It'll be a new experience."

Melik looked Chase in the eye and smiled easily. "I don't take money. . . ."

"Then get lost," Chase said. "Move your fucking car."

"I take him to doctor," Melik said, nodding toward me.

Chase couldn't believe his ears. He started to get out of the car, but stopped abruptly when he found the barrel of Melik's vintage Luger pressed against his temple.

"You stay in car and put hands where I see," Melik ordered. Chase reluctantly grabbed the steering wheel. "You also." Melik looked to Johnson, who raised his arms.

"Hey, no problem, friend," Johnson said agreeably. "We don't want no trouble. Look, why don't you just take the money? How much you figure for the damages?"

Melik ignored him, told me to get out. I pushed the door open and stepped onto the street. My legs were a little shaky, but I managed to step away and close the door without falling over. Feeling a lot better outside the car, I wiped the blood out of my right eye and walked around to the driver's side, where Melik still had his piece against Chase's temple.

"Keys," Melik demanded. Chase handed them over and the Turk tossed them into some long grass by the side of the road.

"Do you know this clown, Teller?" Chase said.

"I'd be careful what you say about a guy who's holding a bullet six inches from your brain," I answered. "He might think you don't like him." Then, to Melik: "He's got a gun under his jacket."

"Give it," Melik instructed.

"You're making a big fucking mistake," Chase said as he eased the Colt out of its holster.

"Don't you make mistake." Melik pushed his gun harder against Chase's forehead. "Because I don't mind kill you." He confiscated the weapon, held it out for me.

"Take," he said, and I grabbed it between my cuffed hands. I was surprised at how light it was, considering its size. The .44 Magnum Anaconda was built for one purpose—to inflict maximum damage on human flesh. The weapon of choice for psychokillers like Chase. I opened the back door and took aim at Johnson.

"Yours, too, cowboy," I said. "Slide it over."

Johnson reached under his jacket, placed his more conventional Beretta nine-millimeter automatic on the seat and pushed it over to me. I leaned into the car to pick it up and almost blacked out.

"You know this is it for you, Teller," Johnson said matter-of-factly. "You're dog meat now."

"I'll take the key for the cuffs, too," I said, dropping Johnson's pistol into my pocket while concentrating hard on staying upright. Johnson dug into his front pocket and came up with a small metal key. He held it up between his index and middle finger, studied it for a second, then placed it in his mouth and swallowed hard. It could've been under his tongue, but a search-and-rescue at that point would've been ill-advised, certainly not desirable.

"Oops," he said with a big "screw you" Texas grin. I suddenly lost any warm feelings I'd felt for him and unloaded a round into the window next to his face. The goddamned thing went off like a cannon and Johnson's smirk disappeared right away. He kept his cool under fire, though, calmly looking over at the six-inch hole in the window, then back at me.

"Let's see the molars," I said. He didn't believe me so I put another one into the seat by his leg and he opened wide. Sure enough, the crazy bastard had swallowed it.

"That's gonna hurt on the way out," I said.

"Anything for my country," he responded with a smile.

"Excuse me if I don't salute."

The shooting had spooked Melik. "Leave him!" he said nervously, probably thinking I was about to blow Johnson away. "Go to taxi!"

"I don't know if that's a good idea," I responded. "I'll stay here while you—"

"Go to taxi!" he insisted. "I come!"

I didn't like it, but it was time to go, not argue. I backpedaled my way to the cab, keeping an eye and the six-shooter trained on Chase. The right side of the taxi was caved in, crushed by the Chrysler, so I opened the driver's-side door, propped myself up against it.

"Okay, let's go," I called out. "I've got you covered!"

Then Melik made his mistake—he looked over his shoulder at me without stepping away first. It was all Chase needed. He got hold of Melik's wrist and yanked him into the car. Johnson leapt forward and grabbed hold, twisted his forearm around, snapping the elbow at the joint and disarming him. Melik screamed, but Chase got him in a headlock through the window and I had no clear shot. It was over before I had a chance—Melik stopped struggling, twitched a couple of times, then went limp. Chase let him go and the poor bastard dropped to the ground, faceup, a four-inch blade buried in his trachea.

Chase and Johnson exploded out of the car. I fired off three rounds, missing everything but making a lot of noise. The boys hit the dirt long enough for me to dive into the taxi, praying to any God who'd listen to please, *please* let the keys be in the ignition. Somebody got the message and I fired up the engine, found first gear, and floored it.

I looked in the rearview mirror, saw Johnson down on one knee, in military posture, emptying the Luger in my direction. One of the slugs came through the back window and lodged in the dashboard, but I didn't see it until later, after I'd stopped.

I drove for about ten minutes, long enough to get out of the area, then pulled into a parking garage and headed down to the basement, where I tucked the taxi into a corner space. I sat in the dark for a few minutes, trying to get my bearings and assess my physical condition. It felt like a nasty gash on my forehead, at the hairline above my right eye. I turned on the overhead light and inspected the wound in the mirror, dabbing it with an oily rag that was in the glove compartment. It wasn't deep and the flow of blood seemed to be abating. I'd live.

I felt bad about Melik. I hardly knew the guy, but if I'd taken control of the situation Chase wouldn't have been able to execute him like that. It was sickening and unnecessary. A few years earlier we would've worked him over for whatever information we could get out of him, stripped him to his underwear, and dumped him by the side of the road, bruised and battered, but still breathing. The times they were a-changing.

Clearly, Melik wasn't your run-of-the-mill cabbie who I just happened to flag down, but I couldn't figure out where he'd come from. My head just wasn't in gear yet, because once the penny dropped, it was too obvious. There was only one way he could've picked me up.

So Horst was a plant. From the moment he'd asked me for a light at the beer hall, he'd been working me. I should've spotted it, and I guess I did have my suspicions, when he showed up at the hotel and when I saw that he'd rifled my pockets and found the Kovinski photo, but even then I'd given him the benefit of the doubt. I wondered if I'd lost my edge, but that kind of thinking wasn't gonna get me anywhere. Horst could wait. Right now I had to figure out how to pick up the thread again.

I spotted a hack license in the glove compartment. The black-and-white photo showed a young student type with long, scruffy hair and the faint beginnings of a beard on his chin. Axel Kindermann, the ID said, eighteen years old. I guessed that Axel had recently left the keys in his taxi and came back to find it gone.

There was half a pack of Turkish nonfilters on the dash. Lifesavers. I looked around for a match, but there wasn't a goddamned one in the car and the cigarette lighter was missing. I guess Axel wasn't a smoker. I dropped the pack into my shirt pocket for later and picked up Chase's Colt, which had ended up on the floor. I was pretty sure I'd used five of its six bullets and I was right; there was still one in the chamber. I stuck the monster in my pocket and took the Beretta out, looked it over. It was compact, more my style, and had a full clip of fifteen ready to go. I made sure the safety was engaged and shoved it into my belt.

The cuffs were the first order of business. I grabbed the car keys, squeezed out through the tiny space I'd left between the taxi and the garage wall, and went around to the back. I was still a bit shaky and it was dark, so it took a minute to pop the trunk, but once I did, I found what I was looking for—a metal toolbox, big enough that it might hold something useful. I flipped the lid and dug through it, uncovering all sorts of screwdrivers, wrenches, ratchets, nuts, screws, and bolts, a hammer, a bicycle pump, a crowbar, and, for some reason, a map of Ireland. About the only thing that wasn't in there was a hacksaw. My frustration eased a bit when I found a box of matches. I pocketed a couple of screwdrivers, which might come in handy at my next stop, then closed the trunk, leaned against the back fender, and fired up one of the Turkish delights. Heaven.

There seemed to be no way around it—I'd have to shoot the cuffs off. I pulled Johnson's pistol out and looked it over, holding the cigarette between my lips, letting the smoke drift up my nose. It might work, but then again, the nine-millimeter slug could easily bounce off the reinforced metal and head straight into my face.

No, if I was gonna do it, I might as well do it right. It would have to be the Anaconda.

I tucked the Beretta away, dropped my half-smoked cigarette onto the floor, and slid into the backseat. Removing the big gun from my pocket, I wrapped the oily, blood-soaked rag around it, then held it upside down in my right hand with my thumb against the trigger, fingers wrapped around the handle. There was only about two inches of chain between my manacles, which I put on the seat and pulled as tautly as I could, placing the six-inch barrel right up against it in order to fire point-blank. The idea was for the bullet to blast through the metal then continue down into the upholstery instead of back at me. That was the theory, anyway.

The barrel was just a little too long and hard to control from that angle. It kept slipping off the chain and pointing at various parts of my body, leading me to seriously reconsider the wisdom of my plan. Maybe I could get by with the cuffs, at least for a while, until I came up with an alternative. . . .

Fuck it. There was no alternative. I closed my eyes, said a quick prayer, and pulled the trigger. The pistol kicked hard and my hands flew apart as the slug blasted through the cuffs like they were ninety-nine cents a pair from Woolworth's. There was a large, scorched hole where the bullet had blown through the seat. I congratulated myself on my ingenuity and stepped out of the car. A brand-new silver Porsche 911 caught my eye. Not the easiest thing on wheels to hot-wire, but worth the effort. Like the ad said, "Just for the Fun of It."

I'd taken a couple of steps when I noticed the pungent aroma of gasoline in the air and a trickling sound coming from underneath the taxi. It didn't take a genius to figure out that the liquid was pouring through the .44-caliber bullet hole that I'd just put in the fuel tank. Just when I was thinking how lucky I was that it hadn't exploded on impact, I noticed that the rapidly expanding pool of flammable fuel was no more than two inches from the still-smoking cigarette butt I'd tossed aside a few minutes earlier.

I got maybe halfway to the exit, running at full tilt, when the blast hit. It picked me up, carried me through the air, and slammed my rag-doll body against a concrete wall. I bounced hard onto the ground, struggled to my feet, and, holding my bruised rib cage, stumbled through the smoke to the doorway. I managed to pull the heavy steel door open and start up the stairwell just as the building's foundation was rocked by a series of explosions, one on top of the other, as car after car on the basement floor took its turn to go *BOOM!*

SIXTEEN

I picked up an old Alfa Spider a couple of blocks from the garage. Very nice, jet-black with burgundy leather inside. I could've had the less conspicuous white Ford sedan parked across the street, but I went for style over substance.

With no idea about my location, I stopped at the first newsstand I came across and bought a map of Berlin. The proprietor, a hulk of a guy who must've been built into the kiosk, gave me a funny look and I realized I'd better get rid of my blood-soaked shirt if I wanted to avoid attention. I paid for the map, along with a copy of *Berliner Morgenpost,* which had Kennedy's picture plastered all over the front page, and headed back to the car.

My left side was pretty sore and I wondered if I'd cracked a rib in the explosion. I gave it a poke, decided it didn't hurt enough to be broken, then tried rotating my arm a couple of times to loosen things up. I thought better of it when a sharp pain shot through my diaphragm and up my arm to my shoulder. Better to leave well enough alone.

Opening the driver's-side door and gingerly removing my jacket, I took the shirt off, rolled it into a ball, and tossed it behind the seat. The T-shirt was relatively free of blood, so I slipped the jacket on over it. It was a bit Miami Beach, but it would do. I sat behind the wheel and looked the paper over. Kennedy's Berlin itinerary was printed in a box in the lower right-hand corner. I spent a moment on it, trying to commit it to memory, then turned to the headline, which translated KENNEDY CONQUERS COLOGNE! The lead article went something like this:

> *Bonn, 25 June — Though the weather was fine this morning, the day got off to a chilly start for President Kennedy as he met with Chancellor Adenauer and other officials in the capital city. But then came the 35-mile drive to Cologne. More than one million Rhinelanders lined the American President's route, chanting and applauding wildly as he passed. In Cologne itself, Mr. Kennedy drew a crowd of at least 350,000 people, who showed their approval with a big roar when he concluded his speech with the words* "Kolle Alaaf!" *("Hooray for Cologne!")*

Not exactly in-depth political analysis, but interesting nonetheless. The West German government might not have succumbed to JFK's charms, but its people seemed to have fallen under his spell. And the enthusiastic reception was just what the president needed to help him with his European problem.

The European problem was a "mutual defense pact" the German government had signed with France. On the surface, it was an historic achievement, two bitter enemies coming together after a century of catastrophic warfare. In reality—at least in Washington's view—it was dangerous stuff and Kennedy's primary mission in

Europe was to scuttle it. Which accounted for his chilly reception in Bonn.

De Gaulle was the troublemaker, as usual. The French president didn't hide his contempt for America's influence on the Continent, and he missed no opportunity to undermine it. With this treaty, de Gaulle was tacitly encouraging the Germans to develop their own nuclear deterrent. He didn't actually want them to have the bomb; he just wanted to put Kennedy in a position where he'd have to veto it, believing that the German people would resent him for interfering. But it didn't look like resentment on the streets—and you could bet that Monsieur de Gaulle wouldn't be getting the Elvis treatment if he turned up in Cologne.

Kennedy had seen in Cuba just how easily the unthinkable could happen, and he knew that even the suggestion of missiles in West Germany would make that near catastrophe look like a walk in the park. After coming so close, he wanted the world to take a step back from the brink, not dive over it. Just two weeks earlier, he'd announced high-level talks in Moscow, saying it was time to negotiate arms control with the Soviets.

And that brought me back to the Black Hand—the ring of military officers and spies who, a half century earlier, had conspired to gun down the archduke as he rode in his open car through the streets of Sarajevo. He had tried for peace, too, and with his death the men of that secret society got the war they wanted. I shuddered to think about history repeating itself in Berlin. Kennedy would arrive in less than twenty-four hours and there were men waiting for him who believed that negotiation with the enemy was nothing short of treason. But if these men got their war, it wouldn't be fathers strapping on their rifles, kissing their wives and children good-bye, and marching off to battle, as my father had done. Not this time. This time the war would come to us. It would come as we slept and it wouldn't discriminate. We would all pay the price—men, women, and children.

I tossed the paper aside, got a fix on where I was and where I was going, put the car in gear, and pulled away.

I parked a block away from Kovinski's building. There wasn't much chance of finding him at home—the boys would have him stashed away somewhere—but I hoped I could pick up some sort of lead in his apartment. I had no idea what I was looking for. A scrap of paper, an address, anything to get me back on track. It occurred to me that he might have a wife or girlfriend hanging around, but having met the guy, it seemed unlikely. It'd be easier if he didn't, but it wouldn't stop me if he did.

I rang the bell a few times until I was satisfied that no one was going to answer, then started down the line of buzzers. I was about halfway through them when an old woman's soft voice came over the intercom.

"Wer ist da?" she said sweetly.

Figuring he wouldn't be on speaking terms with his neighbors, I told her, in German, that I was Herr Kovinski from 5C and I'd forgotten my key, could she be so kind as to let me in? She buzzed the door open without another word. Nice lady, I thought as I stepped into the lobby. It was dark and cool inside, the stark interior consisting of nothing more than painted cinder-block walls and a bare concrete floor.

There was a small elevator on one side, but I took the stairs. If the place was being watched, which was certainly possible, I'd have been spotted and would be a sitting duck in the lift. At least I'd have a fighting chance out in the open. I pulled the Beretta, switched the safety off, and stuck it back in my belt, where I could easily get to it. Carefully opening the door onto the fifth floor, I stepped into a long, empty hallway that smelled of somebody's Wiener schnitzel, making me feel a bit queasy.

All the apartments had basic cylinder locks, easy as pie, and 5C had no extra security. I listened for a couple of seconds before getting started, just to be sure, then pulled out the two screwdrivers I'd taken from the taxi before it went up in flames. I pressed the smaller of the two, a very thin one used for electrical work, against the door frame, bending the tip to a forty-five-degree angle. I then pushed the larger tool into the lock and turned it clockwise, applying enough pressure to slightly offset the cylinder from its housing. Inserting the bent screwdriver, I got under the pins one by one and lifted until I heard the soft click as each fell into place. It took about ninety seconds—like riding a bicycle, I thought. I pushed the door open, looked around, and stepped inside.

By the time I sensed anything, it was too late—the figure flew out from behind the door like a missile, plowed into my back, and took me down with a bone-crunching tackle that would've made Vince Lombardi cry tears of joy. My right cheekbone broke the fall, hitting the floor with a *whack* and bouncing a couple of times as my attacker tried to get me in a half-nelson. My head had been the subject of so much abuse in the preceding hours that I hardly felt a thing, but I'd had just about enough of being knocked around for one day. This was the last straw.

I let out a bloodcurdling scream, grabbed the guy's head, and flipped his body over my shoulder, landing him hard on his back. I jumped up to a kneeling position, whipped the Beretta out, and shoved the barrel up my assailant's nostril.

"Horst!" I exclaimed.

"Jack!" he cried. "I didn't know it was you!"

"Jesus Christ, Horst! You're lucky I didn't blow your goddamned head off! Are you nuts?"

"Yes, I think it must be so," he smiled impishly. I sat there for a minute until he finally said, "May I stand up now?"

I took a deep breath and stepped away. "Sure. Get up. Get up against the the wall so I can search you."

"I don't carry a weapon," he assured me as he scooped himself off the floor. I pushed him against the wall and patted him down.

Once I was sure he was clean, I stowed the Beretta and he collapsed with a sigh onto the single bed that occupied one side of the tiny studio apartment. A filthy kitchenette took up the other side, with a table, chair, and television set in between. There was a box of papers in an open closet, in the process of being rifled.

"What the hell are you doing here?" I said.

"I was about to ask you the same."

"I'm not in a very good mood, Horst, so why don't you just tell me who sent you up here?"

"Why should anyone send me? I'm simply robbing this apartment." He shrugged innocently. "I hope you won't tell Hanna about it. She would be quite disappointed in me."

"Knock it off, Horst. You're insulting my intelligence."

"I suppose it's a bit far-fetched," he admitted. "But it's the best I can think of at the moment."

"For Christ's sake, is everyone in this town a spy?"

"Most have tried it at one time or another," he smiled.

I went to the window and peeked through the blinds, wondering if he was alone. "What were you looking for anyway?"

He shrugged. I picked up one of the documents in the box, which was nothing more than an overdue electricity bill.

"This is dangerous stuff you're mixed up in."

"Perhaps I can take care of myself," he grinned.

"Yeah, sure, like your friend Melik," I said, pulling the box of papers out of the closet. I sat in the chair, grabbed a fistful, and started going through them.

"What about Melik?" he said, looking concerned. I realized that it hadn't been much over an hour since it happened and Horst couldn't know yet. My sense of time was a bit out of whack after the various head traumas of the morning.

"He a friend of yours?"

"My partner," he said. "And yes, I suppose a friend, too. Where is he?"

"Dead," I said flat out, not being in a particularly sensitive frame of mind. Horst's face dropped, like he'd been punched in the gut, then he lowered his head and just stared at the floor. I felt bad, but it was better that he knew how things could go.

"I can't believe it," he said, shaking his head. "How does it happen? Was it an accident?"

"Oh no . . . Very deliberate. One of the bad guys killed him."

"Killed?" he said incredulously. "Why *killed*?"

"Because he was pointing a Luger at the guy's head and he let down his guard."

"But he wouldn't have used it. . . ."

"Then he shouldn't have been pointing it," I said sharply. It was the truth and Horst had better know it. "You don't put a gun to someone's head unless you're capable of pulling the trigger. Especially not when the guy is someone like this guy."

"Melik had a wife and a young child," Horst said softly. "Who will tell them?"

"Nobody will tell them, at least not the truth," I said. "It wouldn't do them any good, anyway." I continued examining Kovinski's papers. There was nothing useful—overdue bills and overdrawn bank statements.

"But he was a hero," Horst said. "Perhaps even he saved your life. Shouldn't they know it?"

"I don't know if he was a hero or not, Horst, and to tell you the truth, it doesn't make a goddamned bit of difference if he was or he wasn't, because he's dead. And whatever they tell you, a dead hero is worthless, no good to anyone. Certainly not to his wife or kid. I'm very sorry for them, but it's done and there's nothing we can do to make it better. That's just how it is. If you don't like it, you'd better walk out the door right now and tell Sam you quit."

He looked at me, thoroughly taken aback. "Since when did you know I am working for Sam?"

"I just figured it out," I said.

"How?"

"You phoned someone this morning to tell them about the picture of Kovinski you found in my jacket. Right?"

"Yes . . ." he reluctantly admitted.

"They told you to arrange for Melik to be there when I needed a taxi, didn't they?"

"That's right, yes," he said, looking more impressed by the minute.

"Well, Melik didn't come after me because I stiffed him for the fare, so someone told him to intercept the car. Since Sam arranged for my transportation, it had to be him. And you just said that Melik probably saved my life, even though I didn't tell you what happened, which means you knew what he was doing. So you're working for Sam."

"Yes, it's logical," he said. "I think."

"Sam told you to watch me, huh?"

"Yes."

"Why?"

"He has told me that you sometimes can be a lost cannon—"

"*Loose* cannon," I corrected him.

"Yes, that's right. So I arranged to meet you at the beer hall. I was only to find out what I could and report it back to Sam. That's all. No one was supposed to get killed. Poor Melik."

Yeah, poor Melik, I thought. It wasn't the smoothest move Sam had ever made. Using raw talent to watch your own people is one thing, but sending them up against trained killers like Chase and Johnson is quite another. It meant he was operating without a lot of elbow room. Unsure who he could trust in the Company, he had to use his own operatives, even if they were a bit green. Sam always had a few handpicked assets on the street, small-time criminals, like Horst, or more experienced reprobates like myself. He felt crooks already had the instincts and some of the skills necessary for the line of work, and he was more confident of their loyalties because they were new to the game. "An old whore might know all the tricks," he explained to me once, "but that's because she's fucking every kid on the block. Give me a virgin with natural talent every time."

Horst was inexperienced, all right, but I wasn't sure about the natural talent. I thought about sending him home. I'd grown kind of fond of him and I didn't want him to end up like Melik. I guess I felt some sort of obligation, maybe in part because of Hanna. But I knew no matter what I said, he wouldn't go home, so I let him stick around. At least that way I could keep an eye on him.

We gave the place a pretty thorough going-over and came up empty. The only thing I got out of his papers was that Kovinski had been in West Berlin since February, had paid none of his bills, including rent, and had seen the 732 marks in his bank account dwindle to less than zero. There'd been a couple of small cash deposits recently, but nothing significant. He seemed to be a voracious reader of newspapers and magazines of all kinds, in both German and Polish, and had a newly issued borrowing card from the public library. There was no address book in the apartment, no employment information, no diary, no photos, nothing at all to help pick up the trail. I sat down and contemplated the big fat dead end I was facing, thought I'd better locate Sam, see what he had in mind when he arranged to spring me.

"Look at this," Horst said, pulling a dozen pamphlets out of a jacket that was lying crumpled on the closet floor. He passed one over to me. "Kovinski has been reading some propaganda."

"Or handing it out," I said, considering the number he had in his possession.

The handout consisted of a couple of badly printed pages on cheap paper, titled *"Die Wahrheit über die Wand"* ("The Truth About the Wall"). It was pretty standard stuff:

> *They panic in West Berlin! But why? It is the aggressive policy of the NATO allies that created the wall which today divides our*

> *city! The imperialist forces, led by the United States, have systematically converted West Berlin into a center of provocation, where ninety espionage organizations attempt acts of sabotage against our socialist brothers!*
>
> *The protective wall serves the cause of world peace! It halts the advance of the neo-Hitlerites toward the East! The imperialist espionage centers, their Fascist solders' associations, their youth poisoners, and their currency racketeers have been walled in! We have erected this wall as a safeguard against the Fascist forces who today dominate Western Europe and threaten our people tomorrow!*

And so on. Typical of the ranting and raving, twisting of facts, hyperbole, embellishment, exaggeration, and downright lies put out on a daily basis by the East German state propaganda machine. Except that this particular piece of nonsense came off a Company printing press. I'd have put money on it.

Why would the KGB put its own asset on the street, passing out anti-American tripe, when he was supposed to be infiltrating the CIA? It didn't make any sense. And Kovinski sure as hell wasn't a committed Marxist standing on a street corner handing out truth on his own time. On the other hand, it was classic Company image building, and it fit right into the profile that was being built for him—a fanatic Communist with a violent hatred for the "forces of imperialism," an extremist who would love nothing more than to put a bullet in the president of the United States. His makers would ensure that people noticed him on the street, too, maybe even have him cause some sort of disturbance so that passersby would remember his face. After the event, witnesses would come forward to testify about their encounter with the crazy leftist. Kovinski probably believed he was infiltrating some Communist student group when, in fact, he was dancing on strings he didn't even know existed. And whoever was putting him together had him right where they wanted him. A crazy Commie with a gun and a grudge.

"Where's Sam now?" I asked Horst.

"I don't know," he lied. I took the receiver off its cradle and put it in his hand.

"Call him," I said. He gave me a look, but he dialed. When Sam got on the line I grabbed the phone.

"When did they put you in charge of the Junior Secret Agent Club?" I said.

"Didn't you get your decoder ring?" he shot back without missing a beat. "You and Horst get together?"

"Sure. He tried out his flying Joe Jitzu move on me," I said. Horst sulked in a corner, but Sam laughed.

"Anybody hurt?"

"The Turk isn't so good."

"Yeah, too bad about that."

"What the hell were you thinking, sending him up against guys like Chase and Johnson?"

"I was thinking about saving your ass, Jack."

"You're going about it in a pretty strange way," I said.

"I don't have a whole hell of a lot to work with, you being public enemy number one and all."

"Why did you go along with Powell's bullshit?"

"Because at this point I don't know who's doing what to who. This thing could lead anywhere."

I wanted to make sure I heard him right. "So you accept that there's a conspiracy?"

There was a pause. If I hadn't heard him breathing, I would've though we'd been cut off. Finally he sighed heavily and said, "There's some strange shit going on all right. I don't know what's up, but something is."

It was a relief. I was starting to think Sam had gone soft in the head, going along with all that crap Powell was shoveling.

"What've you got there?" he asked.

"Nothing."

"You sure about that?" He sounded surprised.

"Sure I'm sure."

"Nothing?"

"The apartment's clean, Sam. Just some unpaid bills and a library card."

There was a pause, then he said, "Gimme a couple of hours, maybe I can get to Kovinski."

"Where is he?"

"That's what I need the couple of hours to find out. Hang tight and call me back on this number," he said, then hung up.

Naturally, I was happy to learn that Sam hadn't cut me loose after all, but something didn't sit right. Maybe I was reading too much into it, but it threw him when I said we'd come up empty in Kovinski's apartment, like I'd gone off script or something. And in all the years I'd worked for him, Sam had never put a shadow on me—at least not that I was aware of. I knew that he never played anything straight up the middle, but up until now I'd always known where he was coming from.

Anyway, there was nothing to do but wait, so Horst and I went back to the Alfa. He started reading Kovinski's pamphlet out loud, translating as he went, and I pulled out the Turkish smokes, offering him one. He turned it down then went quiet, and I realized in midpuff that it was because the cigarettes had belonged to Melik.

"Did you know him long?" I asked.

"Not so long," he said. "Just a few months. We had a business together."

"Stealing cars," I said, and he gave me a wary look. "Don't worry, you're sitting in one." I pointed out the wired ignition cables and he looked impressed.

"Perhaps you can teach me this."

"What the hell kind of thief can't hot-wire a car?"

"It was a new venture," he explained. "We took only cars which had the keys inside. You'd be surprised how many that is." He paused a moment, then said, "Perhaps I will smoke one of Melik's cigarettes. As a tribute."

"Why not?" I said, and lit him up.

We smoked quietly for a moment. Horst absentmindedly stared at one of Kovinski's pamphlets, then said, "You know, I think I will speak with Melik's wife. If it was me, I would want my child to know for what cause I died."

"What cause did he die for?"

"Freedom," he said without hesitation.

There were a million cynical responses to that, but I thought I'd let it stand. What the hell, maybe he was right. Maybe that was the cause Melik had died for, even if he didn't know it. And maybe in Berlin you couldn't afford to be cynical about freedom because you only had to look over your back wall to see what it meant not to have it.

I wondered how much Horst knew about what was going on. Not much, I guessed, and found out I was right when I probed a bit. I decided to keep him in the dark, at least for the moment. He started reading the pamphlet again, then stopped.

"Strange," he said.

"What's that?"

"This address. It's an unusual neighborhood for a group like this."

"Let me see that," I said, grabbing the paper out of his hand. Sure enough, the back page of the pamphlet was stamped with an address:

Kommission für Wahrheit
Lagerweg, 455
Haselhorst, Berlin

SEVENTEEN

Horst made himself useful as a navigator, breaking us loose from midday traffic with a few choice shortcuts and finding the out-of-the-way industrial park where Lagerweg 455 was located with relative ease. The building itself was a shabby, three-story brick warehouse of late-nineteenth-century vintage, situated at the bottom of a cul-de-sac beside one of the canals that ran through the northwestern corner of Berlin. Horst was right. It wasn't the sort of place you'd expect to find the "Commission for Truth."

There was a fair amount of activity in the street as workers made their way back from lunch hour, but the Alfa was a bit out of place among the beat-up vans and delivery trucks, so I swung around and parked back on the main road, a couple of blocks away. I tried to get Horst to stay with the car, but he was already out the door and I could see he wasn't going to be dissuaded.

"Two is better than one," he said, but I wasn't so sure about that. Maybe there was nothing to this place, just a bogus address plucked out of thin air for the brochure, but my gut said otherwise. And if there was something going on in there, I'd have enough to worry about without adding Horst to the mix.

There was a bend in the road where a small crowd was gathered around a lunch wagon. I told Horst to get a sausage and make himself inconspicuous. "Keep an eye on the building."

"But—"

"If I run into trouble, I'll need you out here."

"How will I know that you're in trouble?"

"If I'm not back in twenty minutes, I'm in trouble."

"What then shall I do?"

"Call the cavalry," I said.

"What is the number of the cavalry?" he called after me as I headed for the warehouse.

I approached from the opposite side of the street in order to get the widest view possible of the building. The entrance seemed to lead onto a stairway that ran up to the roof, presumably providing access to each of the three floors along the way. I walked to the end of the cul-de-sac, still on the opposite side of the road, to get a look at the building's far wall, which faced the canal. There was a loading dock on the ground floor, fed by a large freight elevator. Tied up at the pier was a thirty-foot Interceptor speedboat with a 215-hp V-8 engine. Not exactly your standard canal cruiser, it was the same setup we'd used for hit-and-run raids into Cuba.

I crossed in front of the waterway and then back across the front of the building to the entrance. When I saw the newly mounted sign listing EISBERG TECHNISCHE DIENSTLEISTUNGEN as the building's sole occupant, I knew I was in the right place. "Iceberg Technical Services" pretty much said it all. If it hadn't been Kovinski who'd stamped his pamphlets with an actual company address, I might have been more skeptical. But he was just dumb enough, and the truth was that I'd seen worse.

The door was ajar, so I stepped inside. There was a steep flight of stairs in front of me and a passageway on the left that led to a row of offices. I could hear voices coming from inside the offices, so I headed up. The old wooden steps creaked, probably not as badly as I thought they did, but I stepped lightly anyway. I was about halfway up when I heard a door on one of the upper floors open and slam shut, followed by footsteps coming quickly down the stairs. There was nowhere to go, so I adjusted the Beretta in my belt, held my breath, and kept moving. If enough people were in and out of the building, my presence might not be questioned. That's what I told myself anyway.

As the figure made the turn on the landing, my hopes faded because I saw that I'd walked straight into none other than the weasel Aleks Kovinski.

He didn't see me at first. I reached under my jacket, got my fingers around the pistol's grip, certain I could take him out but not so sure whether I'd make it to the exit before anyone reacted to the shots. Then he looked up. I was about to pull the Beretta when I realized that he didn't recognize me—he just slowed down and looked at me, slightly perplexed. A couple more steps and he was close enough for me to see that, in fact, this wasn't Kovinski, at least not the one I'd met. He was almost a dead ringer, if I can use that term, but slightly taller, with a broader face and a more athletic build.

"Could use an elevator in here," I mumbled as we crossed. He didn't respond, just stared at me and kept going. I was aware that he stopped at the bottom of the stairway and looked back up. I kept moving, made the turn at the second-floor landing before stopping. After a tense moment I heard the street door open and close and I was pretty sure he'd gone out.

If I was gonna turn back, this was the time. It seemed like the smart move—I could be walking into anything. I had almost talked myself into going back down the stairs when I thought, What the hell do I do then? Fuck it. I wasn't gonna turn back just when I was finally getting somewhere.

I climbed to the third floor and stopped on the landing to catch my breath. Iceberg, I thought with a chuckle. As in the tip of. Josef had said it was the "public relations" arm of ZR/RIFLE, which was the Company's Executive Action Group (or, in plain English, the assassination squad). Harvey King's domain until he was kicked out by the Kennedys for cavorting with the mob. I wondered who was running it now.

Iceberg's job was to divert blame by creating false evidence, or at least cause enough confusion that no one would be sure what had happened. The "plausible deniability" team. The Kovinski double was a nice touch. He'd probably been all over West Berlin creating witnesses who could testify to Kovinski's erratic behavior. The photo would've been manufactured here, too, along with the propaganda pamphlet, all part of the program to establish their stooge's credentials as a Commie menace.

I pushed the door open and stepped into a large, rectangular space, maybe thirty feet wide, three times that in length. The early-afternoon sun was streaming through the south-facing windows, and I needed a moment to adjust to the bright light. There were no walls or partitions on the floor, just row after row of empty metal shelving. Closing the door gently behind me, I went to one of the front windows and looked onto the street to see if I could catch sight of Horst. The food van was too far away and I couldn't pick him out among the crowd, which was probably just as well. If I couldn't spot him, no one else would.

As I surveyed the room, a long white package caught my eye through the rows of shelving. I walked around and, as I neared, saw that the box was tied in red ribbon with a sizable bow on top. There were two plain blue containers, like large laundry boxes, sitting beside it and it was all situated directly in front of the freight elevator, ready for pickup. Using the small screwdriver that I still had in my jacket, I sliced through the packing tape on one of the blue boxes and opened the lid. Inside were three neatly folded uniforms, the type worn by the West Berlin police, complete with badges and sidearms. I replaced the top of the box and put it back on the shelf, looking more or less untouched, then opened the second box in the same manner. It contained three large padded envelopes, which I opened. Inside were wallets and identification badges for Secret Service agents. This obviously wasn't a fly-by-night conspiracy.

I stood back and studied the long white box. I was pretty sure what was inside, but there was no way I wasn't going to look. I undid the bow and slid the ribbon off as delicately as I could, then lifted the top. A gold card sat on top of a couple of dozen long-stemmed red roses. The unsigned note read "Thinking of You." I removed the flowers, put them aside, then extracted the false bottom from the box. And there it was—a Russian-made Tokarev sniper's rifle, complete with telescopic sight, nestled snugly into its molded container. The rifle in the Kovinski photo.

My first thought was sabotage. I picked up the weapon, looked it over. It was heavy, but nicely balanced. I cradled it in my arms, checked the telescopic sight out the window, looked around the street, but still couldn't locate Horst. It would be easy enough to realign the scope, I thought, but the shooter would certainly recalibrate before firing. Even if I could throw the sighting mechanism off, it would probably mean innocent people getting hit. No, the firing pin was the way to go. I was no firearms expert, but I was pretty sure that I could remove the pin. . . . Then I realized that this weapon could be just a decoy and the sniper wouldn't use it. There might even be more than one gunman. . . .

The freight-elevator doors suddenly thumped open behind me, echoing across the empty floor. I spun around, half expecting to be met by a bullet, but instead came face-to-face with the man who, in my mind, represented all the demented lunacy the Company had to offer. Henry Fisher looked every bit the pompous prick I remembered from Nicaragua.

"Hello, Jack." He stepped out of the elevator, followed by Johnson and the Kovinski double. "What brings you our way?"

"I was hoping to join the Truth Commission."

He attempted a smile but it looked painful. "Didn't I hear that you're a wanted man?"

"Consider me armed and dangerous."

"So I see." He walked around behind me in a pathetic attempt at intimidation. "You know, Jack, you almost fucked up the whole show. Kovinski was so spooked after you got to him that he was useless. We had to dump him. Two months prep down the drain."

"I guess I should feel bad about that."

"Don't worry about us, we're back on line now. But look at you," he sneered. "With your fingerprints all over our murder weapon." He nodded to the Kovinski twin, who stepped forward and grabbed the rifle by the barrel. I was already starting to get the picture, but it got a lot clearer when I saw that he was wearing surgical gloves. Johnson patted me down, reclaimed his Beretta, then gave me a gentle shove into the elevator.

"You're suddenly a very important man, Jack," Fisher said, following me in. "You're about to go down in history as the man who shot John Fitzgerald Kennedy."

The doors slammed shut and we started our descent.

The ground floor, with a large sliding door at the back, was being used as a garage for six nondescript, government-type vehicles, including the black Chrysler that had been crushed by Melik's taxi. Chase was sitting at a table near the door with four other men, two of whom I recognized as officers in the Cuban Brigade—men I'd first seen in Nicaragua and then again at the Miami Bowl when Kennedy got such an unexpectedly warm reception. Judging by this crew, his Berlin welcome was likely to be a lot less friendly.

Fisher sat me down in a small, windowless office, swung his size-twelve loafers onto the heavy wooden desk, leaned back in his swivel chair, and gave me a cagey look. He was feeling good.

"We've got a few minutes while things get prepped," he said. "I'd offer you a drink but I'm fresh out."

"Maybe some other time," I said, wondering if I'd forgotten just how big an asshole he was or if he'd gotten worse.

Folding his arms behind his head, he rocked back in the chair. "I'm sorry you don't see the wisdom of what we're doing, Jack. Believe me, it's for the good of the country. . . . The world."

I didn't bother to answer, which seemed to irritate him. He had a big, stupid grin stuck on his face.

"We're in a war, a bitter war that's going to determine the way this world looks in the twenty-first century. Some people don't have the stomach to win it, but I'm not one of them."

"Yeah, you're a real fucking patriot, Henry," I said. He glared at me for a minute, then dropped his feet to the floor and leaned forward. His voice pitched up a couple of notches with emotion.

"Are you one of those people that's so goddamned enamored with this guy that you can't see what's happening? The son of a bitch has got most of the country snowed with his cute smile and his bullshit Harvard speechwriters, but you should be smarter than that."

"I guess I'm just not as sharp as you."

"Don't be an asshole!" He leaned back again, picked up a rubber band, and fiddled with it, stretching it this way and that. "Haven't you noticed that ever since that Catholic bastard got into the White House, the Commies have run rings around us?"

"I think you're onto something there, Henry. He's probably taking orders from the Vatican. I hear the place is crawling with Marxist cardinals."

"Fuck you if you don't take the future of our country seriously! You deserve your fate." The rubber band snapped. "For Christ's sake, Jack, you were on the Cuba team. . . . Doesn't it mean anything to you that the bastard let those brave men die on that beach? That day fucked up everything, I mean everything!"

He left a space for me to say something, but I just stared at him. He shook his head, stood up, and started pacing. There was nowhere to go, so he walked in a circle. I don't know why it mattered so much to him, but for some reason he wanted me to see what a great thing he was doing. Maybe some corner of his mind had a problem with it and he needed me in order to justify it to himself. Or maybe he was just so goddamned full of his own piety that it overflowed out of his mouth.

"It *all* came out of Cuba!" he said, throwing his arms open, imploring me to see reason. "You think Khrushchev would've had the guts to put a wall through this city if our president hadn't been such a weak sister in Cuba? . . . And forget the idea that he faced Khrushchev down over the missiles. Big fucking hero! Ask yourself why they were there in the first place! *Nuclear warheads ninety miles off the Florida coast!* If Kennedy had done his duty at the Bay of Pigs, they wouldn't have been there! He made us look like assholes, so Khrushchev decided he could fuck us. . . . It's just like with that goddamned PT boat. Lieutenant Johnny-boy Kennedy navigates straight into the path of a Jap warship, the only skipper in the whole damn Pacific War to do so, and he becomes a fucking war hero for saving his crew—by writing a message on a coconut! They made a fucking movie about it, for Christ's sake! Well, I'll be goddamned if I'm gonna let that Irish bastard navigate my country into the path of a Soviet destroyer!"

I wish I could say that he was at the edge of sanity, or maybe over the edge, but I'm sorry to report that it wasn't the case. He was in touch with reality, all right, he just saw it all upside down and twisted inside out. Like a lot of other people. In the end, he was no more than a garden-variety fanatic spouting the kind of crazy ideas that you could find in any coffee shop, barber's chair, or executive boardroom in the country. It's just that Fisher, and a few others like him, had been let loose on the world. He was a Company man, and

Company men saw the world in a way that we mere mortals could never understand. They would save the world from communism even if they had to blow it up in the process.

He was looking at me, waiting for a response. "I never thought of it like that, Henry," I said. "Thanks for setting me straight."

"Fuck you, Jack," he said, finding his chair again. "It's all a big joke, right?"

"Do I look like I'm laughing?" He seemed to appreciate that and decided to have one last grumble.

"Meanwhile, Bobby sits up there in the Justice Department indicting outstanding Americans, laughing when anybody mentions the international Communist conspiracy. Actually laughing! You know, I used to think they were just naive, but they're no more naive than you are."

He opened the top desk drawer, removed a group of black-and-white eight-by-ten glossies, and tossed them into my lap.

"You're a menace, Jack."

The first picture was taken at the Markthalle, early on Sunday morning. It featured me standing at a fruit stand, paying a little old lady for a green apple while Josef stood behind me. I flipped quickly through the others: Josef standing, me sitting on a bench near the playground; a grainy night shot of me getting into his car outside the dilapidated house on Berlinerstrasse; the two of us clasping hands as he dropped me outside Hotel Europa. . . .

"Consorting with the enemy," Fisher smirked. "You're a traitor, Jack, an agent of communism who turned on his own country and shot our beloved president. It should play very well. I guarantee the press'll eat it up."

"You know, Henry," I said, passing the photos back, "if it wasn't you, I'd be worried. But I know that you've fucked up pretty much everything you were ever involved with." It was bullshit, of course. Fisher was a screwup, all right, but he wasn't running this show. It was way beyond him.

"That's right, Jack. You just relax," he purred, placing the photos back into the drawer. "Everything's gonna work out just fine. In fact, once I thought about it, I realized that you're much better in the role of assassin than Kovinski. It's more dramatic, you know, an American who's betrayed his country. I think it points up the danger from within. Too bad you don't speak Russian."

I was about to come back with a snappy reply, but I was cut short by Johnson, who walked through the door with a fully loaded hypodermic needle in his hand.

EIGHTEEN

"I hope you're not planning to stick me with that thing," I said nervously.

"Nothing to worry about," Johnson drawled. "Cosmic Cocktail, they call it, won't hurt a bit. In fact, it's kinda cool."

"You've tried it, have you?"

"I used to be a guinea pig," he smiled.

"How about putting it in a glass of water?"

"Sorry, man, it's gotta go intravenous." He held the syringe up to the light, tapped it a couple of times with his forefinger, then gently pushed the plunger up until a drop of liquid squirted out the end.

"You afraid of needles, Jack?" Fisher laughed. "He is. . . . He's scared of the needle. That's fucking priceless!"

I've never been too happy about the sight of a pointed metal spike coming at me. One time in Kansas, I was broke enough that I tried to make a buck by giving blood, but I was out the door before the nurse could get anywhere near me. I even lived through the pain of a root canal rather than face the needle. I'm not embarrassed. Everybody's got a phobia; that's mine.

Johnson promised that I wouldn't feel a thing, told me to take my jacket off and roll up my sleeve. He chuckled when he saw that I still had what was left of his cuffs around my wrists and I recounted the story of how I'd removed them, just to stall the inevitable.

"Christ, you're lucky you didn't blow a finger off," he said, producing the key and removing the manacles.

"I hope that's a spare," I said.

"The original," he smiled. "Little trick I do," and he demonstrated by placing the key on his tongue, showing me his empty hands, swallowing hard and then producing the key out of his shirt pocket.

"Very impressive," I said. "How about sawing Fisher in half now?"

"Why not?" he said amiably as he punched the needle into my arm, pulled the trigger back until blood surged into the barrel, then reversed the flow and injected the solution into my vein.

Things got very strange very quickly. The first thing I noticed was an odd, bitter taste at the back of my throat, followed by a gentle surge, like warm water passing through my inner ear and washing over my brain. The room didn't exactly spin, it just moved, changed shape, kind of stretched itself out, pulling away until I was separate from everything, including myself. My mind was still clear at this point, but that was about to change. I was headed over the rainbow.

Time started to overlap and get disjointed. Johnson was standing back looking me over in the same moment he was in my face pulling an eye open and flashing a light onto the back of my skull. The beam exploded on impact and formed a million fragments of colored glass that became planets floating in whatever universe I was entering. Everything was foreign, including myself, and I wasn't even sure that I still existed. The thought crossed my mind that they'd given me a lethal dose and I was already dead. . . .

The next thing I knew, I was lying on a four-poster bed in a quiet room, looking up at the ceiling, with no idea where I was or how I got there. I didn't know if seconds, minutes, or hours had passed. I tried to sit up, but aside from my eyes, I was immobile. I was back in my body, but not connected up yet.

I looked around the room. Heavy velvet drapes were drawn across French windows and soft flames crackled away in a big stone fireplace. It was first-class accommodation, although a bit bloodthirsty in decor. The heads of various beasts stared down from the walls and the marble floor was covered with the pelts of bears, zebras, tigers, that sort of thing. Above the fireplace was a dark painting of a naked man on horseback firing arrows into a wounded lion. I was having a déjà vu, feeling I'd been there before—not just the place, but the moment. It was the drug, I thought, causing a memory synapse to misfire.

I closed my eyes, exhaled, and tried to relax. There was something I wanted to remember, something important, but it kept slipping away. I let myself drift back into the dark. . . .

Twilight on the canal, the lights of the city coming to life, flitting across the water like playful angels drowning in our wake. I was in the back of the boat, a blanket around my shoulders, feeling safe and calm, at one with everything around me. As the canal opened up into a broad waterway, we picked up speed. The sudden rush of air was exhilarating and I got lost in the moment.

Then I sensed something. I turned my attention back into the boat. Chase was in front, behind the wheel, Johnson in the seat beside me, his head thrown back, eyes closed. But there was someone else, too. . . . I leaned forward, looked past Johnson, and there, sitting head in hands, looking very seasick, was what I was looking for.

Horst. . . .

I sat up sharply. The son of a bitch had set me up. That's what I was trying to remember. Horst had set me up.

Realizing that I was mobile again, I jumped onto my feet too abruptly, went light-headed, and had to catch myself on one of the bedposts. I lowered myself onto the floor and let it pass.

The pamphlets hadn't come from Kovinski's jacket! Horst had planted them so I would find the address stamped on the back and go to the warehouse, where Fisher and friends would be waiting to jump me! Horst had probably been in the middle of putting them in Kovinski's file when I interrupted him. And I'd gone for it, convincing myself that Kovinski was just dumb enough to stamp the Company address on a piece of disinformation. The words *hook, line, and sinker* came to mind. But Horst was just playing spies, doing what he was told. The person who had truly set me up and sold me down the river was none other than Sam Clay.

He was right on cue. The door opened and in he walked. "I see you're back among the living," he smiled.

I pulled myself up off the floor and gave him a "fuck you from the bottom of my heart" look. I felt betrayed in a way that I didn't realize I still had in me. Sam had been my sponsor, my mentor, and even, I thought, a true friend. Not an idealist by any means but, I'd believed, a man with some basic principles. Apparently not.

"You don't seem surprised to see me."

"I saw Horst on the boat."

"No shit? They said you wouldn't remember a thing. I'm impressed."

"I guess I should be, too. I didn't know you had it in you."

He drew a breath and frowned. "It's complicated, Jack."

"No, Sam. It's not complicated. It's simple. It's so fucking simple that I'm not even going to say it."

He turned away and moved to the window, peeked past the drapery into the outside world. It wasn't just idle curiosity. He was looking for something.

"Why'd you bring me here?" I said. "Why didn't you just leave me doped up and put a couple of bullets in me at the appropriate moment? That's the idea, isn't it?"

"Yeah, that's the idea." He dropped the curtain and turned back toward me. His face betrayed no emotion, just a cold hard stare.

"How's it supposed to happen?" I asked.

"No idea," he said with a smile. "Operational details are being held at a lower level."

"Plausible deniability."

"That's right."

"Which was created to protect the president."

"Not this time," he said blithely.

I tried to fathom what would make Sam sell out like this. Was he being pushed aside and didn't like how it felt? He was too much of a player to call it quits and maybe this was his insurance. Without the game he had nothing, so maybe in order to keep his place at the table, he was willing to bet it all, including his soul.

"It's wrong, Sam."

"Sure, Jack, I know. It's wrong as hell." He looked out the window again. "We don't have much time. They'll be here soon."

"Who?"

He moved away from the window, looked around the room. "You almost fucked up the whole plan, you know, spooking Kovinski like that. He went off half-cocked."

"I take it he's history."

"More like he never existed. You're the one slated for the history books."

"So I hear." I was feeling kind of wobbly, but didn't want to show it, so I stayed on my feet. "Whose bright idea was that?"

"Mine."

"Great . . ." The room started to spin. "Always could count on you for a good time. . . ." I was heading for a crash landing, but Sam got hold of my arm, guided me over to the bed.

"That shit really did a number on you."

"You could say that." I fell back onto the pillow.

"You probably need food. I'll order up some dinner when we're done."

"The Last Supper?"

"The Last Supper," he echoed. "Funny. Is that a Judas joke?"

"If the shoe fits . . ."

"You gotta have some faith in me, Jack."

"Faith?!" I laughed. "For Christ's sake, Sam. I've been bitten, punched, tackled, arrested, shot at, drugged, double-crossed, and hung out to dry thanks to you."

"That's why you need faith."

"Excuse me if I say 'fuck you' instead."

"Suit yourself," he shrugged, then reached into his pocket and pulled out a pack of Lucky Strikes. "Smoke?"

I was dying for one, and he knew I would be, but I hesitated. "Help yourself," he insisted, flipping the lid open and offering them. I relented, propped myself up on one elbow, and tried to take one. I couldn't get it out.

"Let me show you," he said with a smile, removing a false top that had the tips of nineteen cigarettes attached to it. Underneath was a small barrel, the diameter of the missing Lucky, protruding from a metal box.

"It's triggered here," he said, indicating the side of the pack, "by this button underneath the wrapping. You have to give it a good push with your thumb. They didn't want it to be too sensitive, for obvious reasons." He held the pack in his hand, demonstrated how to fire it. "The tech boys say it's accurate up to twenty feet, but I'd be skeptical about that. You want to be close in, I'd say, point-blank if you can." He twisted the bottom of the pack open to reveal three pointed pellets—small, probably six-millimeter—stowed in a thin piece of Styrofoam. "They're hollowed out," he said, "and filled with hydrogen cyanide. It's not pretty, but it's quick. Five to twenty seconds, depending where you get your target. The closer you are to a major artery, the faster it'll be. There's one in the chamber already, so you've got four shots to work with. To reload you just drop one down the barrel." He replaced the top and handed me the pack. "That's it," he said.

"What the hell's going on, Sam?"

"Like I said, I know what's supposed to happen tomorrow, but I don't have a clue where or how."

"And since I'm the fall guy, I have to be there, so I can use this to stop it. . . ."

"That's the idea," he said.

"Well, it's a fucked-up idea, Sam. Significantly fucked up."

"You got a better one?"

"Yeah! How about we use these pellets on the assholes who thought this thing up! That's who you're waiting for, isn't it?"

"Some of them."

I paused, took a deep breath. "Just how big is this thing, Sam?"

"I'm not even sure myself," he sighed. "But it seems to go in every which way. Including up."

"How high?"

"I can only guess."

"Christ, Sam. How'd you get mixed up in it?"

He exhaled, and sat down beside me on the bed. "Somebody in special ops came to me a few months ago, felt me out about servicing an outside client. I knew it was iffy, but I went along to see where it was going. I didn't find out who the target was until about two weeks ago and then I realized how big the setup was. To tell you the truth, I didn't really think it would come off until you came back with the information from the Colonel."

I turned the cigarette gun over in my hand. It looked real enough. I put my thumb on the trigger, got the feel of it. "How do you know I'll be close enough?"

"That's one thing I do know. Iceberg's my operation." I gave him a look but he shrugged it off. "As you know, we're providing the cover story, which includes you. You'll be on-site, in the same general vicinity as the shooter. Johnson and Chase will be assigned to you, and a Secret Service agent who's in on it will be close by. As soon as the president's a confirmed kill, they set you loose and shoot you on the run. The Secret Service guy gets to be the hero."

"When the president's a confirmed kill? Jesus, Sam."

"Well?"

"Johnson, Chase, and the Secret Service guy. What about the shooter—is there just the one?"

"Three," he said.

"It gets better all the time."

"They'll be in separate locations. But if you get one, they'll abort."

"And if I do manage to pull it off? What about next time?"

"It'll buy me some time. Maybe I can figure out who's behind it before they put it together again."

"Four bullets, four guys," I said. "Not great odds, are they?" I dropped the pack onto one of the bedside tables.

"I'm sorry, Jack. I haven't got anything else up my sleeve."

I took a deep breath.

"You figure the world's worth saving, Sam?"

"I dunno," he said. "It's fucked up, all right. But it's the only one we've got."

NINETEEN

The last of three cars pulled up outside the house. "That's it," Sam said, turning away from the window. "Everybody's here." I was lying back on the bed, smoking one of Melik's Turkish blends, trying to convince myself that I had a chance of surviving the next twenty-four hours. Sam had told me that these guys were coming to give the final thumbs-up (or down) on the operation, but he wouldn't say who they were no matter how hard I pressed him. So I was surprised when he threw me my jacket.

"Let's go," he said.

"Where?"

"You're on."

"On?"

"It's showtime."

"Nobody knocked on my door and said, 'Five minutes, Mr. Teller.' "

"Put the jacket on, Jack."

I crushed the cigarette in the ashtray I had balanced on my chest, rolled off the bed, and slipped the jacket on over my T-shirt. "I guess they wanna see who you got for the Kovinski role," I said.

"That's the idea."

"I should feel honored."

"Just don't fuck up." Sam was uncharacteristically edgy, which didn't do a lot for my nerves.

"How the hell am I gonna fuck up, Sam?"

"If they decide to abort this thing, you won't be getting that last meal I promised you. So be cooperative."

"Cooperative is my middle name," I said, and Sam opened the door.

An old grandfather clock was striking eleven as we entered the ground-floor library. It was a substantial room, with oak-paneled walls and a twenty-five-foot-high vaulted ceiling. A circular stairway led up to a book-lined gallery around the upper perimeter, interrupted only by a massive stone chimney that was decorated with a variety of antique guns, knives, swords, and instruments of medieval torture.

Five leather armchairs were arranged by the fire at the far end of the room, three of them occupied—by a silver-haired gentleman with his back to me and, to his right, a fat guy with a pencil mustache, who I recognized as agency legend Harvey King. Sitting opposite him was a small, wiry fellow with a gray brush cut, thick glasses, a short-sleeved white shirt, and a red bow tie. He was drinking Pepsi out of a bottle.

"Sit down, Jack," the silver-haired man said. I knew the face, but I couldn't place it. Wide cheekbones and broad shoulders, strong, chiseled features, wavy hair, and full lips, he looked like an aging

Roman god. Dressed impeccably from head to toe in oversize Italian eyeglasses, a silk tie, blue blazer, and two-hundred-dollar shoes, he oozed money.

"Relax," he said smoothly in a slight accent. "Have a drink. I can recommend the cognac. It's one hundred years old."

"Bourbon," I said to a butler type who was hovering in a corner. Sam ordered scotch on the rocks and took the seat between the smooth talker and the Pepsi man. The empty chair with its back to the flames was reserved for me.

"A lot of men in your position would try to bullshit their way out of it," the silver-haired man continued, "but I'm guessing that you're smart enough to know there is no way out. The question for you is not *what* will happen, it's *how* it will happen. I'd like to see you get through it with as much dignity and as little pain as possible."

"I'll go along with that," I said, accepting my drink. The man in the bow tie tapped his empty bottle with a fingernail by way of ordering a new one.

"Fine." The silver-haired man smiled warmly, then paused to look around at his colleagues. They showed no expression, which seemed to mean they were satisfied so far. His gaze landed back on me, and just then I realized why I knew the face.

Johnny Rosetti was a highly successful businessman in South Florida, with interests in numerous restaurants, nightclubs, and hotels. But those were just fronts, used to launder the money he made off gambling, prostitution, drugs, extortion, murder . . . that sort of thing. But as much as Rosetti and his pals pulled in, it didn't compare to what they lost when Castro tossed them out of Cuba. A hundred million a year was a conservative estimate—tax-free, of course. Naturally, they wanted it back and weren't too impressed with Kennedy's efforts in that department, so I wasn't exactly shocked to find him a member of our little group.

"Isn't it great?" I said, unable to help myself.

"What?" Rosetti smiled graciously.

"That a small-time pimp like yourself could rise out of the gutter to reach the very pinnacle of society. Imagine—one-hundred-year-old cognac. What a country, huh?"

The smile froze on Rosetti's face and his eyes went ice-cold. I wished I had the poison pellets because I would've been very pleased to put one in his eye then and there. But if anyone was gonna die in the next few seconds, it was me. Fortunately, Harvey King didn't give a shit about Johnny Rosetti's wounded pride.

"Let's get to the fucking point," the big man said, shifting his considerable weight toward me. He had a funny, high-pitched voice that didn't fit his three-hundred-pound frame.

Harvey and I had crossed paths a couple of times in the lead-up to the invasion, but just in passing. He kept a low profile around the agency, steering clear of anything that smacked of camaraderie. He was a hero to the cowboys he ran in and out of Cuba, who loved the fact that a hard-drinking, gun-toting, whore-chasing son of a bitch like Harvey could roam the halls of power, sticking it to the preppies who ran the place. The leadership, with their Ivy League cool, put up with him as a necessary, if unpleasant, character who was an acknowledged wizard when it came to black ops. Both factions were incensed when he got early retirement courtesy of Bobby Kennedy.

"Tell me about Zapata," he said, referring to the code name for the Bay of Pigs. "What happened with you and Fisher?"

"We didn't see eye to eye," I said, not sure where he was going with it.

"He arrested you, didn't he?"

"He locked me up."

"Why?"

"Like I said, I didn't agree with some of the stuff he was doing." He glared at me for a beat, snorted, then reached into his jacket, pulled out a handkerchief, and sneezed into it. I thought his eyes were gonna pop out of his head. "You were concerned about the Guantánamo operation," he said, wiping his nose.

"That's right."

"How did you know about it?

"Fisher told me."

"What did he tell you?"

"That a bunch of mercenaries dressed as Cuban regulars were going to attack American forces at the base in an effort to provoke the president into sending in the Marines."

"You thought that was wrong?"

"Yeah, I thought it was wrong."

"I want you to give me the names of everyone you discussed that operation with."

I saw what he was getting at now. Once I was a world-famous dead assassin, every hack in the country would be tracking down anybody I ever said hello to. Harvey wanted names so he could make them disappear before some reporter got to them. He was protecting his operation's integrity. (Their word, not mine.)

"Go to hell," I said. He smiled and nodded, looking unexpectedly pleased with my response.

"Did you report your concerns about the Guantánamo operation to anyone in the government?" he continued.

"Yes, I did."

"The name and agency of that person?"

"Sam Clay of Central Intelligence," I said. Harvey turned to Sam, who nodded.

"That's true," he said. "And I told him to forget about it."

Harvey rotated back toward me. "Did you take that advice, Jack? Did you keep your mouth shut?"

"Yes," I said.

"Would you tell me if you hadn't?"

"No."

"Regardless of what we do to you, whatever interrogation technique we might use, is there any way in hell that we could be one hundred percent sure that you told us about everyone you ever discussed the Guantánamo operation with?"

"I might give you names, but you wouldn't know if they were the right ones or if I'd given you all of them."

"That's right," Harvey said. "I agree with you. And what else do you know, Jack?"

"Regarding . . . ?"

"Let's stick to Cuba. Would you say that you're fairly knowledgeable about what went on down there?"

"I was involved in some interesting operations."

"Would it be fair to say that you have quite a few connections with personnel and events that occurred in the Cuba action?"

"That would be fair to say, yes."

"How many people know that you were part of Zapata? What would you guess, if you included everyone you came into contact with while you were assigned to the task force?"

"A couple dozen, I guess. Maybe more."

"So at least two dozen people, probably more, can connect you to the Company's Cuba operations."

"That's right."

"And there's every possibility that you talked to people outside the agency about the Guantánamo operation.You don't have to answer that, I'm just making a point." He turned toward Sam again. "The point being that this is as fucked up a choice for cover as I can imagine! What the fuck were you thinking?!"

"Take it easy, Harvey," Sam warned. King wasn't known for his diplomacy, but Sam wasn't known for taking any shit. "We can make this work."

"It's sloppy," Harvey said. "We're supposed to be using him for cover and we've got our fingerprints all over the fucking guy!"

"A good guy gone bad," Sam said. "We can sell it. We've got pictures."

"It opens up too many doors," Harvey said. "Doors we all want under lock and key. I recommend we abort and come up with an alternative site."

There was a long, heavy silence. I wondered why Sam didn't step in, try to get things back on track, then I realized that one way or another, he was willing to sacrifice me in order to buy a bit more time. I was starting to wonder if I had a way out when the Pepsi man piped up.

"We go," he said in a distinct Texas twang. "If there's some cleanin' up to do after, we do it, that's all."

Harvey and Rosetti exchanged a look. This clearly wasn't a guy they could just shrug off. Rosetti spoke first.

"There are programs in Cuba that are happening at this very moment that cannot be compromised—"

"You mean like assassinating Castro?" the Texan interrupted. "Come on now, that's small potatoes compared to what we're talkin' about here."

"The individuals I represent don't see it as 'small potatoes,' " Rosetti said coolly. "In fact, they see it as very large potatoes."

"Castro's gonna be taken care of once this thing gets done," the man in the bow tie said. "And nothin's gonna come out we can't handle. Jack Teller's an unstable individual with leftist tendencies who was directed by the agents of communism to assassinate the president of the United States. Nothing about his past associations with the CIA—or organized crime, for that matter—will ever reach the public's ears. And I'm not just saying that. I can guarantee it, one hundred percent."

Another uncomfortable silence ensued. Harvey finally broke it.

"You wanna tell us more about that?"

The Texan paused for effect, offered up a catbird smile, and polished off his soda. "My people," he said slowly, narrowing his eyes and enunciating each syllable, "want to rid our great country of this nigger-lovin' traitor before he can do irreparable harm. In that regard, they have come to an understanding with a certain gentleman who I won't name, but y'all know who I'm talkin' about. This individual is in a position to make assurances that no awkward questions will be asked. And that's the way it is. No awkward questions will be asked."

Harvey and Rosetti exchanged a look and so did Sam and I.

"Now we've got a perfect opportunity here," the Texan continued. "One that ain't gonna come along again, not before the election. We've got a foreign locale that's right on the Kremlin's doorstep, we've got pictures of our killer associating with a certified Communist agent, and we've got a promise that the right people will look the other way. I'll tell you truly, boys, I don't know what in hell else you want. Hasn't anybody in this room got any goddamned guts?"

I was dismissed at that point, escorted back to my room by the unassuming butler, who I assumed was armed to the teeth. There was no shower in the adjoining bathroom, so I filled the tub with scalding water and lay there with a hot washcloth covering my face, trying to get my head around what I'd just heard.

This wasn't a bunch of renegade spooks getting revenge for Cuba and it wasn't about payback for double-crossing the mob, either. Both had their reasons to get rid of Kennedy, but this was bigger than the Company or the syndicate. They were just the hired hands.

The man in the red bow tie, he was the insidious face of the true "danger from within." He could've been the local pharmacist, the high-school geometry teacher, or the man behind the screen door explaining why you needed more life insurance. Your good neighbor who mowed his lawn every Saturday, went to church on Sunday, and rooted for the home team, he was a hardworking, God-fearing, full-blooded American who smiled and said "nice morning" over the garden wall as he got into his clean car at seven thirty sharp and drove off, well under the speed limit. His dog never pissed on your grass and his lights were always out by ten o'clock. He was safe and ordinary and he was one of us. And that's why he was so fucking dangerous.

My people, he'd said, *want to rid our great country of this nigger-lovin' traitor before he can do irreparable harm.* Who were these people that wrapped themselves in the flag like they owned it, soiling it with their brutally repulsive conceit? "Give me your tired, your poor, your huddled masses yearning to breathe free and we'll be happy to string 'em up for you," that's who they were. But unlike their emissary, these men didn't live among us. They existed behind a wall of their own—one built with money, power, and, above all, with hatred. You didn't have to know their names to know what to call them. They were the good old boys, red-blooded American Fascists who were sick and tired of watching that Catholic, nigger-lovin' Communist ruin their country, so they were gonna take it away from him and hand it over to somebody they could trust.

And no awkward questions would be asked.

TWENTY

A medium-rare sirloin steak with baked potato, tossed salad, and a bottle of '54 Châteauneuf du Pape were waiting for me back in the room—and so was Horst. He was sitting silently on the edge of the bed, staring at me with heartfelt contempt.

"What's the matter with you?" I said, toweling my hair dry.

"I think you know."

"I'm the one who should be pissed off," I said. "After all, it was *you* that set *me* up."

"I've brought your dinner," he said, standing up. "I can say that I hope you choke on it."

"What did Sam tell you?" I called after him as he headed for the door.

"The truth about you," he said, stopping to give me a bleak look.

"Perhaps I have expected too much, but I thought you might find again your ideals and rejoin the battle."

"I'm not Humphrey Bogart, Horst."

"You can make a joke if you like, but perhaps to be a little bit like Bogie is not such a bad thing."

"Even Bogie wasn't like Bogie," I said. "Nobody is."

"Is this the excuse you tell yourself so you can betray your country?"

"I'm not betraying my country."

"I have seen the photos," he said dramatically.

"What photos?"

"Of you and the STASI colonel in a secret meeting."

"So?"

"Sam has told me—"

"For Christ's sake, Horst, wake up!" I was losing patience. "Sam will tell you what's convenient for whatever he's cooking up. He wanted you to set me up at the warehouse, so he told you I'm a traitor to get you to do it. He's a lying bastard, like the rest of them. And that's coming from somebody who actually likes the guy."

I poured a glass of wine, swirled it around in the glass, and held it up to the light. It was a good, rich vintage, but I didn't have a taste for it. I put it aside.

"Why, then, are you under arrest?" he asked skeptically.

"What do you want me to say, Horst?"

"Just the truth," he answered.

"I'm afraid the truth is kind of elusive around here. Everyone's got their own version of it."

"Then tell me your version," he said, easing back into the room.

"I don't think you'll like it," I said.

"I would still rather know it."

"Okay," I said. "Sit down, because it might take a while. This kind of truth doesn't come in a neat little package."

He sat on the edge of the bed and listened intently as I laid it out for him. I told him about Cuba and why I quit the game, and how

Sam called me back into service to come to Berlin, and what the Colonel had told me about the plot to hit Kennedy. I told him about Kovinski and Iceberg and how he himself had unwittingly helped them set me up as their new patsy, then I explained how Sam was working inside the conspiracy, trying to get to the source, and about my encounter with Johnny Rosetti, Harvey King, and the man with the red bow tie. Finally I told him about "no awkward questions being asked."

He sat there with a stunned looked on his face for a moment after I'd finished. "What can I do?" he finally said.

"Go home," I answered firmly. "And forget about all this. Go back to doing an honest day's work, like stealing cars."

"It must be stopped," he said.

"I'm not sure it can be."

"It *must* be!"

He stood up and paced back and forth a couple of times. "I believed you were an agent for STASI, which is no different than an agent for the Soviets!" he said frantically. "If I believed it, the world will believe it!" He stopped in his tracks and looked at me, an expression of alarm on his face. "What will be the consequences of this?!"

I shouldn't have told him, of course. I'm not even sure why I did, except that I wanted to remove that look of contempt he gave me when I came into the room. I think I probably liked being Bogart in his eyes and I wasn't willing to give it up. It turned out to be a costly conceit.

He dropped back onto the bed with wilted shoulders, looking totally defeated. "How can it be?" he said, more to himself than to me. "How can something like this happen with *America*?"

"What do you think America is, Horst?" I asked, not expecting an answer. He frowned and looked down into his lap, which I took to be an expression of disappointment, or dejection, or something else. In fact, he was formulating his answer. He began softly.

"I was nine years old in the summer of 1948 when the Russians blocked all of Berlin. We had no food, no electricity, and no way to escape. It sounds like a nightmare, I know, but it was the most amazing time for me. Do you know how I spent this summer? Each day I woke at dawn and, with my friends, we ran to the same place, just near the airport, to climb onto a pile of rubble where we could watch the airplanes land. They came one after the other, night and day, American planes filled with not just food and coal, but also with hope. Hope that we could remain free . . . We would stand there, all day sometimes, and wave our arms to each of the pilots as he crossed in front of us, hoping that he would see us and understand that we wanted to thank him. Then one day we saw the most fantastic thing. . . . As one of the planes flew over us there came a shower of boxes, each with its own small parachute, filling the sky. Do you know what was in these boxes? . . . Chocolates! Imagine it! Standing on the rubble of our city, with no food to eat, and the sky is raining with boxes of chocolates!" He paused to reflect on the memory for a moment, allowing himself a little smile before continuing.

"Then the next day came the same plane again and there were more boxes, and again the day after until I think every child in Berlin was getting a box of chocolates from this American pilot! It was the most amazing thing ever I have seen!" He shook his head, still in awe of the idea of the sky filled with boxes of chocolates.

I didn't say anything because, of all things, I had a lump in my throat. What a strange condition for a terminal cynic like me to find himself in. Horst looked up and, I think, sensed my situation. He gave me a schoolboy grin, from ear to ear, and said, "Perhaps one day, when I become a big producer in Hollywood, I can make a movie from this story. It can be quite a tearjerker, don't you think?"

I extracted a promise from Horst that he would slip away and go home in return for my assurance that I had a cunning plan to foil the bad guys and save the world. As we know, people will believe anything if it's what they want to believe. And I believed I was rid of Horst.

I started in on the steak, but it was cold and I had no appetite anyway, in spite of not eating for over twenty-four hours. I managed to force a few bites down and was pushing the tray away when Sam came in. I think he was there to say a final good-bye, which didn't do wonders for my confidence in the cunning plan.

"Where did you find Horst?" I asked him.

"He was after a visa," he explained. "Wanted to immigrate. Turned down because of his police record."

"You told him you'd get him in?"

"That's right."

"Do me a favor, Sam. Leave him alone."

"Sure," he said offhandedly, sitting down and helping himself to my dinner. "I don't need him anymore. Why do you care?"

"I don't know. Can you get him a visa?"

"I don't see why not. Anything else?" Sam's way of asking if I had any unfinished business I wanted him to take care of if I wasn't able to.

"Can't think of anything," I said.

He nodded and we exchanged a brief look. There wasn't anything to say really, and even if there was neither of us was going to say it. It wasn't necessary.

"They'll come for you just before sunrise," he said. "They'll put you in cuffs until you get there, wherever 'there' is."

"It would help to know."

"I couldn't get it," he said. "Harvey would see his grandmother as a security risk. But I do know that there'll be three shooters, at least one in an elevated position, from an upper floor of a tallish building. That's where you'll be, too. Once the hit is confirmed and the president's down, you'll be given a chance to run. A Secret Service agent will be waiting around the corner to put two in your chest. The team'll get out in the confusion and the world will be left with one lone assassin, dead as a doornail."

"Don't sugarcoat it on my account," I said. "When should I make my move?"

"Go for the shooter first. If you get him, they have to abort."

"How close will I be?"

"Not a clue," he said sheepishly.

"How about afterward?"

"You're on your own."

"Jesus, Sam."

"You're gonna have to play it by ear," he said, heading for the door. "Your specialty."

"Do me a favor if it doesn't work out, Sam."

"Just name it," he said.

"Die a slow and painful death."

He chuckled and left without saying good luck. We both knew if I had to count on luck, I'd be out of it.

I lay in the dark, hoping for sleep, exhausted but wide awake, experiencing a strange sense of stillness and serenity. It wasn't that I was filled with confidence about what was to come. Far from it. I think I felt at peace because I'd finally put the pieces of my life together and they seemed to make some kind of twisted sense.

I didn't need Horst to sell me on America. I was sold when I first stepped onto the crowded streets of Manhattan's Lower East Side and was met with a surge of humanity hustling to get their piece of the dream. The America I found wasn't pure or pristine, not by any stretch of the imagination, and the good guys didn't always win. The streets weren't paved with gold and chocolates didn't fall out of the sky, either, but the air was filled with optimism. It was alive with possibilities, with the belief that good people who worked hard would be rewarded with a good life, free from the tyranny and constraints they'd left behind.

I saw America at its best and I saw the worst of it, but I always believed in it and I would always be there when it needed to be defended. And I don't mean the buildings or the roads or the bridges, or even the people. I mean the idea of it. The simple idea that individual freedom is something people are born with—the state can't give it to you, it can only take it away. That's it. Easy to put into words but, judging by the world's history, tough as hell to put into practice.

I'm not talking about the Fourth of July, flag-waving, love-it-or-leave-it kind of freedom. That's something else. I mean the whoever-you-are, whatever-you-do, no-matter-how-you-look or what-you-think, welcome-to-the-party, be-an-American kind of freedom.

And don't let anyone tell you that the Soviet Union didn't pose a threat to that kind of freedom, either, because it did. It was a brutal tyranny that stripped its people of their rights and took away their humanity, and we needed to defend against it. But what I didn't see when I was in the front line of our secret war was the disadvantage we labored under, and the effect it was having on us. It would have been suicide to meet the enemy on the battlefield, so we were forced underground, and in that dark world we had to play the game by their rules.

Subterfuge, deceit, treachery, subversion, betrayal—they were the tried and tested tools of tyranny, not of a free society. The United States didn't even have a peacetime foreign intelligence service until 1947. None. So we were the new kids on the block, and the longer we played their game, the more we became like them. Not the American people, of course. They were blissfully unaware of the creeping tyranny that was growing like a cancer inside their government. It had spread, unseen, until it would strike at the heart of its host, killing the essence of what it was supposed to be defending.

The coup was an inevitable consequence of giving men like Henry Fisher and Harvey King the responsibility for our freedom. They had planned to attack our own troops at Guantánamo. I guess that said it all. We had become our own enemy.

I had turned a blind eye and gone fishing, mistaking disengagement for freedom. Like a lot of people, I saw our dirty war as a necessary evil, something we needed in order to defend against the enemy at the gate. Now I realized that the enemy amongst us was the more dangerous one—and they were already inside the wall.

So I lay in the dark, feeling calm because I was ready, at last, to rejoin the battle.

TWENTY-ONE

I gave up on sleep around five o'clock, went to the window, and watched a soft, gray light slowly displace the predawn darkness. I wondered if June 26, 1963, would be just another day, or if it would go down in history as one of those bloodstained dates that become etched in our minds forever. Either way, I was glad it had arrived.

The door swung open and Chase sauntered in, wearing a suit and tie and carrying a black attaché case. He stopped in the middle of the room when I turned to face him. "What's the matter, Jack? Trouble sleeping?" He chuckled to himself.

"You know, Roy, before today's over, one of us is gonna be dead, that's for sure, but if I was you I wouldn't get too cocky about which one it's gonna be." He smirked, pulled his jacket back to show me his brand-new Anaconda, then walked over to a dresser, opened a drawer, and removed a folded white shirt, still in its packaging. He threw it to me.

"Put this on," he said, then tossed a set of handcuffs onto the bed. "And these."

I unpinned the shirt, slipped it on. I noticed that the dummy pack of Luckys was still on the bedside table, reached over to pick it up, and thought Chase looked at me funny. I was probably being paranoid, but if he checked, that'd be it, lights out.

"Smoke?" I offered him the pack, feeling for the trigger in case he said yes. But he waved it off, so I slipped the Luckys into my shirt pocket, then snapped the manacles onto my wrists.

He ushered me through a series of empty rooms, down a narrow staircase, and through a large basement kitchen, where we exited from a back door onto an expansive lawn that sloped down toward a wide, slow-moving river. A fresh morning breeze and the scent of dew on the grass made me realize how stale the air had been inside the estate. The building was a heavy-handed version of an Italian Renaissance villa, with twin towers connected by a two-story gallery, ceramic tiles on the roof, arched windows, and a terrace with curved steps leading down to a fountain. I wondered about the owner, but it didn't matter, so I let it go.

We followed a gravel path down to a pier where the Interceptor was tied up. Chase freed one of my wrists and cuffed me to a chrome rail in the back while he prepped the boat, leaving the briefcase by the pilot's seat on the upper deck. If I sat down, my arm would've been above my head, so I stood, leaning against the rail.

"What's your angle in all this?" I called to Chase as he turned the engine over. He looked at me warily, like it was some kind of trick question.

"How do you mean?"

"I mean how do you feel about killing Kennedy?"

"I don't feel anything about it," he shrugged, crawling out onto the bow to cast off the line. "He's just another guy."

"He's president of the United States."

He considered that, then said, "They say he'd do all sorts of shit if he got reelected, but what the fuck do I know? . . . I know it'd be a damn shame if they pull us out of Vietnam. . . ."

"You like it there."

"Yeah," he agreed. "I like it. It's a good setup."

"What do you do?"

"Hunt down gooks and grease 'em," he answered coolly, then adding with a perverse grin, "I'd hate to see my license to kill get revoked." He revved the engine, put the boat in gear, and slipped away from the mooring. I decided I would have no qualms about killing him.

He took it easy on the throttle and the boat cut smoothly through the calm waters, just the gentle hum of the engine intruding on the peaceful setting of thick woodland and pink sky on the eastern horizon. We were heading south, so I guessed we were passing through the Berliner Forest in the northwestern corner of the city.

I stared into our wake and tried to recall the itinerary I'd seen in the paper the previous day. Air Force One was scheduled to land at nine thirty—about four hours away—and if I was right about our location, we were heading straight for Tegel. But that didn't make much sense. Sam had said that at least one of the shooters would be in an elevated position and the only elevated position at the airport was the control tower, which was ridiculous. Anyway, security would be too tight there. They needed crowds, where a team could penetrate, do the deed, then disappear in the confusion. There'd be no shortage of crowds once Kennedy hit the streets—upward of a million people had lined the route from Bonn to Cologne, and Berlin would be no different.

After landing, the party was scheduled to travel by motorcade to Brandenburg Gate, where the president would get his first look at the wall. His limousine—it had been open in Cologne—would have to pass through downtown Berlin, where the streets would be filled with well-wishers hoping to catch a glimpse, maybe even shake Kennedy's hand. And there would be plenty of high-rise buildings along the way—private offices and hotels where a gunman could easily set up without being noticed or interfered with. Not a bad scenario, except that hitting a target in a moving car with a long-range rifle is a low-percentage shot, no matter how good the sniper. So unless the president's driver, a Secret Service agent, was part of the team and was going to slow down or stop the car at the critical moment, hitting the motorcade seemed too risky an option.

At the wall, Kennedy would stand on a platform and peer over the concrete barrier into enemy territory. He would be exposed and vulnerable, but with armed East German guards watching over the proceedings, he'd be well protected and crowds would be kept at a distance. It wasn't ideal, but it couldn't be ruled out, either. The theatrics might be tempting, even raising the specter that the president had been fired on from across the border.

There were a couple of off-the-record events scheduled after that. Lunch with West Berlin's popular mayor, Willy Brandt, and a private meeting with some relatives of men and women who'd been killed while trying to escape to the West. Even the press was banned from that one. Late in the day the president was to accept an honorary degree from Berlin's Free University, but I thought the moment of greatest danger would come before that, at about 1 P.M.

That was when the main event of the day, a speech from the steps of West Berlin's city hall, was to take place. It would be the climax of Kennedy's German tour and probably the highlight of his European trip. He'd be on the Cold War's front line, speaking to the world, and Berliners would be there in the hundreds of thousands. I'd walked through the plaza he'd be facing. It was surrounded by buildings and there was ground cover in patches of trees and shrubs that were thick enough to conceal a sniper. Three gunmen—two firing from above, one on the ground—set up for triangulated fire. A large crowd, a stationary target, a symbolic setting. If I was in Harvey King's shoes, that would be my moment.

I caught a movement out of the corner of my eye and looked up. What I saw a few feet in front of me made the bottom of my stomach fall out. . . .

The cabin door was halfway open and Horst's foolish face was hanging out of it, right arm waving back and forth, trying to get my attention. I flashed a *"What the fuck are you doing?!"* look at him, then cast a quick glance up at Chase, who was on the upper deck, sitting behind the wheel with his back to me. The pilot's seat was set forward just enough so that he and Horst couldn't see each other.

When I looked back Horst was proudly displaying the hardware he was going to use to save the day. Goddamn Hollywood, I thought! And goddamn double 0 fucking 7, because in Horst's Dream Factory–riddled mind he thought he could go up against a heavily armed professional killer with a speargun. . . . *A goddamn underwater speargun!*

There could be little doubt about the outcome if I didn't do something. I tried to wave Horst back, but he ignored me and stepped out onto the deck, bent at the waist, speargun gripped tightly across his chest, like some kind of big-game hunter stalking his prey. I felt like I was in one of those terrible dreams where you're helpless, absolutely fucking powerless to do anything—you can't move and you can't even call out a warning, all you can do is watch in horror as the disaster plays itself out to its inevitable conclusion.

I grabbed the Luckys out of my pocket, but Chase was a good twenty-five feet away—five feet over the pellet's maximum range, and the forward motion of the boat was working against me. It was pointless to try. I yanked my cuffed wrist away from the railing a couple of times, trying in vain to get free. No chance.

Horst took another step into the open and spotted Chase. My

heart stopped beating when I saw him raise the spear and take aim. Jesus Christ, I thought, he's not gonna take a shot from there! Standing upright, wobbling back and forth with the movement of the boat, and out in the open with no cover! I saw his finger squeeze the trigger and I knew it would be over in seconds. . . .

I did the only thing I could think of doing.

"Chase!" I called out. "HEY, CHASE!"

Horst whipped his head around and looked at me like I was nuts, but I got the result I wanted—he leapt back into the doorway, out of sight as Chase swiveled around in his seat.

"What?"

"Got a light?" I said, displaying the pack of Luckys. His crack response was to take out his own pack of Marlboros, light one up, and say "fuck you" with a smile.

"For Christ's sake," I pleaded. "You want me to beg?" He was amused, but after a moment of gloating he took the hook—at least partially.

"Catch," he said, and tossed me the Zippo. But I didn't need his lighter, I needed him standing in front of me! I made a feeble attempt at catching it, let it fall to the deck, then looked up at him with my most pathetic look.

"Come down and give me a light, will you? What the hell do you think I'm gonna do?"

He hesitated, but rose to the challenge, pulling back on the throttle and letting the boat drift while he climbed down onto the lower deck. I stole a peek at Horst, saw that he'd slipped back inside the cabin, and I started to feel like there was a chance of salvaging the situation. I'd have to kill Chase earlier than I'd wanted to, and that would leave me hanging as far as Kennedy was concerned, but I'd worry about that afterward. There was no alternative at this point.

Chase bent over, picked up the lighter, and stood there for a moment, looking at me like he was trying to figure out what I was up to.

"Catch it this time," he said. He was standing twelve feet away from me now. I could've taken the shot, probably hit him, but Sam had said it would take up to twenty seconds if you didn't get an artery and you can do a lot of damage with a .44 Magnum in twenty seconds.

"For Christ's sake, Roy," I said. "I'm one-handed here. Can you please light a fucking cigarette for me?"

He nervously flicked the Zippo open and shut a couple of times—some instinct seemed to be telling him that something was up, but he couldn't figure what. Finally he smiled and took a step toward me. . . .

I heard the *thwack* of metal exploding through flesh before I saw anything. Chase just stopped walking and calmly looked down at his chest, where the spear had impaled him, the bloody tip protruding about four inches out of his left breast. He reached over to touch the arrow, let out a low, rumbling moan, then looked up at me. It was shock on his face at first, then confusion took over, like he was trying to figure out how I'd done it to him. Finally—and this all took about two seconds—a trickle of blood ran out of his nose and he went ape shit, reaching for the Anaconda and swinging around, the spear through his torso no more than a minor annoyance. He was ready to obliterate whatever he found behind him.

Horst was paralyzed. He couldn't believe what he'd done and wasn't reacting to the fact that he was about to be blown away. I yanked my manacled right arm hard, pulling away from the rail with such force that I thought I'd dislocated my elbow. . . .

The pain hit Chase now, but he managed to raise his gun and point it at the center of Horst's forehead. I extended myself as far as I could. There was about six or seven feet of air between me and the back of Chase's head. The pellet exploded out of my hand with a *pffftt!* and struck him in the neck, about three inches below the ear. The poison hit his system immediately. I don't think he even knew he'd been hit.

Every muscle in his body seized up, including his trigger finger. The handgun exploded into the air, missing Horst's head by a few inches. The kick threw Chase back against the portside railing. His eyes had already glazed over and I was sure that he was dead on his feet, but he just stood there for a five count before falling back, head over heels into the water.

Horst dropped the speargun and it flew across the deck, dragged by the steel cable that was fixed to the harpoon. The gun's shaft lodged against the rail, holding Chase's skewered body on the surface, floating faceup, a few feet away from the boat.

"Pick it up!" I yelled to Horst, who still hadn't moved. I had to repeat it a couple more times before he reacted, but he finally got hold of it. He looked down at Chase, bobbing in the river, an expanding pool of blood darkening the waters around him.

"I can't believe . . ." He trailed off, shook his head at the sight.

"Pull him back into the boat," I said.

Horst gave me a look. "You want me to pull him up?"

"He's got the key to these in his pocket," I said, displaying my cuffs. "So either he comes up or you go in."

He nodded and got hold of the cable, gave it his best shot, but it was a big fish he had on the other end. The body bounced up against the hull and I watched with disappointment as Chase's pistol worked its way out of his lifeless fingers. My heart sank when it did the same.

"Looks like you're going for a swim," I said to Horst.

He looked down at the dead man. "Yes, okay," he said apprehensively. "In which pocket is the key?"

"Check them all and get whatever he has. And see if he's got another gun stashed somewhere, maybe on his ankle."

"Yes, all right, I will," he replied as he removed his shoes and socks. "I can't believe . . ." He was still shaking his head as he started down the ladder. "It's quite cold," he complained, sticking a toe in.

"Then jump," I said, not feeling particularly sympathetic. He actually held his nose before stepping off the ladder, then paddled over to the body. He hesitated as he came face-to-face with Chase's fixed stare.

"Shall I close the eyes?" he called up to me.

"If it makes you feel better," I replied.

"I think it does," he said, pushing the lids shut.

"Check his jacket first," I said. "Try the inside pocket. . . ." I couldn't see what was happening under the surface, but Horst seemed to be taking a very long time.

"Any luck?"

"No key," he said. "But here is an envelope. . . ."

"Toss it up," I called out.

"Yes, okay," he answered, and a moment later a thick, soggy envelope dropped onto the deck.

"What about the key?" I had a quick look around, concerned that we were pressing our luck. It was just a matter of time before someone came along.

"I haven't found one. . . ."

"Try his pants. . . ."

"If I must," he said.

"You must." Horst ducked underwater. He seemed to stay there far too long, but finally surfaced with a gasp.

"Here is a wallet," he said, holding it aloft. I told him to throw is up, too, and it came over the side.

"Ah . . . I have found a key!" he called out happily. "It was in the shirt pocket."

"Don't drop it!" I said.

"I'll come up."

"Did you check for a gun?"

"Wait a moment," he said, going under again, resurfacing more quickly this time. "No . . . no gun."

"Okay," I said. "Come on out."

He climbed out of the water looking like a drowned rat, handed me the key, then plopped onto a bench. He sat there in shock while I released myself, then unlocked the other half of the cuffs and dropped them into my jacket pocket. You never know what'll come in handy.

"Go up to the bow and detach the anchor," I said. "Bring it back here."

"Why?"

"Just do it, Horst!" I snapped, then added more coolly: "We can't just leave him floating like that. We'll have to sink the bastard."

"Yes, of course," he said, then scrambled up the ladder to the upper deck. I secured the speargun to the rail, then picked up Chase's wallet and the envelope. There was a stack of hundred-dollar bills in the envelope that I didn't bother to count. I stuffed them into my breast pocket and turned to the wallet. It contained eighty-five marks and change and a Polaroid of an Oriental girl in what you might call a compromising position. You might also call it physically impossible, which I suppose is why he carried the photo. I didn't know much about Chase, but I knew enough not to be surprised. The wallet had been stripped of everything else—no ID, receipts, nothing.

Horst returned with the anchor and I went to work attaching it to the cable as close to the body as possible without sending Horst back into the water. I wanted to get moving.

"I can't believe I have killed somebody," Horst said as I removed the cable from the speargun and threaded it through the anchor's eye.

"What you did was almost get yourself killed. . . ." I said, knotting the cable back onto itself. "And me along with you."

"You must admit, though, that it was quite resourceful."

"It was quite dumb, that's what it was." I picked the anchor up and tossed it overboard. "I needed him alive, for the moment anyway."

"Oh," he said, deflated. "Have I made a bad error?"

I didn't see any point in rubbing salt in his wound. "Forget it," I said. "Maybe it'll work out."

We stood at the rail and watched Chase disappear below the surface on his way to the bottom of the river. He'd pop up in a day or two, but that didn't matter.

"Amazing," Horst said philosophically. "To be alive one minute, and the next . . ."

"Don't feel too bad," I said. "He wasn't a real human."

TWENTY-TWO

I eased up on the throttle after putting some quick distance between us and Chase's watery grave. The wooded shoreline had given way to a belt of leafy suburban homes, then clusters of concrete apartment blocks, finally succumbing to the industrial zone surrounding Tegel Airport. I had guessed right about our location.

"Take over," I said to Horst, who was sitting on a bench behind me wrapped in a blanket.

"In which direction?" he asked, slipping into the pilot's seat.

"No direction," I said grumpily. "Just stay afloat and don't hit anything." I grabbed the black briefcase that Chase had stowed under the control panel and climbed down to the lower deck, where I could investigate its contents without Horst looking over my shoulder.

I located a screwdriver and a large wrench in the cabin and knocked the locks off the case. Inside I found a walkie-talkie and a stopwatch along with a Canadian passport, driver's license, and $250 in traveler's checks in the name of Ian Howe. My own passport, which I hadn't seen since Johnson relieved me of it three days earlier, was also there, but two entry visas to the Soviet Union had been added. The only other item was a small medical kit that contained a loaded hypodermic needle, presumably another Cosmic Cocktail meant for yours truly. It was a return trip I'd happily miss out on.

With a little luck—and I thought I must be due some—the walkie-talkie meant that Chase would've been operating independently, in contact with the rest of the team solely by radio. Keeping me isolated made sense, of course. The last thing they needed was for the accused assassin to be connected to the actual assassins. Chase, the only direct link to me, would've been on his way back to Saigon within minutes of the action, and anybody who went looking for Mr. Ian Howe of Toronto would find themselves chasing thin air.

Good news/bad news. Nobody would be expecting to see Chase; that was good news. The flip side was that it was a two-way radio, so they were expecting him to check in. I could probably get by on the voice, but he would have a password, and if he'd committed it to memory, well, it was as gone as he was.

One method black ops uses to secure communications is to designate a control operator, who receives signals from any number of individual satellite operators. He is the conduit for all communications, receiving information and relaying it to the intended recipient. Control can broadcast to any combination of satellites, each one of which has its own prelocked secure frequency. If one is compromised, as Chase's would be when he didn't check in, the control operator would simply remove that frequency from the relay. Literally cut him out of the loop. Whoever was running the op—presumably Harvey King—would then have to choose between aborting the mission or proceeding with a possible security breach. I couldn't be sure which way he'd go, but based on what I'd witnessed the night before, I'd put my money on a green light. If that was the case, I wouldn't be able to do a damn thing to stop it. Without the password, I might as well go home and watch it on TV. My best, and maybe my only, shot was if the code word was stashed somewhere in the briefcase.

I looked through the papers again. It could be anything, of course. It might be "Tulip," the street that the nonexistent Ian Howe called home, or his birthplace of "Hamilton," or even his mother's maiden name, "Davis."

I noticed a piece of paper, folded over twice and taped to the inside back cover of my passport. When I opened it I found three typewritten lines in the center of the sheet:

VICTORIA HOTEL, SCHÖNEBERG
11 am check-in
confirm EZECH13V10

It wasn't the password, but it was a location and a timetable, which gave me some breathing room. I shut the case and climbed back up the ladder.

"What time is it?"

"Nearly six," Horst said. I wondered what Chase was supposed to do with the five hours before he checked into the hotel. It was unlikely that there would be any contact planned, so it wasn't too important, but it was strange. Why not go directly there?

"Do you know the Victoria Hotel in Schöneberg?"

"Yes, I've been for a drink," Horst answered. "It's quite nice."

"How close is it to city hall?"

"Directly in front. You can see it—" He stopped short. "Kennedy speaks there today. . . ."

"That's right."

"It's where they will attempt to shoot him?"

"Looks that way," I said.

I had to admit, it had a certain flair. The leader of the free world, murdered in front of hundreds of thousands of witnesses—millions if you count the television cameras that would beam the moment around the globe. It was a hell of a thought. An event that could very well take the world over the brink, unleashing the nuclear nightmare we'd been flirting with for fifteen years. The whole world would see it, but no one would ever have a clue about who did it or why.

A guy named Adolf once said: "The great masses of people will more easily fall victim to a big lie than to a small one." Well, this was one goddamn major-league monster of a lie.

"What shall we do?" Horst asked, his teeth chattering from the cold, and maybe a little excitement, too.

"You're not gonna do anything except drop me off and go home," I said firmly. "You've done more than enough already."

He thought for a moment, then said, "You have not much choice but to have me with you." I was about to set him straight, but he said it with such conviction that I decided to listen.

"You'll go to the Victoria Hotel?" he said.

I nodded.

"And this is where they expect you to be, correct?"

"Get to the point, Horst," I said.

"If you walk in alone, they must know that something goes wrong. . . ."

"And if I walk in with you, they won't?"

"Are you sure they'll know it's me? I'm more or less the size of this dead man and we have something of the same color of hair. . . ." He smiled. "And as the fat lady has said to the man at closing time, it's better to have me than to have no one."

I gave him an unhappy look. It was unhappy because he was right. There would be spotters placed throughout the plaza reporting the action to Control, and there would certainly be a couple stationed outside the hotel or in the lobby. In order to maximize security, they'd be men or women that neither Chase nor I knew, spotting us based on photos. But they'd be concentrating on me, not Chase. If I went in alone, alarm bells would go off, but there was a decent chance that they wouldn't have a good look at the guy I came in with. I took a deep breath.

"Do you own a blue suit?"

He grinned like a kid who'd been told he could go to the circus. "Of course I do."

I didn't expect to see Hanna at the apartment, Horst having told me that she'd be on her way to work by seven o'clock, so I was taken by surprise when we found her sitting at the table with a plate of toast and a cup of tea. She looked pleased to see me at first, but something changed her demeanor right away. Her female radar sensed trouble.

Horst asked what she was doing there and she explained that the factory had been closed for the day so the employees could attend Kennedy's speech.

"Will you go?" he asked anxiously.

"I haven't decided," she said, and he suggested that she'd see more on television, reminding her that she hated crowds anyway.

"Yes, I expect I'll watch from here," she said, satisfying Horst, who went off to find his suit. I took a seat across from Hanna. She offered me coffee and started to get up, but I told her I was fine. She nodded and sipped her tea, avoiding my look.

"I'm sorry that I didn't phone you," I said.

She shook her head and looked up at me. "I told you I didn't expect anything."

"I meant to, but . . ." I trailed off as she got up and carried her plate of unfinished toast to the kitchen. I followed her in, found her wiping down a perfectly clean counter.

"Is something wrong?" I asked innocently.

"What could be wrong?"

I was amazed that we'd managed to get to those two sentences in two short days. On the surface, I was mystified as to why she was acting this way, although I think deep down I must've known. I went with the surface.

"I would've called, but—"

She gave me a look and cut me down to size. "Do you really think I'm upset because I haven't heard from you in twenty-four hours? Are you that egotistical?"

"I have no idea what I've done to make you angry." I said flatly. "I'd appreciate it if you filled me in."

She drew a breath and slowly exhaled it. "I don't know what you do, Jack, and I don't think I want to know. But I do know that you won't be here for long, one way or another. I knew it from the moment I saw you and I accepted it." She paused and I waited. "You're dangerous," she said. "That's who you are, it's what you do. But my brother, he's not the same as you, although he thinks he is. Don't take him with you."

I don't know how she knew, but she did. Not what we were facing, not exactly, but she sensed that something was up, something that might end badly. I could've walked out the door right then, of course, leaving Horst safely out of it. But things don't work that way, do they?

"I won't let anything happen to him," I said.

"Is that a promise?" she mocked. I didn't get a chance to answer because Horst strode into the room at that moment.

"How do I look?" he said, doing a turn in his dark blue conservative best.

I could read Hanna's dark thoughts as he waited for an answer, but she forced a smile and said, "Like a respectable businessman."

"Jack and I have an important meeting," he said, kissing her cheek. "I must look my best."

"Jack always seems to have an important meeting," she said. "He must be a very important man."

"We are both," he said with a wink. "Someday you'll know it."

The look she gave me as we went out the door was one I'll never forget. It was one of hope and fear, supplication and scorn, all at the same time.

TWENTY-THREE

The clock on the bombed-out Kaiser-Wilhelm Church hadn't struck eight yet, but the street below it was in full swing. Like some great migration of humanity, the citizens of Berlin were converging on Strasse des 17 Juni, the broad avenue running through the Tiergarten that would carry President Kennedy to his first stop. They wanted to see him in the flesh, maybe shake his hand, but even more than that, I think they wanted *him* to see *them,* to reach out and touch *them*. Spirits were soaring, the atmosphere charged with high expectations.

Horst convinced me to abandon breakfast and join the crowd advancing up Kurfürstendamm. Armed with American flags and homemade signs, they spilled out onto the street—young ones held above the fray by shoulders that would give them a clear view of history, construction workers in hard hats who'd spontaneously downed tools to join the parade, schoolchildren shepherded by anxious teachers, bearded professors expounding on the day's significance to wide-eyed students, housewives with freshly teased hair, old men in old hats, and young boys in crisp blue jeans. . . . The whole damn city had declared a holiday and was on its way to greet the American president.

"It's nuts," I said to Horst as we were swept up by the sea of euphoric faces. "He's the president of the United States, not the goddamned Second Coming."

"I don't think Berliners would be so interested in the Second Coming," he grinned. Horst was proud of the welcome his city was about to bestow on Kennedy. "Understand," he continued, suddenly looking very serious, "we in Berlin have feared more than anything being forgotten by the world. And now comes Kennedy, and the people know that he doesn't come to tell us that we are on our own. He comes to say that America won't forget us, even if sometimes our own leaders might like to."

I nodded and we continued on in silence, letting the surge of happy people carry us forward.

The atmosphere was infectious, but in the back of my mind I was trying to get inside Harvey King's head. I'd been on the money about city hall—maybe Harvey and I were on the same wavelength. The key to figuring out the operation lay in the fact that the whole world would witness the event and they'd all have to come away believing that one man had pulled the trigger.

It would go something like this:

Kennedy is at the platform, speaking to a rapt audience, when shots ring out—two quick blasts echoing through the plaza. Each volley has been counted down by Radio Control so that the two bursts of three simultaneous shots sound like the report of one rifle reverberating off the buildings that surround the square. Some witnesses say the shots came from the Victoria Hotel, while others claim they emanated from elsewhere—another building or from behind a group of trees. But that would be later, when it didn't matter anymore. The lone-gunman story would've taken hold by then. Now, in the seconds following the shots, a wave of horror and disbelief fans out across the plaza. Some in the back don't realize what's happened, while those closest to the stage can't believe their eyes. Except for one—an individual who is positioned at the front of the crowd or even on the platform itself. He calmly speaks into a hidden radio, sending a damage report back to Control in the form of one prearranged word. If Kennedy has taken a lethal hit, the "all clear" word goes out. If the president has escaped injury or is judged to be capable of surviving his wounds, the "hit him again" word is sent and Control calls for another volley. But with up to nine shots fired by expert marksmen in triangulated, coordinated fire, chances are that the job is done. Kennedy is dead.

All hell breaks loose. Confusion followed by panic on the platform, nobody sure what to do. Secret Service radios are buzzing with "shots fired, the president is down," but they're acting like chickens with their heads cut off because the Secret Service has only one mission in life—to protect the president—and they've just fucked up beyond their worst nightmare. Local police go into overdrive. Uniformed and undercover German cops rush to secure buildings in the vicinity and to lock off the plaza, but it can't be done in less than five minutes, probably more like fifteen—long after three unassuming men have melted away from the scene, never to be heard from again.

Back in the Victoria Hotel, Roy Chase shoves poor old drugged-out Jack Teller into the hallway, where a Secret Service agent puts two bullets in his chest. A pistol is fired into the wall—or better yet, into the agent's leg—and then placed in Jack's lifeless fingers so self-defense can be claimed. Who's going to question this hero's story when the recently fired Tokarev with my fingerprints on it is sitting in a room registered to me? Then, within hours, the photographs of Josef and me, the Soviet visa in my passport, and who knows what else is made public. Whatever happens after that, as far as the JFK assassination is concerned, it's case closed. . . .

We had almost an hour before we had to check in to the hotel and I needed some thinking time, so I was happy to hang back while Horst wormed his way to the front of the crowd, determined to get a close-up look at the Kennedy magic. Once the motorcade passed, I'd bring him down off his cloud, prep him as best I could for the various sticky situations we might find ourselves in.

If we beat the odds by making it past the lobby and into the room, we'd still be up shit's creek unless we found Chase's password. I'd convinced myself that it would be waiting for us at the hotel. It would be a needless security risk—one that Harvey was too smart to take—to hand out codes until the last possible moment. If I was right, it was just a question of finding the password once we got there. It might even find us: a message at reception or a note on a complimentary basket of fruit; or it might be harder to find; written on the back of a bar of soap or inside the wrapping of a chocolate bar. It could be in a hell of a lot of places and we wouldn't have much time.

Then a thought occurred to me: We might not need the password at all. What if we slipped through the lobby, headed upstairs, and opened the door to find the shooter waiting for us in the room? I liked that scenario because it meant I could walk in, kill him, and inform Control what I'd done as we made a fast exit. It seemed like a long shot, too easy, but there was some logic to it. In fact, the more I thought about it, the more it made sense.

I knew that one of the three shooters would be positioned somewhere in the hotel. Looking at it with my Harvey King hat on, it seemed to me that you ran the risk of casting serious doubt on your cover story if you didn't put your shooter in the room with me. After all, it was a virtual certainty that in a crowd of half a million or more, a fair number of people were going to witness the shots being fired. If they all agreed that the gunman's window didn't match up with the room that was registered to me, you've got a problem. On the other hand, if it was the same window, those witnesses would be a plus, confirming your story for you. In fact, you could create a series of photos—not obviously directed at the window, but shot from behind the president, so the hotel window would be visible in the background. When blown up and enhanced, the pictures would tell your story: In the first shot, Jack Teller stands at the window as Kennedy takes the podium. He's gone in the second photo, but moments later the photographer catches the barrel of a rifle protruding from the window—you can't see the gunman's face, but you can see the same white shirt that Teller had been wearing. In the last image, the president is down. The series of photographs would make the front page of every newspaper across the planet with a caption that read "The assassin sizes up his target, takes aim, and a president is dead."

I didn't see how Harvey could pass it up.

A buzz of excitement ran through the crowd and the ground started to vibrate with the drone of police motorcycles—a distant rumble at first, like rolling thunder, then closer and stronger until you could feel the vibrations under your feet and in the pit of your stomach. Then, drifting in from the west, the muffled chorus of ten thousand voices chanting "KEN-NE-DY . . . KEN-NE-DY!" building in intensity and growing louder as a wave of unbridled fervor worked its way up the avenue ahead of the motorcade.

I couldn't see a damn thing, and before I knew it I was hanging off a traffic light, craning my neck for a view of the approaching cortege. In the crisp, clear June air, the scene played out in full Technicolor glory, as if Berlin had been transported from its dull, black-and-white existence to the gates of the Emerald City. The lead car—Stars and Stripes flying on the right fender, the red, black, and gold of the German standard on the left—was a half mile away, close enough that you could see the pandemonium it was carrying with it. People were running along the sidewalk as the open limousine passed, trying to get ahead of the procession and join the crowd again, swelling the number of spectators to the bursting point.

I could see Kennedy now—standing in the back of his car, a wide grin on his tanned face, hair blowing in a gentle wind as he waved to the countless faces calling out, even screaming, his name. As glamorous and charismatic as he was, I don't think the people lining that avenue were cheering the man. They didn't know the man. What they knew was his youth, his energy, and his inspiring, sometimes electrifying words. They were cheering the promise that he offered for the future.

You only had to look at Adenauer, standing on the other side of the car, to see what it was all about. The German leader looked stunned, as if he'd been ambushed by his own people. He stood there, stiff and grim-faced, offering a halfhearted salute while he wondered, in God's name, when he would be able to sit down. He had served his country as head of state for fourteen years and now he was old and tired. He was the past and his people desperately wanted to look forward. Maybe that's what Willy Brandt was thinking as he stood between the president and the chancellor. Roughly Kennedy's age, the mayor seemed satisfied, and a bit bemused, by his city's unrestrained welcome.

Twenty white-jacketed motorcycle cops escorted the president, ten on each side of the sleek Lincoln Continental. Eight gray-suited Secret Service men jogged alongside, two stood on the rear bumper, and a whole carload followed, along with a couple of buses for aides and the press. The convoy was proceeding so slowly and Kennedy was so completely exposed that the thought crossed my mind that it actually wouldn't be a bad kill zone. I took a quick look around and saw that the only perch a sniper could use on this route would be a tree, and being up a tree with a rifle wouldn't give you high degree of confidence in your shot, and even less in your escape route. But on a different road, one surrounded by buildings . . .

When I turned back to watch the motorcade pass, I saw, out of the corner of my eye, some activity on the sidewalk—a quick flash of movement followed by a figure streaking toward the car, his right arm extended . . .

"Jesus Christ . . ." I whispered aloud when I realized it was Horst making the dash across the concrete. He headed straight for Kennedy, weaving successfully between two motorcycles, then giving a Secret Service agent the two-step shuffle and ducking under his arm. He pressed on, calling out what looked like "Mr. President! . . . Mr. President!!" as he shot forward, his outstretched arm pointing at the president's midsection. Kennedy, who had been waving to the other side of the road, turned back toward Horst, looked at his hand, then reached out to shake it.

The crowd went wild, releasing a colossal cheer into the atmosphere as the president leaned over to shout something in my crazy friend's ear. Horst released Kennedy's hand, then stood there in the street a moment, watching the car move away. A Secret Service agent stepped up and gently led him back into the crowd. Horst acknowledged the applause he was getting with a wave of his hand, then he was swallowed up by the masses.

It opened the floodgates. Two middle-aged women rushed the president next. Four agents pushed forward to hold them back, but Kennedy, who was taking great pleasure in this unbridled adulation, leaned out of the car so far that it looked for a moment like he might fall out. Brandt grinned and grabbed the president's jacket, holding him in the car while he reached his hand out to the ladies. No sooner were the ladies ushered away than a man carrying a young boy on his shoulders ran forward to touch the hand, then a man in sunglasses, and a woman dragging a young girl, and so on. . . .

"Quite a welcome," I said to Horst once I'd tracked him down and separated him from a gaggle of admirers.

"I should say so," he beamed. "People will remember this day for as long as they live." We'd found a quiet street that would take us most of the way down to Rudolf-Wilde Platz. It was pushing eleven o'clock, when we needed to check in, so I set a healthy pace.

"What did he say to you?" I asked.

Horst grinned broadly, paused a beat for dramatic effect. "He has told me that in his three days in Germany, I'm the only one who has broken out of the crowd!"

It was a badge of honor for Horst, and why not? I couldn't think of a better compliment than that one.

TWENTY-FOUR

"Mr. Teller, to check in," Horst whispered.

"Could you repeat it, please?" The pretty young receptionist was doing her best to deal with the morning's chaos. She leaned across the counter in order to catch Horst's words the second time around.

"Mr. Teller," he repeated softly. The girl cocked her head and gave him a quizzical look.

"I'm sorry . . . ?"

I had coached Horst to keep his voice down so that no one would pick up his accent, but the din in the lobby was making it impossible for the poor girl to hear him at all. There was nothing I could do about it, though. I was in the middle of my zombie act. After a third attempt Horst finally pushed my passport across the counter, open to the attached sheet with the reservation number typed on it. The girl looked at the paper briefly, then turned to the photo page.

"But you are not Mr. Teller," she observed.

"That's right," Horst answered, gesturing toward me as we had rehearsed. "Mr. Teller is my employer, who has asked me to check in for him." I could feel her glance over at me even though I was facing into the lobby. I wanted to make it easy for the spotters who were bound to be hanging around to see me, hoping they'd assume that Horst's back belonged to Chase. It helped that the place was so chaotic.

I couldn't help speculating about who was in the game with us. The man hiding behind the newspaper was the obvious choice, but good operatives don't make obvious choices. It was more likely to be the skinny lady with the barking poodle on her lap or the busy young bellhop. It didn't really matter. Even if they'd been wearing a sign across their back saying SPY, it wouldn't have changed anything.

The receptionist checked her reservation book, found my name, and turned her attention back to Horst. "I must have Mr. Teller's signature on the registration card," she said, pushing a pen and a three-by-four index card across the counter.

"Yes, of course," Horst nodded, relaxing into his role once he realized that she wasn't going to give him a hard time. "I'll have him sign it." He ambled over, waited for the girl to look away, then quickly forged my signature on the card, as I'd shown him. It was far from perfect, but I couldn't very well be seen signing autographs when I was supposed to be riding a Cosmic Cocktail.

"So far, it's so good," Horst whispered.

"If you say another word, I'm gonna stab you in the eye with that pen," I whispered back. "Hurry up and get the key."

He nodded and returned to the desk, where the girl was already involved with her next customer, an obese gentleman wearing a tweed jacket over a sweater vest with a raincoat slung over his arm.

He was sweating profusely and I wondered why anyone would dress like that on a day like this, and then I realized that he was English. He claimed to have a reservation, she claimed he didn't, and he was ready to fight the war all over again if he didn't get a room. Horst stood back and waited patiently while I started to boil over. I wanted to pummel both of them. Finally, after running out of steam, the jumbo Brit went away angry and Horst stepped up to the counter. He handed the receptionist the signed registration card.

"Yes, Mr. Teller's room," she sighed, sounding a bit frazzled now. Retrieving a key from the board, she handed it to Horst, along with the piece of paper with our confirmation number. "Room 417," she said, and I was starting to feel like we were gonna make it through phase one. Then the bottom dropped out.

"Mr. Teller was expected some time ago," she scolded. "We were told it was essential to have his room ready by eight o'clock."

"We were detained," Horst explained offhandedly. "I apologize." He clearly didn't get the implication of her statement, but I did. The implication was that we were fucked. Completely and utterly fucked . . .

DAMN!

If they'd been watching the lobby at eight o'clock, they knew Chase was missing in action. How could I be so fucking *dense*?! I had even wondered what he was supposed to be doing with the spare time! Why didn't I check it with the hotel?!

What would the move be? Damage control, that's what. But how? A disposal team waiting in room 417? Whether they aborted or not, they needed to make me disappear.

But something didn't fit. . . . I hadn't checked with the hotel because the reservation sheet attached to my passport had read "11 A.M. check-in." Why would it say that if Chase was supposed to check in at eight?

Jesus Christ, I was an idiot. . . . I looked at the clock behind the reception counter: 11:04. I needed that fucking password, like now! The girl was asking Horst if we had any luggage.

"Just this," he replied, holding the black briefcase up for her to see.

"The lift is to your right," she said, ready to move on to the next person in line. Horst thanked her and stepped away, forgetting to do the one thing I had told him not to forget. But my drug act didn't matter anymore—if anyone had been waiting for Chase, they'd be long gone by now, so I stepped up to the desk, pushed a startled customer aside with enough force that he wouldn't ask questions, and smiled at the receptionist.

"Could you check messages for room 417?" She froze, startled at first, then angry. "If you could wait—"

I couldn't wait, so I jumped the counter and checked the box. Empty. I hopped back over, telling the startled girl, "Nope, no messages!" as I walked away.

There was no time to explain to Horst, so I grabbed the room key and the briefcase from him. "Stay here," I said, then headed for the elevators, elbowing my way through the crowd.

"Why have you blown our cover?" he fretted, following in my wake.

"Forget it," I said curtly. "Just wait for me down here." The elevators were mobbed with people, so I went for the stairs. Horst stayed with me as I took the steps two at a time.

"What has happened?" he puffed when we hit the top floor.

"The '11 A.M. check-in' had nothing to do with the hotel. . . ." I said, trying to figure out which direction the room was in. "Chase is supposed to check in *on the radio* at eleven!"

He looked at his watch.

"Don't say it, Horst!" I barked.

"So then we must find the password. . . ."

"That's right," I said, trying to sound calm even though my heart was racing and I was gulping air. "We need the password." I took a deep breath and had a last shot at getting rid of Horst. "I'm gonna check the room out. . . . You head back to the lobby. There's a lady with a poodle in her lap down there. . . . She's been watching us."

His look said he wasn't buying it, but I'd committed to the story. "Watch her," I said. "If she leaves the lobby, stay with her."

"A lady with a poodle?" he said skeptically. "Are you sure?"

"Positive. Don't let her out of your sight."

"What about—?"

"For Christ's sake, Horst, do what I tell you!"

It did the trick. He hesitated but he started back down the stairs, tail between his legs. It was for his own good. If there were people waiting for me, they wouldn't know about Horst unless we walked in together. Anyway, his job was to get me past the lobby and he'd done that. The rest was up to me.

I found the room and stood at the door for a moment, gathering my thoughts. The strange thing was that if I had second-guessed Harvey King correctly, and one of his shooters had been waiting in the room, then I'd be as good as dead when I opened the door. But if they knew, I was as good as dead whether I opened the door or not, so there was nothing to lose. There was a thin ray of hope—and it was toilet-paper thin—that I'd been wrong and the room would be empty.

I dug into my pocket to retrieve the pack of Lucky Strikes, thinking the least I could do was take one of the bastards with me. I was about to slip the key into the door when I realized that I hadn't reloaded after putting one in Chase's neck. I took a step back, leaned against the wall, and twisted the bottom of the pack open. After carefully removing the molded Styrofoam container that held the cyanide missiles, I flipped the top of the pack open and, holding my breath, removed one of the pellets. I carefully dropped it down the barrel, as Sam had demonstrated. After replacing the Styrofoam holding the last two shots, I stepped up to the door again, slipped the key into the lock, took a deep breath, and turned it. The door swung open and I stepped into a completely empty room.

I had to laugh because I realized that as relieved as I was, I was also a little bit disappointed that I'd got it wrong about Harvey's game plan.

"Can we make a deal?"

I spun around and almost fired a cyanide pellet into Horst, who was standing behind me in the doorway.

"Jesus Christ, Horst! If you keep sneaking up on people like that, you're gonna get yourself killed!"

He stepped in and closed the door.

"What kind of deal?" I said.

"That you don't bullshit me again."

"What's the other half?"

"Other half?"

"There are usually two sides to a deal. I don't bullshit you again is one side, what's the other side?" He looked quizzically at the pack of Luckys I was aiming at him and I put them back in my pocket.

"I'm not stupid," he said.

"I don't think you're stupid, Horst. Just a little inexperienced."

"Is this why you have tried to get rid of me?"

I started the search with a basket of fruit that was sitting on the table. The note said "Welcome to the Victoria Hotel" in German, English, and French.

"Look, Horst," I said, "the only thing I want right now is to find the goddamned password. . . ."

"I can help," he said. I gave him a look. He wasn't going to go away, so I suggested he check the bathroom.

"Of course!" he said enthusiastically, and went in.

"Look for anything unusual or out of place," I called after him. "Writing on a bar of soap or a bottle of shampoo . . . Look in the bath, on the mirror, unroll the toilet paper, open up all the towels and washcloths, check the pockets of the bathrobes. . . . Check it all! If there's a shit floating in the goddamn toilet, see if it spells anything!"

I started going through the desk—hotel stationery, envelopes, room-service menu. . . . I flipped through a *Welcome to West Berlin* magazine and turned the ink blotter inside out in case something was written on the back. The clock by the side of the bed read 11:18. If it wasn't too late already, it would be soon. I pulled the sheets off the mattress and was taking the pillows out of their cases when Horst walked in, absorbed in a piece of paper he was reading.

"Did you find something?" I asked.

"No . . ." he said slowly. "I was just thinking—"

"Don't think, look!"

"I was thinking," he repeated, "that if this instruction referred not to an eleven o'clock check-in at the hotel, perhaps this number of confirmation is also not for the hotel. . . ."

He handed me the typewritten page that had been folded into my passport. I reread it:

VICTORIA HOTEL, SCHÖNEBERG
11 A.M. check-in
confirm EZECH13V10

"Can it be that it has something to do with the password?" he speculated.

"Horst," I said. "I think you might be a genius."

"I suppose it's possible," he smiled. I picked up the phone and dialed reception. It rang several times before the girl's harried voice came on the line.

"Reception."

"This is Mr. Teller."

"Yes, Mr. Teller," she said wearily.

"Did you get the confirmation number for my reservation?"

"I'm sorry?"

"My employee gave you a piece of paper with the confirmation number for my reservation. Did you use it?"

"We have no confirming numbers in our reservation system, Mr. Teller."

"That's what I thought," I said, and hung up. I heard a sarcastic "You're very welcome" as I put the receiver down.

"You get a gold star, Horst," I said, sitting down at the desk, picking up a pen and a piece of hotel stationery.

"It's a strange password," Horst said, studying the page. "Quite difficult to say."

"It's not the password, but it just might tell us what the password is." I wrote the letters and numbers down as they were configured:

EZECH13V10

"It makes no sense," Horst said, looking over my shoulder.

"It's not supposed to make sense," I said. "It's a code. The whole point is that it doesn't make sense unless you know how to read it." I started writing the digits down in every possible combination.

Backward:

01V31HCEZE

Dropping alternate letters:

EEH31 or ZC1V0

Replacing letters for their numerical equivalent in the alphabet and vice versa:

5-26-5-3-8-M-21-J

None of it helped. The only word I could squeeze out of the letters was *CHEZ* but that didn't go anywhere, so I tried different groupings:

EZ/ECH/13/V10

EZ could be *EASY* . . . ECH could be *ECHO*. . . . That gave me the idea to try the marine radio alphabet. It would read:

ECHO-ZULU-ECHO-CHARLIE-HOTEL

Hotel. Now I was getting somewhere. . . . And *V* would be *VICTOR* in radio speak, which might as well be *VICTORIA,* so you had *HOTEL VICTORIA*. . . . But what about the rest of it? I didn't like it, it was too fucking sloppy. I crumpled the paper, tossed it aside, grabbed a fresh sheet, and started over:

EZECH13V10

"Perhaps he had a book with the key to the puzzle," Horst said. "A codebook of some sort."

"He didn't have any books on him."

"Perhaps it's here, in this room somewhere."

"If you can find a book—" I stopped short, looked back at the letters. I wrote out what I was thinking:

EZE CH13 V10

"That's it," I said, reaching across the bed, pulling the side-table drawer open.

"I don't understand," Horst said, examining my writing.

I grabbed the book that was in the drawer, sat on the bed, and flipped through it.

"Know your Old Testament, Horst?"

"Not so well," he confessed.

"It's a good thing I do, then. How about Ezekiel, chapter 13, verse 10?" I found the passage. "Ever read that one?"

I displayed the book for Horst. Across the page was scribbled the word:

BABYSITTER

TWENTY-FIVE

I opened the briefcase, fired up the walkie-talkie, and threw the Bible to Horst. "Now would be a good time to learn how to pray," I said.

Flipping the television set on, I pulled a chair up to the screen and waited for it to warm up. A picture finally emerged of JFK and a couple dozen dignitaries standing on a temporary platform that looked like something they'd erect in Dodge City for a public hanging. The structure was intended to let the president and his entourage look out over the wall into East Berlin, but they weren't seeing much since the authorities on the other side had overnight hung giant banners with anti-Western propaganda from the Brandenburg Gate, effectively blocking the view.

Dialing around until I found a channel without a signal, I raised the volume of the static noise, then leaned into the speaker and hit the send button on the radio.

"Babysitter, checking in . . ." I said, doing my best to re-create Chase's macho monotone. "Do you read me? . . . Over." I released the button and waited.

"This is Big Daddy. . . ." Henry Fisher's voice came back loud and clear. I hadn't really thought about it, but I wasn't surprised. Henry was the logical choice for Control. "You're late, Babysitter," he said. "What's the problem? . . . Over."

I put the mouthpiece directly in front of the television's speaker and pressed *send* without saying anything.

"I'm getting a lot of interference here, Babysitter. Are you on line? . . . Over."

"It's the goddamn radio. . . ." I said. "What'd you do, get a deal from the Japs? . . . Over."

"What's your location? . . . Over." I was afraid he was going to ask that question. Since it was reasonable to assume that the hotel had a designation, and I didn't know it, I stalled.

"Didn't get that . . ." I said. "Can you repeat? . . . Over."

"Are—you—at—home? . . . Over," he said slowly, enunciating each word and handing me the hotel's designation. It wasn't a mistake on his part. Unlike my "Babysitter" designation, which was an internal security precaution, location designations were a safeguard against eavesdroppers, which you had to assume were out there in spite of the secure channels.

"Yeah, yeah . . . I'm at home. . . ." I confirmed. "Over."

"How's the kid? . . . Over."

"I gave him his medication and he's fast asleep . . . Over."

"Okay, stand by, Babysitter. . . . Over and out."

I sat back in the chair and exhaled a lungful of air. The fact that we'd made it that far was as close to miraculous as it gets, at least in my experience.

"What shall we do now?" Horst asked.

"We wait," I answered.

Horst tried to sit still, flipped quickly through the *Welcome to West Berlin* magazine, then threw it aside and flitted around the room, ready to explode. He started to say something, but I guess my look told him I wasn't interested in conversation.

I didn't mind that Fisher was running Control. In fact, it could be a bonus—at least I knew what I was dealing with. Henry was the kind of guy who would see aborting a mission as a personal failure, so he'd filter his risk assessment, ignoring anything that didn't stare him in the face. It was how I got away with the static-noise ploy.

Harvey was the exact opposite—he always assumed the worst. He had big ideas, but lots of guys have big ideas. Harvey's genius lay in being able to pull them off and that was the result of his obsession with detail. Like a grand master of chess developing his game, he would've spent weeks, probably months, thinking this operation through, putting it together, studying it from every conceivable angle, then taking it apart again until he could see no flaws. It was why he had argued so strongly for a postponement. The last-minute change from Kovinski to me made him nervous. Without properly vetting the deviation from his carefully worked-out plan, letting all the possibilities and potential pitfalls sink in over a period of time, he couldn't predict the problems it might create. The only solid argument he was left with was that my past with the Company might blow the cover story, even though he knew there were any number of elements that I might upset. Had he written the plan with me in mind, for instance, he probably would've arranged for more security than just Chase.

In all his plotting, Harvey had seen something that prevented him from placing the gunman in the same room with the patsy—originally Kovinski, now me. If I could get at that, maybe I could get at where he did place him. I was close, so damn close to spoiling these bastards' day, but I needed to know where to find that shooter. . . .

"Come in, Babysitter, this is Big Daddy. . . . Over." The walkie-talkie crackled to life. I picked it up, raised the volume on the television, and signed on.

"Babysitter here . . . Over."

"We'd like to get some photos, Babysitter. . . ." Fisher said. "Go ahead and draw the curtains. . . . The window should already be open. . . . Put the kid in front of it and I'll let you know when we've got what we need. . . . And keep out of sight. . . . Over."

Horst was already standing beside the window, the drawstring clenched in his fist. "Not yet," I said, getting into position behind the drapes.

"Okay . . ." I put my zombie face on again. "Open. . . ."

Horst pulled the curtain, revealing a crowd of somewhere close to a million people jammed into the plaza below me. I felt like the pope standing there in the window, except that the faithful were facing the wrong way. All eyes were focused on the stage that had been set up in front of city hall and the star-spangled pulpit where Kennedy would stand in less than two hours, a twelve-foot-high American flag below him, a massive red, white, and blue ribbon spanning the width of the platform behind him.

Horst and I had entered the hotel through a back door, so it was my first look at Rudolf-Wilde Platz and it was a hell of a scene—a sea of faces filled the long rectangular space, spilling out into the adjoining streets in all directions as far as I could see. The more dedicated had claimed a spot near the stage by staying overnight in tents and sleeping bags; others were spending hours up a tree to ensure their view.

The Victoria, five stories high and L-shaped, was one of several buildings overlooking the plaza from the west side of the square. The facade curved ninety degrees around the corner of a narrow street that fed into the plaza. The southern half of the building, where we were, was parallel to city hall and directly across from the speaker's dais, about a hundred and twenty yards away. Well within the bull's-eye range of the Tokarev in the hands of a good marksman. Combined with a second gun placed in the apartment complex on the opposite side of the narrow road, there would be a forty-five-degree convergence of fire onto President Kennedy's head.

Ideally, you'd want your third gunman firing at the target from ground level. Given that almost every square foot of the area was filled with spectators, it would be tough to conceal the third man, but I noticed a patch of trees to my left that was unique in that it hadn't been invaded by spectators. I couldn't see who was securing the area, but there was an ambulance parked next to it with a clear path through the crowd. A perfect setup for escape and weapons disposal.

"Babysitter, this is Big Daddy. . . . Over." I could feel Horst freeze up. "Hello, Babysitter . . . Over."

"What shall I do?" Horst asked urgently.

"This is Big Daddy, Babysitter. Please acknowledge. . . . Over," Fisher said impatiently.

"Answer it," I said, trying not to move my lips.

"How can I? He will know! He will hear my accent!"

"Do Bogie," I said.

"Babysitter, are you receiving?! . . . Over!" Fisher's blood pressure was on the rise.

"What do you mean, do Bogie?" Horst said, closing in on panic. "I'm not an actor!"

"You are now. . . ." I said. Horst drew a breath, picked up the radio, and leaned into the television speaker.

"I hear ya, Big Daddy. . . . Go ahead. . . . Over." He sounded more like John Wayne than Bogart, but it seemed to do the trick. I was starting to believe in God.

"We're not seeing the kid's face too well, Babysitter," Fisher said. "Push him up a little closer to the window . . . so he catches the light. . . . Over."

I stepped forward.

"How is that? . . . Over," Horst said into the radio. I wanted to tell him to keep quiet, but I was pretty sure they'd have a telephoto lens on me now and might see me move my lips. I'd been half-right about the photographs anyway. They were getting me on film standing at the window—I just couldn't see why Harvey wouldn't want a shot of the rifle hanging out of it at the crucial moment.

There was a slight delay before Fisher came back on the line. "Okay, Babysitter . . . That's fine." Then another voice, in the background, came on over the open mike. I couldn't be sure, but it sounded like Harvey King himself:

"Who's that on the roof?" he said.

"One of ours, I think . . ." Fisher answered.

"Don't fucking think!" the voice barked. "Find out and get it cleared! I don't want anybody on that roof until—!" Then Fisher remembered to take his finger off the send button.

Until what?! . . . Until the shooter turns up? . . . Was Harvey going to place the sniper on the roof above my window? . . . Why? . . . What advantage was there?

Did he think it would be a better escape route? Maybe he didn't want to risk the possibility that the gunman would get caught up in the hallway "shoot-out" that was supposed to leave me dead. That made some sense. Witnesses would appear as soon as they heard shots in the hallway. Since they would be well aware of exactly how much time had passed between the president being hit and the Secret Service man gunning me down, the two events would have to happen within, say, thirty seconds of each other. It wasn't enough time to ensure that the gunman would get away cleanly. If he had fired from the roof, on the other hand, he could slip out of the hotel while everyone converged on the fourth-floor hallway. . . .

"Okay, that's it, Babysitter. . . ." Fisher's voice came back online. "Put the kid back to bed and keep out of sight. . . . I'll buzz you when we start the countdown. . . . Over and out."

Horst pulled the curtains shut, then fell back onto the bed and stared at the ceiling.

"This was a close shave," he finally said.

"We're fine," I said. "But I'd work on that Bogart impression if I were you."

"What is the meaning of *dow-bed?*" Horst asked a few minutes later. He was pacing again, this time with his nose in the Bible.

"What?"

"D-a-u-b-e-d," he spelled, then sounded it out. "Dow-bed."

"Daubed," I corrected him.

"What is the meaning?"

"Well . . ." I started to say, but came up short. "What's the context?"

"Context?"

"Read the whole sentence."

" 'They have seduced my people, saying, Peace; and there was no peace; and one built up a wall, and, lo, others *daubed* it with untempered mortar.' Also 'untempered mortar' I don't understand."

"To daub is to plaster, I think, and untempered mortar . . . I guess that's some kind of soft cement." Horst shrugged and went back to his walking and reading.

"Is that the Ezekiel passage?" I asked after a while, my curiosity getting the better of me. He displayed the page with "Babysitter" written across it.

"Let's hear the rest," I said.

"From the beginning?"

"From what you just read me."

"Okay," he said. "It's going like this: 'They have seduced my people, saying, Peace; and there was no peace; and one built up a wall, and, lo, others daubed it with untempered mortar.' " He gave me a knowing look before continuing: " 'Say unto them that it shall fall:

there shall be an overflowing shower; and yea, O great hailstones shall fall and a stormy wind shall rend it.' Rend it?" he asked.

"Blow it up," I said. Horst nodded and continued.

" 'Therefore thus saith the Lord God; I will even rend it with a stormy wind in my fury; and there shall be an overflowing shower in mine anger, and great hailstones in my fury to consume it. . . . So will I break down the wall that ye have daubed with untempered mortar, and bring it down to the ground, so that the foundation thereof shall be discovered, and it shall fall, and ye shall be consumed in the midst thereof: and ye shall know that I am the LORD. . . . Thus will I accomplish my wrath upon the wall, and upon them that have daubed it with untempered mortar, and will say unto you, The wall is no more, neither they that daubed it; . . . to wit, the prophets of Israel which prophesy concerning Jerusalem, and which see visions of peace for her, and there is no peace, saith the Lord GOD.' "

TWENTY-SIX

"This is Big Daddy to all units. . . . Repeat, this is Big Daddy. . . . All units please acknowledge, over." I grabbed the radio.

"Babysitter acknowledging, over," I said, clicking on. A long minute passed, just the static noise of the television filling the space. Then Fisher's voice came crackling back.

"Okay, we're looking at a green light. . . . Countdown begins on my signal. . . . Get set for ten and stand by. . . ."

I opened Chase's briefcase, which was lying on the bed, and grabbed the stopwatch. It was a Company special, the first digital timepiece I'd seen. I set it for ten minutes and we waited.

Fisher came back after a short delay. "Okay, we're ready to roll," he said. It was a big moment for him and you could hear in his voice that he was enjoying it. "Stand by . . . three . . . two . . . one. . . ."

I hit the start button and the seconds started ticking off. The clock by the bed showed it was a couple of minutes short of one o'clock, when Kennedy was supposed to appear on the dais. It occurred to me that only the Germans could keep things on schedule in the midst of all this insanity.

"We're operational," Fisher announced. "All systems are go!" He sounded more like he was blasting a rocket into space than murdering his president. "Stand by. . . ."

We were on the clock now. No more theories or conjecture, no time for maybe this or maybe that. Whatever was gonna happen was gonna happen *now* and it was gonna determine whether the world kept turning on its knife's edge or went spinning out of control. Everything was plugged in, switched on, and, like Fisher said, all systems go. I could see that Horst was pumped up, too. He had that look—the slightly deranged, supercharged look that I'd seen on the faces of too many boys. Boys who were so juiced on adrenaline that they were prepared to rush headlong into a machine gunner's nest with bayonet fixed. Whenever I saw that look I knew chances were pretty good that I was looking at a soldier who wouldn't come out the other end.

Horst said something but it was drowned out by a sudden deafening roar from outside. The thunderous cheer shook the entire building, rattling doors and windows in their frames and twisting the butterflies in the pit of my stomach into a tangled knot of nervous energy. Kennedy had arrived on stage.

"NINE MINUTES!" Fisher barked out.

Time to make my move, but I needed to do it alone. I knew the odds were against me, and making a casualty out of Horst wouldn't improve them any.

"Stay here!" I shouted over the din.

"No!" he yelled back. "We go together!"

There wasn't time to think, let alone argue. I grabbed Chase's handcuffs out of my pocket, quickly slapped one manacle onto his wrist then locked the other to the metal bed frame.

"I'm sorry, Horst," I said, clipping the radio to my belt and heading for the door. "But it's better this way."

The cheering built to a fever pitch, then the crowd started to chant: "KEN-NE-DY! . . . KEN-NE-DY! . . . KEN-NE-DY!"

Horst gave me this parting look—a combination of hurt and anger that I can still see clearly to this day. He felt betrayed and offended, but I dismissed it then, partly because there was no time to do anything else, but also because I believed that I was doing him a favor, maybe even saving his life. And, in some feeble way, I think I was thinking about Hanna.

The hallway was unnervingly quiet. Another great cheer went up, muffled by the hotel's thick walls, then evaporated, leaving an expectant hush in the air. I guessed that Kennedy had stepped up to the podium.

"EIGHT MINUTES . . ." Fisher's voice called out over the radio.

I spotted a "Fire Exit" sign and followed it up the long corridor. Walking quickly at first, then breaking into a run.

Kennedy's familiar voice cut through the silence:

> *I am proud to come to this city as the guest of your distinguished Mayor, who has symbolized throughout the world the fighting spirit of West Berlin. And I am proud to visit the Federal Republic with your distinguished Chancellor, who for so many years has committed Germany to democracy and freedom and progress, and to come here in the company of my fellow American, General Clay, who has been in this city during its great moments of crisis and will come again if ever needed. . . .*

I tried to ignore the second thoughts I was having about leaving Horst behind. I told myself that no matter how humiliated he felt, he'd be safer where he was than tagging along with me. If it all worked out I'd retrieve him before anyone knew what had happened. If it didn't work out . . . well, he was still better off handcuffed to the furniture than being teamed up with a dead patsy. By the time things went sour, he'd probably have figured out that I'd left the key to the cuffs in Chase's briefcase and, I hoped, have the good sense to make a quick exit. Anyway, it was done, so I had to let it go and I did.

"SEVEN MINUTES . . ." Fisher announced.

I hesitated at the emergency exit. I knew I'd run into security somewhere along the line, wondered if this was the place. I put my ear to the reinforced door, but all I could hear was my heart pounding like a jackhammer and the president's voice:

> *There are many people in the world who really don't understand, or say they don't, what is the great issue between the Free World and the Communist world. Let them come to Berlin! . . .*

The crowd roared its approval. I grabbed the Lucky Strikes out of my jacket pocket. . . .

> *There are some who say that communism is the wave of the future. Let them come to Berlin! . . .*

More applause and I reached for the handle. . . .

> *And there are some who say in Europe and elsewhere we can work with the Communists. Let them come to Berlin! . . .*

Wild cheers and I almost bounced out of my skin as "SIX MINUTES!" blared out of the radio. I jumped back, threw myself against the wall. Fumbling around, I managed to hit the off switch on the radio, then froze. Didn't move, didn't breathe. I clutched the Lucky Strikes, ready to pop anyone who tried to come through the door.

> *And there are even a few who say that it's true that communism is an evil system, but it permits us to make economic progress. Laßt sie nach Berlin kommen. Let them come to Berlin!*

The crowd went wild. . . . A drop of sweat rolled down my forehead, burning as it filled my eye. I drew a breath, reached for the handle again, but stopped short when I heard a radio sputter to life on the other side:

"Big Daddy to Hero," Fisher's voice crackled out. "What's your position? Over."

"The north stairwell, fourth floor, over," came the response from behind the door.

"Okay, Hero . . . Stand by," Fisher instructed him.

I didn't recognize the voice, but it wasn't hard to figure out that "Hero" was the Secret Service agent who'd decided that instead of protecting the president today, he'd help knock him off. He was also my executioner and I was sorely tempted to open the door and put a poison pellet up the bastard's nose. I thought better of it, slipped away, and doubled back, jogging the length of the corridor. I was hoping, but not really expecting, to find an unguarded stairwell in the south wing.

The cheers faded away and Kennedy's voice filtered through again:

> *Freedom has many difficulties and democracy is not perfect, but we have never had to put a wall up to keep our people in, to prevent them from leaving us. . . .*

Kennedy had to pause, unable to continue over the frenzied response that this statement elicited. It was a simple enough observation, almost a cliché, that would get polite applause anywhere else in the world. But this wasn't anywhere else; it was Berlin, and the wall was more than an abstract idea to them. It was a desecration of their city and a violation of their lives, separating them from family and friends. They abhorred it and Kennedy had said the words they'd been waiting for. The words they'd come to hear.

I reached the end of the hall and ducked into a doorway across from the exit. Even if the stairs were covered, I was out of options. I'd have to go in and take my chances.

The timer read 04:22.

I decided to wait for Fisher's four-minute announcement to see if there were any more "Heroes" behind this door. At least I'd know what I was walking into.

The crowd finally let Kennedy continue:

> *I want to say, on behalf of my countrymen, who live many miles away on the other side of the Atlantic, who are far distant from you, that they take the greatest pride that they have been able to share with you, even from a distance, the story of the last eighteen years. I know of no town, no city, that has been besieged for eighteen years that still lives with the vitality and the force and the hope and the determination of the city of West Berlin. . . .*

The four-minute mark came and went with nothing from behind the door. I wiped the sweat off my palms, slipped the Luckys into my palm, and grabbed the door handle. . . .

Locked. . . .

Goddamm it! Kennedy would be lying on a slab at the morgue by the time I picked the dead bolt. I didn't have the tools anyway. I tried kicking it in, but it wasn't gonna give. Desperation creeping up on me, I looked around, spotted a fire extinguisher attached to the wall. Above it, behind glass, was just what I needed. I ran over, punched the window out, and grabbed the ax.

I noticed halfway up the hall that I was trailing blood. Locating a gash in my right palm, I hastily tied a handkerchief around it as I ran the rest of the way and went to work on the door. After a few solid blows, I was able to kick the bastard in.

Racing up the steps, I found the door leading onto the roof wide open. I dropped the ax and stepped back into the shadows, needing a minute to catch my breath and think things through. I drew a mental picture of the building's L-shaped layout, placing myself at the southern end. The gunman would be above my room in the north wing, just past the ninety-degree turn. I'd have about sixty yards to cover.

I peeked out, trying to get a sense of how open the terrain was. An elevator support unit—a ten-foot-high brick structure at the center of the building—stood between me and where the sniper's nest would be set up. I'd be exposed for about forty yards, but once there, I could locate the shooter and lay low until the right moment, when he was focused on the plaza with the president in his sights. About the only thing I had going for me was the element of surprise, so I'd damn well better make the most of it, I thought. I'd rush him at full speed, come up from behind before he had time to react. I'd go for a head shot from point-blank range.

I turned my radio back on before stepping out onto the roof, just in time for the three-minute warning. Time was running out.

I slipped in behind the open door, scanned the area up and down. I was too far from the front of the building to see the stage, but now that I was out in the open, Kennedy's voice was coming through loud and clear:

> *While the wall is the most obvious and vivid demonstration of the failures of the Communist system, for all the world to see, we take no satisfaction in it. . . . For it is, as your Mayor has said, an offense not only against history but an offense against humanity, separating families, dividing husbands and wives and brothers and sisters, and dividing a people who wish to be joined together. . . .*

I couldn't see any security from my position, but it was impossible that the shooter would be out there naked and vulnerable. If there was one of them, I might have a shot—a long shot—at killing him and still getting the sniper. If two guns were up there, well, the fat lady could start warming up.

I ducked out from behind the door and sprinted across the asphalt surface, hitting the safety of the brick wall sooner than I'd expected. I hadn't seen anything, but I'd been moving, not looking. I edged around the structure and peered out toward the retaining wall at the front of the building. Still nothing. Not a sign of anybody or anything along the entire length of the wall. Or on the entire roof, for that matter.

I started to get a sinking feeling.

"TWO MINUTES . . . !" Fisher barked.

I stepped into the open, turned in a complete circle, surveying the whole area. I was alone, completely fucking alone. I walked toward the front of the building, where I'd expected to find the assassin. As the plaza came into view, I could see President Kennedy gesturing emotionally from the speaker's platform:

> *. . . real, lasting peace in Europe can never be assured as long as one German out of four is denied the elementary right of free men, and that is to make a free choice. . . .*

Jesus Christ, I thought, it's gonna happen. I'd got it wrong and they were gonna murder the president right there in front of me and a million other witnesses.

> *In eighteen years of peace and good faith, this generation of Germans has earned the right to be free, including the right to unite their families and their nation in lasting peace. . . .*

"BIG DADDY TO BABYSITTER!" Fisher's voice crackled out. "COME IN BABYSITTER! . . . OVER!"

I grabbed the radio like it was a life preserver. "This is Babysitter. . . . Go ahead, Big Daddy. . . ." Come on, Fisher, I prayed, give me something! Give me a fucking clue!

"STAND BY TO RECEIVE SHADOW ONE! . . . REPEAT, I'M SENDING SHADOW ONE IN TO YOU NOW! . . . OVER!"

I went numb, actually numb in the face and hands. He was going to fire out of the window of my room, exactly the way I'd figured it. He hadn't been waiting for me because they were sending him in at the last minute. Into my room, where Horst was locked to the bed like a lamb waiting for slaughter.

"FISHER, IT'S JACK TELLER!" I yelled into the radio. "CHASE IS DEAD, I KILLED HIM! . . . THE OPERATION'S BLOWN! YOU HEAR ME, FISHER, IT'S OVER!"

"Jack?! . . . What the fuck's going on?"

"CALL IT OFF!"

"Where the hell are you, Jack?"

"YOU KNOW WHERE I AM!" I bluffed desperately. "AND I'M TELLING YOU, HENRY, IF YOU SEND THAT KILLER IN HERE, I'M GONNA DROP HIM OUT THE FUCKING WINDOW!"

There was a short pause, then Fisher came back on the line.

"Look to your left, Jack," he said. "The building across the street. . . ."

It was a six-story apartment block, recently built.

"The balcony on the top floor, the one nearest to you." I scanned across the face of the building until I found the one he meant. And there he was—Big Daddy, Henry E. Fisher, radio in his right hand, the left fully extended, giving me the finger.

"Fuck you, Jack," he said with a smile, forming his hand into a gun. "Bang, bang, you're dead. . . . Over and out, amigo."

I was already sprinting toward the north exit when he finished his sentence. Hero would be on his way up and I'd be exposed, a sitting duck on the open roof. If I could get to the door before he did, I might have a fighting chance.

He beat me to it, stepping out onto the roof, pistol drawn, when I was still twenty yards short. He pivoted toward me and I launched myself as he lined me up in his sights. . . .

"HRUMMPHH!" I could hear the air go out of him as I plowed into his midsection. We bounced off the door and went flying back into the building, landing in a pile at the top of the stairwell. He pulled himself onto his knees, doubled over, holding his gut, struggling to draw a breath. I stood up, held the pack of Luckys to his ear, and pressed the trigger. . . .

Click . . . Nothing.

Either the damn thing misfired or I'd shot the pellet off into space during my flying tackle. Either way, "Hero" was getting his wind back and his pistol was moving around toward me. I kicked him hard in the gut, then again across the side of the head, sending him tumbling backward down the stairs. I don't know if it was the kick or the fall that did it, but he landed with his head facing the wrong way on his shoulders. It looked very odd and I must've hesitated a moment at the sight before snapping out of it and hastily looking around for his gun. It was gone, lost in the shuffle . . .

"SIXTY SECONDS . . ." Fisher announced. "STAND BY. . . ."

I exploded into the hallway and up the corridor. Kennedy's voice rose above the spellbound plaza as he built to a climax:

> *So let me ask you, as I close, to lift your eyes beyond the dangers of today to the hopes of tomorrow, beyond the freedom merely of this city of Berlin, or your country of Germany, to the advance of freedom everywhere, beyond the wall to the day of peace with justice, beyond yourselves and ourselves to all mankind. . . .*

I burst through the door and found myself looking straight into the long barrel of a silencer-fitted .22. Shadow One was a big, Mediterranean-looking guy, athletic, with short dark wiry hair, a broad nose, and a thick black mustache. I saw from his position that he'd been a hairsbreadth away from putting a slug into Horst's forehead and had swiveled the gun toward the door at the last moment when he heard me coming through it. And I was trapped, as good as dead.

But he hesitated.

I don't know why he did, and it couldn't have been for more than a fraction of a second, but it felt like a damned eternity. There's nothing like staring death in the face to make you feel alive. Every sound is amplified, every detail is crystal clear, every twitch catches the eye. I became aware of Horst's movement in the same moment that I saw the killer's finger squeeze down on the trigger. It happened quickly, more quickly than should've been possible—Horst stretched his long frame across the bed, grabbed something out of Chase's briefcase, then shot to his feet. Extending himself as far as the handcuffs would allow, he brought his arm around and stabbed the killer in the jugular with the hypodermic needle.

A look of complete and utter shock replaced the killer's detached expression. He managed to say *"Merd—"* just before Horst drove the plunger home, sending the Frenchman on what must've been the Cosmic Cocktail ride of all time. He stumbled backward for a few steps, then his legs gave way. He landed hard, his back propped up against the wall where he'd left the Tokarev. Hard to say whether the blank look in his eyes was that of a dead man or a vegetable, but either way the guy was traveling on a one-way ticket.

Horst and I shared a "Holy Shit!" look.

"THIRTY SECONDS!"

Freedom is indivisible, and when one man is enslaved, all are not free. . . .

I grabbed the killer's radio.

"FISHER!" I screamed into it.

". . . Jesus Christ, Jack . . . Aren't you dead yet?!"

"No, but your shooter is!"

When all are free, then we can look forward to that day when this city will be joined as one, and this country, and this great Continent of Europe, in a peaceful and hopeful globe. . . .

"Give it up, Jack!" He clicked off then came back on, announcing "TWENTY SECONDS! . . . STAND BY FOR FINAL COUNTDOWN. . . ."

When that day finally comes—as it will—the people of West Berlin can take sober satisfaction in the fact that they were in the front lines for almost two decades. . . .

"WAKE UP, HENRY! I'M USING YOUR SHOOTER'S RADIO, FOR CHRIST'S SAKE! . . ." I grabbed the killer by the collar and propped him up against the window. "LOOK AT THE HOTEL WINDOW! . . . SEE HIM, YOU STUPID FUCK?! AND I'M GONNA THROW THIS PIECE OF SHIT AND HIS RIFLE OUT THE WINDOW IF YOU DON'T CALL IT OFF!"

All free men, wherever they may live, are citizens of Berlin . . .

"TEN SECONDS . . ." he announced. "NINE . . . EIGHT . . ." I drew a deep breath and spoke into the radio again—quietly, absolutely calm.

"If you can hear me, Harvey, I want you to know that I'm dialing the phone. . . . I'm calling the West German police. . . ."

"SIX . . . FIVE . . ."

". . . And the first name of the many that I'm going to give them is Harvey King. . . ."

"FOUR . . . THREE . . ." Then it stopped. Nothing for a moment, then . . .

"ABORT! . . . REPEAT . . . ABORT ACTION AND DISENGAGE! . . . ALL UNITS ABORT AND DISENGAGE!"

. . . and, therefore, as a free man, I take pride in the words "Ich bin ein Berliner."

The wall wouldn't hold back the cheer that filled the plaza with those words.They probably heard it in Moscow. I let the killer drop to the floor and freed Horst. He didn't move, just sat there on the bed with a dazed look on his face.

I pulled him up and said, "Let's get the hell out of here while we can."

"Yes . . . yes . . ." he said, and headed for the exit. I stopped to pick up the killer's handgun and looked up as Horst was going through the doorway.

"Wait!" I yelled, but it was too late, he was in the hallway. I heard the shots—three of them—and saw Horst fall away.

Christ. I get the same sick feeling now that I got then, even after all these years. Sudden shock and alarm, like you just stepped off a cliff.Then your stomach drops out and dread takes over as you wait to hit the ground.

I flew out the door, laying down fire wildly, killing Andy Johnson in a hail of bullets. *POP! POP! POP!* went his flesh.

Horst was lying on his side, holding his gut. He was bleeding badly and I could see he wasn't going to make it, so I didn't try to move him, I just rolled him onto my lap and held him. I didn't care that they were coming for me. I wasn't going to let him die alone.

"Don't move," I said.

He didn't try to speak, just nodded. I could see that the pain was receding, but he was scared.

"You'll be all right," I said.

He coughed up some blood and said, "I thought we did win."

"We did," I answered. "We won . . . and you were the hero." But I think he died without hearing it.

TWENTY-SEVEN

"There was no shooter, Jack. No Roy Chase, either . . . No Andy Johnson, no dead Secret Service agent, and no Aleks Kovinski. Poof, like magic, they all disappear. It never happened."

"What about Horst?"

"Shot and killed while resisting arrest for the murder of a Canadian businessman named Ian Howe—who was found floating in a canal with a spear through his lung."

I gave Sam a look, but he kept his eyes focused on an open field where an impromptu game of soccer was in progress. I was too worn out, too depressed, too drained to protest. It wouldn't change anything anyway. The whole thing had already been cleaned up and swept under the rug. Except for me, of course. I was a loose end. I'd been walking aimlessly for hours, going over the events of the last five days, trying to fit the pieces together. Sam had been waiting for my call when I finally got the full picture and we were standing in the Tiergarten a half hour later.

"Why'd we have to go through all this?" I said to him. "Was there a point?"

"What's the matter, Jack? Don't you know you just saved the world?"

"You could've gone to Bobby Kennedy with what you had. He would've been all over it."

"I needed some pressure," he said, finally looking over at me. "To find the weak points." He shrugged and turned back to the soccer game. "Anyway, you know me. I'm a backdoor kind of guy."

"I've been thinking about how this all went down."

"Sounds like you came up with something."

"Maybe."

"Wanna spit it out?"

"You know how the Colonel learned about the plot?"

He looked at me out of the corner of his eye. "I'm all ears."

"A high-level source at Langley told him about it."

"The elusive mole, huh?"

"That's right."

"What makes you think that?"

"He told me." Sam forgot about the soccer game, gave me his full attention.

"Did he give you a name?"

"I didn't ask him."

"I see," Sam said with a smile, then went back to the soccer. "Got anything to go home to, Jack?"

"A leaky boat and a sticky typewriter."

"Might be a good idea for you to get lost for a while. Until I can get a handle on things, anyway." He handed me a British passport. "Use this," he said with a smile. "And let me know when you get settled."

"You can count on never hearing from me again," I said.

"Maybe that'd be for the best."

"You gonna go after these guys?"

"Let me tell you something you might not know, Jack." He kept his eyes focused on the game. "I hate those bastards. . . . I hate 'em with a passion. Not because they tried to kill Kennedy. I hate 'em because they're the scum of the earth. . . . You bet I'm gonna go after them."

"I might just miss you, Sam. As ridiculous as that sounds, I just might."

"Yeah, I guess I'm something of an enigma all right."

"You're being kind to yourself."

"Maybe so," he laughed and produced a manila envelope out of his pocket. "It's the Kovinski picture. Give it to your brother when you see him."

"I wasn't sure if you knew."

"Didn't you know?" he said with a wink. "I'm a master spy. Watch your back, Jack."

And he turned and walked away. The soccer ball got loose and he kicked it back into play, but he didn't look back. That was the last time I saw Sam. He died two weeks later of sudden heart failure, although as far as I know, he never had a heart problem.

As hard as they tried, nobody ever unearthed the Langley mole. You don't need all the facts to know the truth.

I was still registered at the Kempinski, so I thought, what the hell, I was owed a last night of comfort. I was sure nobody would look for me there, but I was wrong.

The doorbell rang early, just after dawn. I was already awake after a mostly sleepless night and wasn't all that surprised to find Josef standing in the hallway.

"You should have left Berlin by now," he greeted me.

"I haven't seen all the sights yet," I said, leading him into the living room. He didn't sit down at first, just stood in the middle of the room looking uncomfortable.

"I thought I should see you before you leave," he said.

"You make it sound like your Socialist duty."

He shrugged, but didn't disagree. "You'll disappear?" he asked, although it sounded like more of a hope than a question.

"Seems like the thing to do," I said, pouring two lukewarm coffees from a carafe I'd ordered an hour earlier. He sat down and put the cup aside. I felt that he wanted to say something, but was having trouble finding the way in.

"How'd you figure I'd be here?" I asked, just to fill the space.

"Your unpredictability has become predictable," he smiled, shifting his weight and leaning forward. "I thought you might have stayed in Berlin because you hoped . . . well, that I could offer—"

"Thanks anyway," I interrupted, saving him the embarrassment. "But spending my golden years in Minsk isn't exactly what I had in mind." I knew Josef had acted independently, which was even less tolerated on his side of the wall. The last thing he needed was me showing up at his doorstep, so he was here to head me off. I couldn't believe that he actually thought I'd consider defecting, but I guess he had to cover all his bases. Anyway, he seemed relieved that I dismissed the idea out of hand and relaxed a little bit after that.

I wish I could say that we came to some conclusion about our relationship over the course of the next hour, but, of course, we didn't. We had so little in common and what we did have was too far in the past to really matter. Seeing him had brought back memories that stay with me to this day, and I was grateful for that, but it wasn't something I wanted to talk about. I did wonder, though, if seeing me had brought something of that lost time back for Josef, too.

We talked politics, disagreeing on pretty much everything, and exchanged gossip about world leaders. He told me that he was going to be posted to New York in the near future, attached to the GDR's delegation at the UN. I wrote down the name of a couple of good restaurants and said the best spot to see what America was all about was from behind first base at Yankee Stadium. When he stood up to go, there was a good feeling between us and that was enough to make me feel a little bit lighter.

"I wish you the best of luck," he said.

I handed him the envelope containing the Kovinski photo. "From a mutual friend," I said.

He smiled. "You know, most of us don't have the opportunity to choose our side. . . . It chooses us. And those who do choose usually do so for selfish reasons. Once in a while, though, there's an exception who chooses out of principle."

"What if he makes the wrong choice?"

"He lives with the mistake," Josef said with a shrug, then reached into his pocket. "I have something for you, too." He extended his palm and revealed two faded toy soldiers. Much of the color had worn off in the forty-five years since they appeared under my Christmas tree, but you could still see that one was in red uniform, one in blue.

"For you," he said.

"For as long as I keep our secret?" I smiled, taking the figures and looking them over. They were like old friends.

"If ever I can be of help . . ." he said, with a shrug.

"There is something," I said, recalling the photograph Hanna had showed me. "A man named Alfred Mann. He's a mathematics teacher in East Berlin. He could use an exit visa."

"It shouldn't be a problem," Josef said, then we shook hands and parted.

I went to Horst's funeral, but watched from a distance, mostly out of regard for Hanna, but also because there was a pretty good chance that someone would be keeping an eye on it in case I showed up. It was a short service, with a good crowd of mostly young faces, but Hanna kept to herself. I caught up with her as she waited at a bus stop outside the cemetery gates.

"Don't say you've come to say you're sorry," she said evenly. "I couldn't stand it."

"I thought you should know the truth," I said.

"Why? Will it change anything?"

"Maybe," I said.

"He trusted you," she said.

"He had no reason to," I responded, having no wish to justify anything.

She smiled bittersweetly. "Horst saw the world in black and white, like one of those films he always talked about. He thought you were some kind of hero."

"Your brother saved a lot of lives before he died, including mine," I said. "If anybody was a hero, it was him."

"In the movies, the hero never dies," she said as the bus appeared and opened its door for her. She was about to get on, but paused and turned back to me. "It doesn't change anything," she said. "But perhaps someday it will."

I slipped an envelope containing forty-five one hundred dollar bills into her jacket pocket before she stepped on board. It was the five grand that had been in Chase's envelope, minus five hundred to get me where I was going, wherever that was.

As the door closed behind Hanna and the bus pulled away, I hoped she would marry her mathematics teacher and live happily ever after.

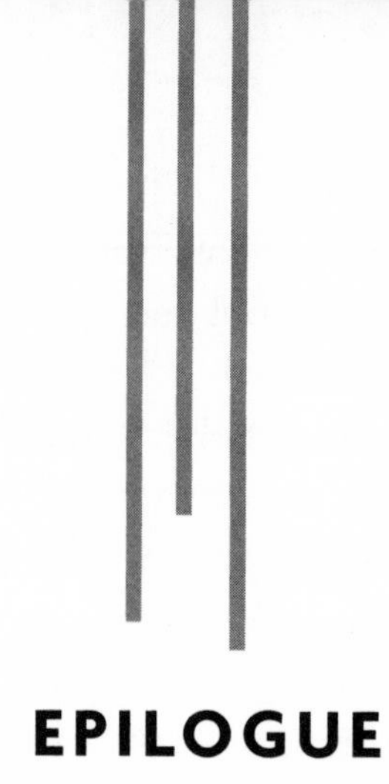

EPILOGUE

I was drifting in the waters off British Honduras on a balmy afternoon in late November when I turned on the radio:

> *. . . Shots have been fired at President Kennedy's motorcade as it left downtown Dallas this afternoon. . . . The president was taken to Parkland Memorial Hospital, where he was pronounced dead at 12:50* P.M. *. . . Police have arrested Lee Harvey Oswald, a known Communist sympathizer, who is believed to have fired from an upper-floor window of the Texas School Book Depository. . . . Authorities are seeking no further suspects. . . .*

Within three hours of the assassination, fully loaded American bombers were on their way to hit targets inside Cuba and all U.S. forces were placed on DefCon 3, which is a telephone call away from launching an all-out nuclear attack. The Soviet Union went to full alert, also, and the party was ready to get into full swing when somebody at the Pentagon took it upon themselves to call the planes back, just seconds before they entered Cuban airspace. No one could say in the confusion following the assassination who had ordered the planes back or—more to the point—who had ordered the attack in the first place.

Dallas was a poor substitute for Berlin. The public will swallow a lot, but asking them to buy Dallas, Texas, as the breeding ground for a Communist conspiracy was too much. I used to wonder if those planes would've been called back had the president been shot in Berlin instead of Texas. But history has a way of writing itself in stone. Once it's happened, it's hard to imagine it occurring any other way, and it's pointless to speculate. Still, I like to think that maybe Horst and Sam and Josef and me, maybe we did change the course of history, after all.

The men who killed Kennedy lit up cigars that day in November and slapped each other on the back, but they didn't get the country they wanted. America's strange form of democracy survived, as vibrant as ever—probably a lot more vibrant. The real coup took place not with bombs or bullets, but with ideas, and the irony is that the social revolution of the sixties probably wouldn't have happened, at least not in the same way, had Kennedy lived.

When Johnson created the Warren Commission to look into the assassination, he told its reluctant chairman that there was evidence of Soviet involvement in Kennedy's death. Unless people were convinced that Oswald acted alone, he said, the country might have to go to war, putting forty million lives at stake. Johnson was a first-class operator.

The FBI, under the watchful eye of Johnson's friend, neighbor, and ally J. Edgar Hoover, was the sole investigative body for the commission. Six weeks after the president was killed, Johnson exempted Hoover from mandatory retirement, making him director for life. The Warren Commission found that Lee Harvey Oswald, acting alone, killed John Kennedy.

No awkward questions were asked.

ACKNOWLEDGMENTS

My mother was a librarian, my father a history teacher. When my brother and sisters and I were young—and I mean very young—our bedtime stories consisted of tomes like *The Iliad* and *The Odyssey*. When I was ten years old, my father handed me Churchill's *War Years*. Well, he didn't actually hand it to me because it was six thick volumes. I eventually made my way through three and a half of them and produced my first "book," a significantly condensed account of the conflict that I called *Hitler's War.* It took me four decades to get around to my next effort—this one—but I'm certain that I owe Homer and Churchill a thank-you. And Mom and Dad, of course. Thank you.

Henry Ferris, at William Morrow, has been everything I could've hoped for in an editor—enthusiastic, supportive, honest, creative,